IN THE TUNNELS
OF DOCTOR SUN SUN

The voices drew nearer.

There could be no question that the midgets were lethal. Not only were they armed, Sam well knew, but in the tunnels they were virtually invincible in hand-to-hand combat. They were another of Sun Sun's devious resources. Seemingly innocuous, amusing, the mere playthings of a madman, they were in fact a deadly weapons system.

Sam reached behind Honey, took the flashlight from her and put it head down against the floor of the tunnel. He needed time. He needed to think. He needed to compensate . . . Honey stared wide-eyed, panicked.

She knew something Sam didn't.

Valor consists in the power of self-recovery, so that a man cannot have his flank turned, cannot be outgeneraled, but put him where you will, he stands.

Ralph Waldo Emerson

THE NINTH DRAGON

CHAPTER ONE:
SHORTSIGHTED

Paris
August 15

It was time. Turner checked his watch, then tossed a few more francs onto the saucer and stood up. In front of the café terrace a guitarist slurred folk songs in mangled French redolent of Algeria. It was time to move now, time to meet his contact. Turner threaded his way through the closely packed tables and chairs and walked off quickly, heading down the busy Boulevard St.-Germain in the direction of the Rue St.-Jacques. He weaved in and out of the crowds of strollers, stopping only once for a good look at the object of a large crowd's attention. They were ogling an escape artist. A bikinied assistant was binding the artist in chains. Turner moved on.

Marshall Turner was a seasoned agent. He'd been in the Company for years, since graduation from Dartmouth in the late fifties. Over the past quarter century he'd been in many world hot spots, from the Far East through the Middle East to the Near East. He'd helped overturn a government or two in Latin America; he'd shaped the fate of more than one emerging African nation; he'd spent the better part of a decade intriguing in Eastern Europe. He was an old hand, and a good one. Twice the Company had commended him for bravery, in Angola and in Cambodia. He was one of the Company's best, so they'd tapped him again. He was in Paris to lure a man into a trap that wouldn't close till the entire turncoat operation the man worked for was crushed utterly, half a world away.

At the Rue St.-Jacques he turned toward the river. As he approached the little church of St.-Julien-le-Pauvre, he slowed his step. Out of the shadows stepped a small Asian dressed in a white linen suit. Turner walked up to him and nodded. The man nodded back. He had a white crescent scar on his left cheek. The little man spoke up in perfect English.

"Welcome to Paris."

"Thank you."

"Shall we have a drink?"

"No. I'd like to get to our business."

"As you wish. Follow me."

The man turned and started off, and Turner fell into step beside him. They walked in silence along the Rue Galande. In the little park surrounding the church, *clochards* stretched out on benches and on the ground. Through the leaves of the trees the street lamps cast geometric patterns onto the street, wet from a shower earlier that evening. At the Rue des Anglais they turned away from the river and crossed the Boulevard St.-Germain. They entered the immediate neighborhood of the Sorbonne. A quick turn down a side street brought them to an imposing town house with a highly polished black double door. The right door sported a brass knocker like the handle for a giant samovar. The little man hit the knocker lightly and the door opened.

Turner stepped into a brightly lighted foyer. The floors and the walls to the level of his shoulders were covered in elaborate Delft tiles with an intricate floral pattern running throughout. In each corner elegant palms stood in burnt orange urns. The little man stepped past Turner, and the retainer closed the door behind them. Turner followed his escort down a short hallway to a set of doors on the right. The man pushed the doors back and motioned Turner into a large room. The room was decorated austerely, as an office. To the right was a delicate desk on scrolled legs, obviously an antique. In front of the desk were two armchairs.

Turner cased the room carefully. There was no other furniture besides the desk with its two chairs in front and one behind except a beautifully polished red commode set against the left wall. There were no bookcases lining the walls. Turner concluded there could be no moving panels or secret entrances to the room. All this he analyzed in a flash. He proceeded across the room and sat in the farthest chair from the entrance. From this chair he had an excellent view of the doors leading to the room. He was positioned perfectly. He felt secure.

"I will join you momentarily," the little man said from the doorway. "Please make yourself comfortable."

"Thank you. I will."

"Would you care for a drink now?"

"No, thank you."

"If you so desire, there are cigarettes in the box on the desk."

"Thank you."

The man left the doorway, pulling the doors closed behind him. That meant anyone entering would have to at least open the doors. Turner relaxed back into the chair, his eyes on the doors. He felt the weight of his 9mm MAS automatic against his left breast. Its nine rounds gave him comfort. He felt he had the situation well in hand. He leaned forward, opened the hinged lid of the cigarette box on the desk, took out a long unfiltered cigarette and reached out for one of the blue-tipped stove matches fanned artistically in a cut-glass holder beside the box.

The doors silently opened on the commode. An Oriental midget stepped down onto the plush Persian carpet and sighted along the silenced barrel of a Walther model P1.

As Turner reached down cowboy style to strike his match on the sole of his shoe, he felt another presence in the room and whirled around in his chair, reaching inside his jacket. Before his hand found the butt of his MAS, a bullet shattered his cranium between and slightly above his eyes. His head exploded. Another parabellum shell tore into his right shoulder as his twisting body flew out of the chair and banged heavily into the desk before landing on the parquet floor with a thud louder than either shot.

The double doors opened and the little man in the linen suit looked from Turner to the midget and back.

He smiled and the midget bowed.

CHAPTER TWO:
BACK IN THE RACE

Sam Borne was bored. He was always bored when he ran, but it was part of his job, so he ran. He ran to stay in shape, just as he pumped out his push-ups and sit-ups to stay in shape. Not all agents did, but then Sam was not like other agents. He was special.

To the east the sun crested the horizon. Sam ran toward it. The air at dawn was tangy, clean and clear. The white-washed houses along the road stood out plainly, the muted orange tiles of their roofs contrasting sharply with the deep green of the trees dotting the plains and hills spreading out behind them. Sam ran on the hard surface of the asphalt berm, not in the middle of the road. At this hour there was little traffic, but Sam held that the one immediate consolation of running was the time it gave you to think, and he didn't want to distract the free flow of his mind with attention spent listening for the hiss and hum of occasional trucks or cars carrying their passengers on their rounds of early morning deliveries or to their destinies as hotel maids or clerks, cooks or waiters. Thinking while running was fine; it allowed Sam to trace out his days, to plan his reading, to take stock. It was not equivalent to the states of clarity and mellowness he achieved in meditation, but this side of a first-stage transport, it helped.

But he was bored. He had been in Ibiza, earthly garden

that it was, for over a fortnight now. At first he had entered the spirit of the place, tooling around in one of the
rented dune wagons one saw everywhere on the island,
but lately he needed more. He was restless. A sure sign
that he was ready to move on showed itself three days
earlier when he traded in the yellow dune wagon for a
silver Porsche. He had blown the 911 Carrera Cabriolet
out around the island, snapping the tight gearbox to its
limit, whipping into curves and surging on the straight-
aways, looking for the outside of the envelope, but it
wasn't to be found. The roads of Ibiza couldn't truly
challenge the Porsche, and Sam found himself yearning
for the lower corniche along the Riviera or for some of
the better race tracks the Committee had arranged for him
to test during the off hours when he had them all to himself with only the ghost of his own nerve to keep him
company. There was nothing to match the sweet tension
of ultimate risk, just for the hell of it. It was a major
charge to strap yourself into a wild machine and spool it
up tight. It took something special to wind it up and go
the limit, your own obituary only a millisecond's hesitation away from going to press. The difference between
chance and risk, Sam knew, was profound; if you understood it, you understood it instinctively; if not, not. He
understood it.

　　Ahead lay the traffic circle on the outskirts of town. In
a matter of seconds Sam would loop it and head into town
along the Avenida de España, with its shops, stores and
bars, one amusingly enough advertising topless dancers.
Only a few kilometers away everyone swam nude. Irony
amused Sam, no matter what manifestation it took. With
Sam, nude swimming was a passion. It was natural.
When he did it he felt as though he were in direct connection with nature; he felt part of the larger order, part of
the cosmos. And the Mediterranean was made for swimming bareback. With a mask and a snorkel, you could see
everything. You could see the ghostly white fish coast

by. You could see the patterns the sand made from the currents on the bottom. You could explore the rusts, the browns, the oranges of the rock formations. It was a good feeling. Snorkeling around like that, Sam could feel at one with nature.

He hit the circle, looped it and shot off down the avenue. Then he cut right and up the hill, heading for the steep staircase that would carry him to his room at the summit with the wide sea view. And Ina.

Ina he'd met in the buff on the beach. She was a statuesque German girl; tall, blonde, willowy; self-possessed and athletic. She spoke several languages, including a fair, if husky English. In conversations on a wide range of topics, she could hold her own. Like Sam she loved to snorkel. Like Sam she loved sex. At all hours, under any and all circumstances, without qualm or inhibition, she loved sex. But she didn't like the way things had gone lately. She didn't like to drive with Sam in the Porsche. She didn't like the way Sam withdrew into himself. She couldn't abide the recent intensity with which Sam had begun to read, exercise or brood. She found his habit of stalking about the living room, slamming about the kitchen and skulking about the bedroom irritating. His habit of roaming about town at night she found unsettling. The way he stared at the setting sun from the terrace until the bright disk slipped behind the central ridge of hills she found unnerving. He was altogether too intense for her.

Had she known Sam better, Ina would have recognized the signs. Sam was bored. Sam was doubting himself. Sam was beginning to think he was in mothballs for the duration. He was beginning to wonder where he fit in the scheme of things. He was starting to itch in a way that could be cured only with that most stimulating of tonics: direct and dangerous action in a cause he believed in. He needed a cosmic adrenaline rush.

Toward the top of the stone staircase, a tawny lizard

scooted across Sam's path. There was something erotic in the motion of a lizard; the way they shot along on their stomachs made Sam ache to be so horizontally agile. There was no purity like the purity of animal motion. In a few strides he was at the summit, in the little circular courtyard around which the Hotel Cenit's apartments clustered. From his wristband, he fished out his key and inserted it gently in the keyhole. Ina was a luxurious sleeper and he didn't want to wake her.

Sam entered the living room, crossed to the terrace and went outside. The terrace was in shade. He checked his watch. He had run the twelve kilometers between Ibiza and San Rafael in an eyelash under forty minutes. He hadn't pushed himself, but he'd breezed it pretty good. It would do to keep him tuned, if ever, he thought, I get another assignment. Before his mind had time to trick him away from duty, he fell forward and slapped, hands outstretched, onto the red clay tiles of the terrace. With blinding swiftness he started to pump out push-ups, first with both hands, then swiftly with one and then the other, hanging in midair as he switched hands. When his count reached a hundred, he flipped onto his back and, hands linked behind his head, started to snap off sit-ups, touching his kneecaps with outthrust elbows in a quick and sure rhythm. When he reached a hundred this time, he decided to hell with it, he'd done enough for one day, especially for a guy on the shelf.

He went back into the living room, crossed to the counter separating it from the kitchen, went around it and plucked from the refrigerator a large bottle of mineral water. He drank several huge drafts before heading for the reward of a stinging shower.

Pleasure was on his mind when he emerged fresh and energetic minutes later. He tiptoed into the bedroom, latticed with morning light from the louvered twin doors leading to a small balcony, and crawled softly into bed with the sleeping Ina. Gently he turned back the light counterpane covering her and started to kiss her delicately, starting ever so tenderly with her eyelids. She didn't move or stir a muscle. The game was on.

For as long as she could, Ina would feign sleep. And for as long as he could, Sam would feign indifference. Whoever moaned or sighed or stretched luxuriously, whoever did this or anything else overt first, lost. This was a game made to order for Sam Borne. As hard as he'd been drilled in the martial arts, as hard as he'd been trained as a commando, as hard as he'd been tutored in the theatrical arts of acting and dissembling, just as hard had he schooled himself in the arts of lovemaking.

With the ardor of the truly talented, Sam set to work, sculpting Ina with his lips, first here, then there, ever lower, ever more gently, with an increasing vigor, a mounting intensity. His lips traced the cinnabar tips of her breasts, caressing the nipples, teasing them ever so lightly between his teeth and tongue. Instantly they tightened.

Sam knew, and Ina knew that Sam knew, that she was awake. But she could play the game a little herself. She gave no outward sign of pleasure. She moved not a trifle. Only her breathing quickened involuntarily. Like all Westerners, Ina had never really mastered her body, had never gained the control of it as an instrument for pleasure that Sam had.

Sam had her, and knew it. With a feathery touch he traced her spine with his one hand, his other caressing her breast. His hand moved lower, molding the curves of her magnificent body. His mouth traveled softly down her stomach, marking its spoor with kisses and subtle little suctions against her buttermilk skin. His tongue licked languidly the filigree of hair that descended in a peaked line to her golden thatch.

She moaned.

After their passion had subsided, Sam slowly grew aware of a giggling sound in the still room. He opened his

eyes gradually and saw that Ina had hunkered back on her
haunches between his legs. She looked like a mermaid on
a rock. Only, she was giggling triumphantly. She was entitled to her moment. Sam shot out a hand, grabbed her
by the shoulder and pulled her down on top of him. He
rolled her to the side and hurled himself atop her. Peals of
laughter filled the room.

"Sam, you are crazy, like all Americans," she said,
laughing. "You are a crazy and wild people."

Sam looked down into her face, his strong hands pinning her shoulders to the mattress.

"And what are you going to do for this crazy American
this glorious morning?" he asked.

"What more can I do for you?" Again she let loose a
loud laugh.

"You can get your fabulous ass out of my bed and fix
me some breakfast. You can make coffee. You can show
me you appreciate me for more than my body. You can
do all of this and more. Am I right?"

"Yes, Sam. You are right. But you are a chauvinist pig
all the same."

"A hungry one."

Ina's invigorating laughter filled the room as Sam
rolled off her and she climbed out of bed. He lay on his
back. He enjoyed the way morning light played about the
room, and he enjoyed, despite his mounting boredom,
the freedom he had, on days between assignments, to
think of what he might do, to plan what he might read, to
anticipate the fun of sunning, swimming and snorkeling.
He was reading as usual in the writings of Emerson and
other American Transcendentalists. As always he was
trying to reconcile this school of American writing with
his studies in Zen. For relief he had been reading, as was
his habit in whatever country he might be stationed, the
literature of that country. This trip had brought him to the
great novel of Spain, *Don Quixote*. Intrigued by the old
knight and his faithful companion, he was nevertheless

appalled at times by the turn his mind took in reading of their misadventures. He especially feared that he would end up like Quixote, mad and jousting at windmills. God knew there were enough real villains in this world to keep Sam Borne busy from now till Judgment Day, but he was beginning, as always when his time between assignments mounted, to question his own worth.

Whenever this happened, all the rest was predictable. He would begin to map a new strategy to get himself permanently out of the Committee's grasp. He would start to think of ways to get the Committee to grant him his freedom. He would think of a new argument why he should be allowed to retire from his role as the free world's ultimate secret weapon. All of his training by the Japanese as the world's deadliest ninja, all of his training by the Americans as the world's fiercest commando, all of his training by the British as the world's greatest unacknowledged actor—at times like these all of it weighed on Sam like a marble cross. He wanted to plead with the Committee to retire him, to find a replacement for him, to let him slip off with a neatly ordinary identity into a teaching job at a college in the American Midwest where he could settle down and teach literature and raise a son who could light up the heavens with his play at shortstop.

All of this pointed up the central paradox at the root of Sam's existence. On the one hand, he wanted out of his life of adventure; on the other hand, he needed the rush the dangerous assignments gave him. On the one hand, he wanted to serve a purpose teaching the beauty of literature; on the other hand, he felt like the world's most essential being when he wrapped up a Committee assignment. Then there was the war within him between appetite and meditation.

With this thought, he reached out and pulled back the hemp handle on the drawer of the night table beside the bed. He snatched up a pack of Gauloises and shook one out, spilling the pack's loose tobacco onto the sheets, where it formed a random pattern of light and dark browns like a Mondrian. He struck a match and inhaled deeply. The hit as the smoke rushed into his lungs was sweet. With one hand cradling his head, he lay back and mellowed out. Fuck it all, he thought, fuck self-reliance, fuck self-understanding, fuck discipline, fuck satori, fuck transcendentalism, fuck it all and hurrah for satisfaction.

From the direction of the kitchen, Sam heard Ina's footsteps approaching and braced himself. She stood in the doorway, hands on hips, her earlier grin replaced by a frown.

"Sam, you are smoking."

"Yes."

"They are no good. From the kitchen I can smell them even."

"They're very definite, Gauloises."

"They make you die."

"Not yet."

"You will see."

"No. I'll be dead."

"You are stubborn."

"What's with breakfast?"

"It is coming. I must go down to the store and get some cream for the *Kaffee*."

"Okay."

"You will please listen for the water to boil."

"I'll listen."

"Good."

Ina pulled on white shorts and wriggled into a red halter. She looked daggers at Sam and left. He heard her close the door and then he heard the scrape of her sandals as she walked away across the concrete. Each time he smoked she smoldered. It was nothing more than usual; Ina was a health nut in an age of health nuts. Sam inhaled lustily, heard the teapot whistle, took a last hearty hit on the Gauloise, stubbed it out in the ceramic ashtray on the night table. He climbed out of bed and headed off to get the kettle.

No sooner had Sam turned off the flame under the tea-kettle than the buzzer on the door sounded. It was a bit early for the maid, so he was slightly startled. In a few strides Sam was at the door, pulling it open expectantly. He had a hunch.

One of the boys from the hotel's central office stood on the patio. He smiled at Sam and launched into an apology in halting Spanish for the early hour. Among themselves, Sam knew, the natives spoke Ibicenco, so their Spanish was not always polished. In the boy's hand was a packet that was all too recognizable to Sam. It was word from the Committee. In a flash Sam reached out and snared the packet and in another flash retreated into the room and scooped up a handful of change from the counter. This he thrust on the boy and slammed the door.

Back in the room Sam ripped open the thick envelope and read rapidly. The top page, as always, detailed his travel plans. By instinct and training he checked it first. This time it was more than necessary. Sam was to be on the 9:30 Swissair flight from Ibiza to Madrid, where he'd get a connecting flight to Zurich. From there it was on to Hong Kong.

There was just enough time to catch the flight. The Committee, Sam thought wryly, was always demanding, always exact. He could get out to the airport and check himself in and, if lucky, grab a cup of *café con leche* and a croissant and call it breakfast. Ina's would be wasted. This pained Sam. But even more than the lost breakfast, so carefully and lovingly prepared, Sam would miss Ina's energy, her tenderness, her spontaneity. He'd miss everything about her.

Taking leave was always hard. Sam knew from long practice and bad experience that the best break was the fastest break, that the cleanest break was the disappearing act. So he hurried now into the bedroom. He quickly

packed, then dressed. Wearing a raspberry polo shirt over
his white ducks, he carried his fully packed lightweight
suitcase of parachute material back into the living room.
He was adjusting his blue blazer and tucking the packet
from the Committee under his arm when he caught the
faint sound of approaching footsteps on the stone staircase leading up the hill. Without a moment's hesitation
he grabbed the keys to the Porsche and was out the door.
He threw everything into the car and then slid in himself.
He inserted the ignition key and turned over the engine.
He was in reverse and easing back out of his parking spot
when Ina appeared at the head of the stairs. Sam smiled at
her and threw the car into forward. Before he could accel-
erate out of the courtyard, Ina, womanly instinct alert,
dropped the package she was carrying and ran over in
front of the car. Sam stopped. He was trapped. She would
see the luggage. She would know he was off somewhere.
As always, Sam had been vague with her about his line of
work, telling her only that he was in imports and exports.

Ina came toward Sam, leaning as she did so on the
fender of the car. She knew that Sam would tear out and
leave her with a backward wave if she didn't somehow
appeal to his sense of chivalry. If Sam wheeled out now,
Ina would go sprawling. Possibly she would hurt herself
badly. The situation left Sam no choice. She came along-
side the driver's window and looked at Sam with big, hurt
eyes for a moment. He took the opportunity to reach out
and pluck his aviator shades from the visor. He put them
on.

"Sam, what are you doing? Where are you going?"

"I have to leave. It's important."

"But why?"

"Business."

"Please, Sam, tell me. Was it something I did?"

"No."

"We are on vacation. Please explain."

"You are on vacation. I've been called back to work."

"Wait. I will come with you."

"You can't."

"Why not?"

Sam almost laughed as he bit back the natural reply, "It's too dangerous." If ever he had to speak a line like that, he'd move to Hollywood and pick up big change as a matinee idol.

"Why are you like this, Sam? Leaving me like this."

"I have to go immediately. It's crucial to my business."

"Nothing is so crucial as us, Sam."

He hated when they turned to mush. One minute a beautiful Valkyrie, the next, Gretel lost in the forest. He debated a lie to let her down easy; he considered telling her he'd be back in a day or two. He never got the opportunity.

"Well, fuck you, Mr. America. Fuck you, Mr. Sam Borne."

Ina stood straight up from the car's fender, took two steps back and stared at him. Sam searched his mind for something nice to say, something soothing, something that would carry Ina through life with nothing but pleasant memories of him. He hated this part; he hated seeming like a bastard. Brevity, he decided, was the better part of gallantry.

"Auf wiedersehen."

Sam blasted down on the accelerator and the Porsche shot forward, coiling out of its turn and spinning out of the circular courtyard. He glanced into the rear-view mirror only briefly, but it was enough for him to spot Ina standing where he'd left her, her middle finger shooting him the bird in fluent international sign language. He smiled. She would be fine.

He had himself to worry about now. He had to get to Madrid and on to Hong Kong. At the foot of the hill, he stopped at the light, reached down and snapped the Sinatra tape into the deck. When the light changed, he shot forward, heading out of town toward the airport, his ears filled with the rough but liquid sounds of that fabulous voice. By the time Sam reached the traffic circle, Frank had blasted his way into the bars of "That's Life."

Yes, Sam thought, I've picked myself up and I'm back in the race.

His blood jumped.

CHAPTER THREE:
IN A CAT'S EAR

Cholon
August 16

In the darkness, rain fell steadily. Night had descended on Cholon like a shroud. This was the notorious twin city of what used to be called Saigon and was now called Ho Chi Minh City. No matter what you called it, Cholon was an annex of hell. For hundreds of years it had been the center of corruption in a corrupt country and headquarters for the Vietnamese underworld. Everything here was closed, shuttered, clandestine.

Through the slick streets a caravan slowly threaded its way, the headlights of the lead vehicle piercing the darkness. The lead vehicle was a black Cadillac limousine, a stretch model such as movie stars used. This particular limo had been nothing less than the official car of the American ambassador to Vietnam before the debacle of 1975. The Americans had left it behind, and like much else they had left behind, it had fallen into the hands of the man who occupied its back seat at this very moment.

He was a large man, peculiar beyond words. He was dressed now like a mandarin, in yellow silk pajamas and a green silk robe with dragons on it. In the dim light of the passenger compartment, he sprawled like an emperor. Clutched in his fist was an Old-Fashioned glass full of Scotch. From time to time he took huge gouts from the glass, all the while fondling the nape and hair of the beau-

tiful Vietnamese woman nestled against him. She was
delicate and magnificent. Dressed in a dark blue dress
with golden peacocks embroidered on it, she was an
Asian beauty of the first rank, with lovely, high cheekbones framing jet-black eyes above a sensual mouth and
small, straight nose. Her features when she smiled were
radiant, her skin glowing and dusky. She was returning
the man's affection by stroking his cheek slowly.

"Why are we coming to this godforsaken spot?" the
woman asked.

"You will see."

"I want to know now."

"It is necessary to make an example."

"But why?"

"It is simple," the man said. "Someone has talked.
Someone has let the cat out of the bag. I have to make
sure that things like this do not happen. Therefore, an example will be made."

"But why the girls?"

"You will see."

"They should be working. They should be hustling in
the hotels. They should be learning what they can of the
foreigners in the city."

"All I want you to know is that I have discovered a
leak and I intend to fix it like any good plumber."

"I don't like coming here at night. This section is
spooky. And ugly." She was pouting now. She was
playing her strange sugar daddy for all he was worth.

"Be still," he said. In the light of the passing street
lamp, the woman could see that his face had the stern and
brutal set it always took when he was angry with her. She
knew he would have no more patience. Her questions
would only enrage him. Theirs was not a relationship of
equals. The man was clearly in power, and she was just
as clearly subservient to him. He had about him the aura
of a despot, the sinister power of a dictator. The woman

could study his face for hours and it would reveal not one clue to the man.

The big man was an enigma. He was odd. His face was all askew, contorted, ugly. Something about the eyes was all wrong. They were folded over like the eyes of an Oriental, but they were somehow distressed. Nothing about them was natural. Then there was the mouth. It was full and fleshy and cruel. His skin was pitted and pasty, not at all smooth and dusky like an Oriental's. He was a freak. There was absolutely no natural way an ogre like him could attract a woman of superlative beauty like the one beside him.

The limousine splashed through a big puddle, fanning water out on both sides as it turned sharply to the right. They were nearing the river now, with its dilapidated warehouses and rickety docks and rusting tin huts. In the beams of the headlights, shadows fled. Street urchins and refugees of every stripe huddled here in the abandoned buildings at night, seeking what scant shelter and comfort they could squeeze from such slums. Occasionally a stray dog scrambled into an alley, or a scraggly cat slipped back against the walls. The Cholon docks offered an urban Asian landscape at its eeriest.

Suddenly the Cadillac pulled to a stop before a cyclone fence with a double gate leading onto a dock. The gates were held fast with a chain clamped with a lock the size of a grenade. To the side and just within the gates was a small shack. From it a man emerged carrying a flashlight the size of a small plunger. Its beam shone like a strobe light into the eyes of the limo's chauffeur. The chauffeur rolled down the window, stuck out his head and said something rapid and short in Vietnamese. The guard lowered the light, shook his head and went directly to the large lock on the gates. Taking a key from a big ring of keys fastened to his waist, he opened the lock and swung back the gates. As the limo pulled through onto the dock, the guard raised his flashlight in salute and bowed low.

Behind the limo came a three-wheeled lambro and a jeep. The three vehicles moved gingerly down the dock, bouncing lightly in and out of the big potholes in the pavement. The Cadillac drew up beside a large corrugated-tin warehouse. The lambro pulled to a stop behind it with the jeep bringing up the rear.

From the jeep stepped four sentries holding M-16s. In the dim light from the caged bulb over the entrance to the warehouse, one of them stepped up to the corrugated door and pounded on it with the heel of his hand. The sound from within had a hollow, echoing quality. A latch could be heard to snap, then the door rolled back on its track. A small man dressed all in workman's blue walked the door back to its limit. A large square of light fell out onto the dock. The sentries motioned with their weapons, and the four women in the open back of the lambro stepped down and were quickly herded into the warehouse.

In the Cadillac the strange-looking man turned to his companion and gestured with his glass of Scotch. "I think," he said, "that it wouldn't be a bad idea for you to have a big drink of Scotch with me. What you will see in a matter of minutes may leave your nerves unsettled."

"You know I don't like whiskey."

"You're making a mistake. Like it or not, you'll need whiskey for this."

"What do you plan to do?"

"You will soon see."

"Please don't hurt the girls."

"How do you make an example if you don't make it strong?"

"I don't like you when you're like this."

"I don't think you like me anyway."

"You're wrong."

"Then you like me?"

"Of course."

"Honey, you are too sweet."

"Let's leave then. Let's go back and make mad love till the sun comes up."

"That sounds great. But first I must make an example. And you must have some whiskey."

"No. I will wait here in the car. Please hurry."

"You will not wait here. You will come and you will watch. I want word of this to spread quickly. I want everyone in this town to know about this by tomorrow, and to be warned."

The man stretched forward to the bar, took a bottle of Black & White Scotch and poured two huge amounts into Old-Fashioned glasses. He handed one to the woman and drank a heavy draft from the other. Raindrops beaded on the car's windows cast black freckles onto his already hideous face. He smiled.

"Why are you doing this?" she asked.

"I am doing this simply because the only information I have on my leak is that she is a whore."

"So you are going to hurt these girls."

"You'll see."

"I wish that I wouldn't."

"You will see how economical I am. While I make an example, I will also make a profit. I am going to make myself a movie star for tonight. I will send this film out over the decadent capitalist networks, and it will bring a fortune to us and to our cause."

"You are depraved."

"I am not nearly so depraved as the swinish capitalists who will pay to see this."

One of the sentries came back out of the warehouse and knocked on the window of the passenger compartment. The man rolled the window down slightly. In staccato Vietnamese the sentry announced that everything was ready. The big man did not deign to answer. He merely pressed the button again and the window rose. He took a big swallow from his drink, finishing it off with a smack. He turned to his lovely companion.

"Bottoms up. Let's go."

"Do I have to? Please don't make me watch."

The man grinned maniacally, his face speckled with the black dots of the reflected raindrops. "How do I know," he asked with a leer, "that it's not you?"

The woman maintained her composure, straightening with forefinger and thumb the fall of her sleeve. She took a discreet sip from the whiskey before handing it to the man, who finished it in one gulp. When he put the glass down, the woman looked him straight in the eye, matching nerve for nerve.

"I once heard a great line in an old Charlie Chan movie," she said. "It occurs when Charlie looks at his son and says that it's a foolish mouse that builds its nest in a cat's ear. I think that about covers the implications of your insult, don't you agree?"

"Yes. I agree. But you still have to watch."

CHAPTER FOUR:
MORE THAN A DAY

Zurich
August 16

It was midday. Sam Borne had an hour to kill while he waited to board the Hong Kong plane. At the desk they had told him in clipped and succinct English that his Swissair flight would board in an hour. When the Swiss said an hour, they meant an hour. All of the old saws about this country were true; it was spotless, efficient and staid; it was spectacularly beautiful, and the people were greedy beyond belief. That's what Sam liked about old saws; they were old and they were true.

So he sat in the coffee shop and studied his dossier. He had already studied it on the flight from Ibiza to Madrid and on the flight from Madrid to Zurich, but he wanted to study it more. He would study it now and he would study it again on the flight to Hong Kong. There was a simple reason for this. About your friends it was prudent not to know everything; about your enemies it was foolish not to know everything. Sam could never know enough about his targets. At rest they were dangerous; enraged they were lethal. It always befell Sam to meet them at their worst, to take them on when they were on the alert. No matter how powerful the Committee was—and it was more powerful than anything Sam could imagine—it still could not preempt the management of the world. This being so, as far as Sam could make out, the Committee functioned as a free-lance world policeman, as a free-lance universal vigilante, coming in to troubleshoot and fix where all else had failed. Usually what had failed was the CIA, that bumbling coterie Sam was forever picking up after. Not surprisingly, they had fucked up yet again. Only, this time their feinting and stunting could have dire consequences for America, and as usual it was Sam Borne's job to make sure that this didn't happen. The CIA reminded Sam of nothing so much as a spastic shadowboxing in the shade.

This time the Committee was onto a nefarious piece of work named Doctor Sun Sun, an improbable but all too real madman plotting and scheming to destroy the moral fiber and strength of America by flooding the country with uncut heroin. Why was it, Sam wondered, that the most bizarre plans, the most outrageous villains, always ended up on his agenda?

Doctor Sun Sun's dossier was an in-depth study of one of the greatest American traitors. He was no more Doctor Sun Sun than Sam Borne was Mickey Mouse. He was in fact a rogue United States Army general who had played both ends against the middle during the Vietnam conflict, and after the defeat of the United States military, he had set himself up as Ho Chi Minh City's biggest gangster. The dossier made clear that Doctor Sun Sun had taken control of all aspects of crime in Vietnam, which covered a lot of ground under the heroically inefficient Communists. He controlled prostitution, gambling, the black market. He had smashed the power base of what was left of the Corsican Mafia from the old days of French rule. He had cut into the power base of the old river pirates. He had subjugated the opium networks formerly controlled by the Chinese syndicates, and he had watched with glee as the Communists smashed the corrupt grip of the former military leaders of South Vietnam. Doctor Sun Sun was a world-class ass-kicker, one with no compunctions, no scruples, no conscience to speak of. His relationship with the government since the Communist takeover was a combination of official sanction and unofficial license. He functioned as a government within a government, surreptitiously supported but officially unrecognized. The official government took no overt part in his heroin operation, yet it placed no obstacle in its path. His mad revenge scheme had every chance of succeeding.

Doctor Sun Sun's real name was Loftus R. Laidlaw. The R stood for Randall. He was descended from one of the finest families of Virginia, one with a military pedigree stretching back beyond the Civil War to the American Revolution. Laidlaws had served everywhere, from Mexico to the American West, to France twice and to the Pacific once, to Korea. Finally, with the posting of U.S. General Loftus R. Laidlaw to Vietnam, they had served in the first defeat of the United States military in a police action. It always annoyed Sam to hear that Vietnam was the first war America had lost. It wasn't a war; it was a police action. In a war you acquired or relinquished real estate. In a police action you fought your ass off, maybe you got killed, maybe you didn't, while some half-ass politician with a shoe-size IQ sold you down the river for a footnote in history and a Swiss bank account.

So General Loftus R. Laidlaw had come to Vietnam in the early winter of 1964 in an ideal position to advance his career. Placed in charge of the entire operation at Da Nang, he was the number-one man, the supreme honcho in an operation where billions in supplies and matériel passed under his jurisdiction daily, hourly, every minute, around the clock, seven days a week, fifty-two weeks a year. He had overseen the buildup of that base to where it was huge, sprawling, nearly out of control—but not quite, for Loftus R. Laidlaw had his finger in every pie.

That's when he got greedy. There was just too much of everything to be accounted for. And Loftus R. Laidlaw had always held that the government was just a sheep waiting to be shorn. So he started to filter millions upon millions of dollars worth of equipment, supplies and matériel into the black market. His distribution network reached everywhere. Did you buy a six-pack of good American beer in Saigon? You bought it indirectly from General Laidlaw. Did you pick up a Japanese transistor at a price that couldn't be beat in Bangkok while on R&R? You bought it indirectly from Loftus R. Laidlaw. Did you get an unbeatable deal on the Rue Catinat on a Leica? You bought it indirectly from the man who was on his way to becoming Doctor Sun Sun, archgangster.

And what did General Loftus R. Laidlaw do in 1970 when he saw which way this asinine police action was going to go? He decided, when the big boys back in the Pentagon passed him over for supreme commander of all United States forces in Vietnam, that he'd had enough. He decided he'd been passed over one time too many. He simply made up his mind that selling his country's bounty, that violating its spirit was not enough. He sold the whole country. He sold its soul. He sold the American fighting man down the drain as surely as any President or national security adviser or secretary of state. He shook hands with the devil and made a deal with the North Communists.

At the time, the United States brass believed he'd been kidnapped and assassinated. There seemed no other explanation. One day when he was the kingpin at Da Nang, he took a field trip and never returned. The only assumption that made sense was that a Vietcong patrol had ambushed him and he was no more. Not even his command vehicle was found. Nothing of General Laidlaw was left behind.

In truth, he'd quietly gone over to the other side and quickly gone underground in Saigon, where he began immediately to build the massive and far-reaching power base that made him, at the time of the fall of Saigon in the spring of 1975, the strongest strongarm in that most elegant city. If Saigon was the Pearl of the Orient, he was its oyster, so surely did he hold that city in his grasp. He controlled it top to bottom, front to back. He controlled its people and its life. When the troops from the North rolled into town, he was at the head of the reception line. He had paved the way for the so-called victory, and now he had devised a scheme that would wreak even greater revenge on the land and people he thought had wronged him in not making possible his secret dream to be known as the Patton of the Orient. Had he got control of United States forces in Vietnam, had he been named the supreme commander, Loftus R. Laidlaw had had plans.

General Laidlaw had planned to put his name right up there with George Patton. He had planned to eclipse "Vinegar Joe" Stilwell and to make Doug MacArthur just another dogface leader who'd had his moment in the sun. Laidlaw was going, on his own recognizance, to ship limited tactical nuclear weapons into the South and to launch an all-out attack on the North, perhaps not a bad idea. On the contrary, it might have won the police action. But the way Laidlaw planned to do it was sure to make matters worse. He was going to burn and destroy innocent women and children as examples, for the sheer hell of it. He was going to make the scorched-earth policy look like a land-improvement movement sponsored by the Camp Fire Girls. He was going to make General Sherman's march to the sea look like a candlelit procession.

General Laidlaw planned an amphibious landing at Haiphong that was slated to make MacArthur's stroke of genius at Inchon pale by comparison. Of course, its projected casualty rate was over ninety percent, but Laidlaw didn't give a good intercontinental fuck about that. If he made "Butcher Joe" Hooker look like Tiny Tim, so what? He was going to enter his name in the hall of fame, and that was that.

His plans gradually became known to the Pentagon brass. That was why he was passed over. There were also heavy suspicions about Da Nang, about the shortages despite the abundant shipments coming in. Things were starting not to make sense. Then there were the leaks about Laidlaw's secret plans—about the amphibious landing, doomed for sure; about the invasion over the DMZ, which would be undertaken without the proper air and offshore naval support; about his policy to make examples of innocent women and children. The long and short of it was that General Loftus R. Laidlaw was mad. He had clearly gone round the bend.

"Excuse me. May I share your table?"

Sam Borne looked up into one of the sweetest smiles in Switzerland, or anywhere else for that matter. Above him stood a svelte blonde with an infant in a harness cradled on her chest. The baby stretched and kicked. The woman made no move to sit down. She only stood there, a study in politeness and good manners.

"Of course."

"Thank you."

"You're very welcome." Sam started back into his dossier when he noticed that the woman was having difficulty shifting her baby and settling her luggage. He was on his feet and around the table in a flash and instantly had the situation in hand. He helped the woman settle herself, then started back to his seat. On the way, he introduced himself with a smile and learned that her name was Daphne Wells.

"It's nice to meet you," Sam said, resuming his seat. He picked up the dossier, but before diving back into it, he noticed Daphne looking off in the distance. He followed her gaze to a bar.

"Is there anything else I can do for you?" he asked.

Daphne hesitated. "Well," she said, "I would like some orange juice for the baby. I wonder, would they have any?"

"I'm sure they do. Would you like anything else?"

"No, thank you."

"Be right back." He crossed to the bar, grateful for the chance to busy himself, to get his mind off Doctor Sun Sun. He had hours ahead of him on the long flight to the East to think about his newest assignment. It was good to divert himself.

The bartender came over and he placed his order. While he waited, an older man leaning against the bar asked him in English, the way so many American tourists did, assuming the entire world spoke English, where he was going. The man was dressed completely in pastel polyester and looked like a refugee from the Sunbelt.

"I'm going to Asia." Sam wasn't sure he wanted to be part of this man's conversation. It wasn't wise to talk to too many tourists when he was starting an assignment. He always tended to close down the social part of his personality when the chips were down and the cards had been dealt, but it probably wouldn't do to huddle with himself like a mad bomber. It probably would help to keep one foot in the everyday side of things for at least a few more hours. Still, concentration was the key to success in many ways, and Sam had not worked to achieve his startling capacity for concentration just to keep it on the shelf. He was definitely in the grip of the steep rush he got whenever he went on a real challenge, whenever the Committee tapped him for a tough assignment. There was always the possibility against enemies the caliber of Sun Sun that he wouldn't come back, so it was good practice to shut down the hale and hearty side of his nature and go into a fighting stance out of which he could coil like a striking cobra when the time was right. Modulated intensity, Sam knew, was the key at this stage.

"I'm going back, praise Jesus, to the land I love, the good ole U. S. of A.," the man replied. "The wife and I have been dragged around Europe on this goddamn church tour for about as long as I can stand it—two weeks to be precise—and I can't wait to plant my ass and watch a good ball game. What the hell do these people do for entertainment, I wonder. Do you know? Do you live here?''

"I live all over." Sam decided to humor this old codger. He was harmless, and meant well. He was only one of countless things Sam loved about America and Americans. The man was direct. He knew himself. He didn't give a damn if a monastery was built two hundred or four hundred years ago. He was bored, and he was brassy enough to say so.

"Christ, I had my fill of living all over when I went through this part of the world in the forties—infantry, wouldn't you know—and it's no goddamn treat to me. Can't hold a candle to the States, but try to tell that to my old lady. C'mon over and try to tell her. She's sitting right over here."

The man started to take Sam's arm. Sam stopped him.

"Excuse me. I'm in a hurry."

The bartender arrived with the orange juice and Sam paid in pesetas. There was no point in changing money to Swiss francs for an hour layover, and Sam knew the Swiss loved to handle currencies of other countries, to weigh them against their vaunted franc and find them wanting. Leaving the change in the dish for the bartender, he nodded quickly to the old veteran. "Have a good time at home. Safe trip to you."

"Thank you. Same to you. And if you ever get to Arizona, stop by and say hello. We're the Bateses, Harry and Rhoda. Live right in Tucson. We're in the phone book. Drop in and have a beer."

"I just might do that."

Sam smiled and moved off toward Daphne Wells and her infant. Back at their table, he refused Daphne's offer to pay for the orange juice, then chatted with her, learning that she was on her way to Hong Kong on the same flight he was taking and that she had a husband there, English like her, who'd gone out on assignment for Barclay's Bank. They would try living there now that the husband had found a proper apartment, but Sam could detect that Daphne was apprehensive about the whole arrangement. She was obviously a girl from an insular background and the Orient was full of mystery and intrigue for her, an impression she'd no doubt picked up from reading paperback novels and watching old B-movies.

The public address came on and announced their flight in French, English, German and Cantonese, a nice touch the thorough Swiss would rather have died than omit.

Sam helped Daphne gather herself and the baby together and got them moving toward the gate, commandeering their luggage, since as always he was carrying only his small takeoff bag of parachute material. They were through the gate and stepping onto the plane when Daphne turned to him.

"You know," she said, "it's funny. Traveling to the Orient, you lose a day."

"Oh, in the Orient you can lose more than a day."

CHAPTER FIVE:
SANDS OF TIME

Cholon
August 16

The entire makeshift studio was flooded with light from the kliegs posted around the stage setting, umbrella reflectors intensifying the light even more. The setting looked like a seraglio. Along the walls were striped coverings like those on Arab tents. Here and there were poles like the ones that support large tents. Placed carefully along the back wall and along the two sides were banquettes strewn with pillows. Incense burned in a brazier off to one side. In the corners elaborate golden candleholders held burning tapers.

Out in front stood a camera and a cameraman, surrounded by two men serving roughly as grips, and the sentries, who were grinning at one another and making short, snappy statements in Vietnamese that almost always brought sniggers and laughs from the others. The grips were fussing with the lights. Behind them in a wicker armchair, the woman in the pretty blue dress with golden peacocks on it sat smoking apprehensively. A small man dressed in white linen trousers and a black silk shirt, Western and very chic, suddenly stepped up in front of the camera and waved his arms.

Everyone fell silent. The man in the casual clothes then hollered in the direction of the set. He picked up a clapboard and held it still for a second before smacking it shut. The camera started to whir. It was dead quiet.

Off to one side, part of the cloth covering the wall, representing the tent flap, was pulled back and into the setting stepped a huge Negro wearing Aladdin pants of bright gold with a red sash around his waist. He was bald. His torso was bare. Under the hot lights sweat popped out on it immediately and his flesh gleamed. He looked like a genie. He held the tent flap back, and into the room stepped the four women from the back of the three-wheeled lambro. They were dressed in sheer and flowing wraps that covered them from head to knees. The wraps were of various colors, all beautiful pastels, one powder blue, another a sandy beige, another a soothing light green, the last a soft cerise. All of the wraps were edged with gold.

From somewhere out of sight Arab music started and the four women began to dance, undulating their hips and waving their hands on extended arms in free-flowing and graceful patterns. They tripped lightly around the huge Negro, who stood stock-still, in the middle of the room with his arms crossed, moving not so much as an eyebrow. The women danced in rhythm with the music.

Then the music stopped and the women stopped, holding themselves on pointe like dancers. They looked like figures on a fountain. In the stillness the Negro clapped loudly. From the tent-flap opening a midget entered the room, then another. The two midgets stood expectantly, holding the flap back. After a dramatic interval, a large man entered dressed in a flowing white burnoose with the hood up. Before him he held the burnoose closed tight. He looked up, smiled at the women poised in a tableau, then moved off to the side and lounged on a banquette. He flourished his hand in the air, whirling his index finger, and the Negro clapped again.

The music resumed. The women again started to slither around the room, arms waving, hands flowing, the two midgets circling them like sheep dogs. At another clap from the Negro, the midgets reached up and pulled the strings on the wraps. The wraps of two women fell loose and the midgets whipped the garments off. The Negro clapped again. The midgets reached up and pulled the strings on the other two women. The wraps loosened and the midgets snatched them away. All four women writhed about the room stark naked. Like magicians, the midgets flung the wraps to the side, where they floated to the floor.

The midgets went to the flap and held it open. Into the room came two nubile girls, one bearing a salver on which fruit was piled high, the other carrying an earthen amphora and a bejeweled chalice of beaten gold that gleamed under the bright lights. The girls went over to the man in the burnoose and kneeled before him. On extended arms, they proferred to him the salver, the amphora and the chalice. He took an orange from the salver, bit into it and spat out the rind. Then he took another big bite and sent juice squirting over his burnoose and over the girls, who didn't flinch. With a flick of his wrist he tossed the orange off camera.

The big man then took the chalice from the one kneeling girl and held it out for her to fill. She did. He took a long gulp, spilling a little wine down the front of his burnoose. Belching loudly, he wiped his mouth with the back of his hand before taking another big gulp. Resting the chalice on his bulging stomach, he watched intently as the women danced about.

After a short interval, the Negro looked toward the man in the burnoose, who nodded. The Negro clapped. The music and dancing stopped. Everything was still and quiet. The Negro clapped again and the women arranged themselves with the help of the midgets in extremely provocative poses along one banquette. At another clap from the Negro, the music resumed, this time slower and softer.

Prompted by the midgets, the pairs of women began

gradually to caress each other. They stroked each other's arms, then began to peck kisses onto each other's throats, shoulders, faces. Soon they were fondling each other's breasts as they kissed long and sensually on the mouth. They embraced, stroking and caressing.

One midget scurried across the room and out through the flap. In a moment he returned with two huge ostrich feathers and gave one to the other midget. The midgets then began to run the feathers over the embracing bodies of the women. The music played on slowly. From the center of the room the Negro stood, stock-still, arms crossed, watching.

The man in the white burnoose leaned back on his elbow, drinking wine and eating handfuls of fruit, watching impassively. He might have been observing a deliberate game of chess. As the women became more passionate, he started to respond, fondling himself desultorily through the folds of his burnoose. A smile began to light his face. Then he clicked his fingers, and the two kneeling girls rose and opened his burnoose. They folded it back carefully and began to massage him, using oil from a small vial the Negro handed them. There was a determination and an avidity about the actions of both the nubile girls and the four women that made for an eerie feeling. They were somehow desperate.

The woman in the blue dress sitting in the director's chair knew this. Chain-smoking, she folded back her fingers and checked her nails. But when she looked away, toward the back of the warehouse or to either side, a sentry stationed behind her with his M-16 would nudge her in the back and she would look up again and direct her attention toward the set. The other sentries stood about, quietly elbowing each other and exchanging maniacal grins, long and leering. The cameraman and the grips and the man in the white linen trousers and the black silk shirt attended solemnly to the equipment and to the actions on the set.

The Negro looked toward the fat man being massaged
by the girls. The fat man raised his hand toward the Negro as though in benediction. The Negro clapped. The
midgets stopped fluttering the ostrich feathers. They put
down the feathers and waited expectantly as the Negro
crossed to the four women and started to arrange them
along the banquette.

He then strode across the set and, stooping low, left
through the flap. In a minute he was back. He walked
over and stood above the fat man, holding aloft in his
hand, between index finger and thumb, a tiny gold hourglass slightly smaller than an egg timer. He twisted it to
show that the sands were running. It was not an hourglass
but a minuteglass. It took the sand one minute to run from
one-half of the glass into the other. In his other hand he
held a sinister-looking instrument shaped of heavy-gauge
cable wire with a ring at the end the size of a collar. As its
handle, it had two heavy cable strands running parallel
with a slip-knot device on it for tightening the collar-
sized ring at the end. It was shaped like a tennis racket,
only smaller, and unstrung.

The fat man sat up. He pushed the girls away from
him. Both girls stood at attention, waiting for instructions. He nodded to the Negro, and the Negro took the
girls by the shoulders and led them to the flap and out of
the tent. He returned and stood beside the fat man, who
was enormously pleased. The fat man stood up.

The Negro stepped behind the fat man and deftly removed from his shoulders the white burnoose. The fat
man stood in all his naked glory. While the Negro carefully folded the burnoose into a pile and settled it on the
banquette, the fat man grinned suddenly in the direction
of the camera, full face, before the Negro took him by the
elbow and led him across the room.

When they reached the other side of the tent, the Negro
put the cabled instrument under his arm, the minuteglass
in his teeth, and clapped. The midgets came forward,

grinning. The Negro handed the minuteglass to one midget and the cabled instrument to the other. He then clapped repeatedly for the attention of the caressing women. They broke their embraces and sat back individually, intent on obeying but overcoming sharp anxiety to do so. With a gesture, the Negro indicated for the women to turn and face the striped cloth wall of the tent. They did as he bid. He then arranged them just so.

The fat man was grinning. The Negro turned back from arranging the women and took the cabled instrument from the one midget. He positioned himself behind the first woman lined up along the banquette and gently placed the ringed end of the instrument over her head, adjusting the slip knot on it so that the woman could feel it bite into her flesh. He stepped back and nodded to the fat man and to the other midget, the one holding the minuteglass filled with sand.

The fat man instantly stepped forward and was guided into the first woman. He threw back his head and thrust forward, eyes closed, blind with pleasure. The midget holding the minuteglass watched the sands smoothly fall from the upper section to the lower one. When the sand was all gone from the upper section, the midget nudged the Negro on the elbow and he lay the cold steel handles of the garrote on the first woman's back and clapped.

The fat man opened his eyes and stepped back. The Negro then took the ringed section from about the woman's neck and stepped backward down the banquette to the next woman, the midgets and the fat man following. The Negro slipped the ring of the garrote carefully over the head of the next woman and stepped aside.

The process was repeated for the third and fourth women, the sands running safely down, until the hideous ritual entered its second round, with the fat man returning to the first woman. But she was spared. He moved away from her and the garrote was calmly slipped around the neck of the second woman in line.

There was tension now. The fat man was breathing
heavily. Out in front of the set, the sentries were nudging
each other excitedly and leering. There was an air of ex-
pectancy. The beautiful woman in the blue dress with the
gold peacocks smoked rapidly, enveloping herself and
her nemesis sentry in a cloud of heavy blue smoke. The
sharply dressed man in white trousers and black silk shirt
patted the side of the camera like the flank of a racehorse
and leaned in to observe the action.

The sands of time would soon expire.

CHAPTER SIX:
NINE DRAGONS

Hong Kong
August 17

Hong Kong was hot and humid. On the way in to the Kai Tak airport on approach pattern, the view of the fabulous city was spectacular. They flew over the narrow channel between the islands of Lantau and Lamma before dropping over Kowloon, that densely populated and mysterious area that shared one of the world's greatest harbors with Hong Kong Central across the water. The Swissair 747 glided down on the runway built out over the Kowloon Bay and Sam Borne was in business.

Like the other first-class passengers, Sam was ushered politely through customs and passport control and whisked on his way into town by the waiting limousine from the Regent. The limousine was nothing less than a dove-gray Rolls-Royce stretch model, and Sam was reminded once again of the generosity and concern for his comfort the Committee often showed. It touched him. There were always reminders of the less fortunate in this life, and on the way into town, the limousine passed crowded and dingy tenements and street urchins, vendors, hustlers and beggars of every type. The Orient was full of sharp contrasts and probably nowhere was this more the case than in Hong Kong, arguably the world's most cosmopolitan city and surely the most pronounced nexus on this earth between East and West, between the

Orient and the Occident. Sam always got a charge from
Hong Kong, and this time was no different.

He checked into the Regent and was shown to his room
with courteous dispatch. The room was on the ninth floor
and had a good view of the harbor and across it to the
downtown splendor of Hong Kong Central's closely
bunched skyscrapers with the green hills and mountains
looming up behind them. Sam had no more than tipped
the bellhop than his phone rang. He reached down and
snatched it up from the desk against the glass wall of his
suite.

"Hello, Mr. Borne. Welcome to Hong Kong."

"I'm in Kowloon." Sam recognized the omniscient
tone of a Committee contact.

"So you are. Your grasp of geography is impressive."

"Eat shit."

"The heat and humidity of Hong Kong—pardon me,
of Kowloon—have been known to make visitors irrita-
ble."

"What do you want?"

"I want to know how you feel. We know that you slept
on the plane."

It never failed to bite Sam's ass when the Committee
showed off how well they monitored him. They had certainly had somebody watching him all the way from
Ibiza, and of course somebody on the plane had kept
close tabs on him, but it still griped him when they
showed it off to him this way. It was one more way they
had of asserting their proprietorship: they never tired of
underlining for him the fact that in their unique contract
they owned him outright—lock, stock and barrel.

"I feel grungy, sweaty, shitty. What's it to you?"

"We knew as much. Therefore we have set aside an
hour for you in which to take a leisurely bath in your
sunken marble tub after an invigorating shower. Perhaps—"

"My bathroom habits are my business."

"True enough. But we prefer that you not leave your room right now. You can have a massage if you like. Would you like?"

"No."

"Good. Then we suggest the shower, the relaxing bath and perhaps a catnap of a few minutes."

"That's what you suggest, is it?"

"Yes, because the tailor and his assistants will be there in an hour's time, and we'd like you fresh and pleasant for their sakes."

"I wouldn't dream of being anything but fresh and pleasant to a tailor."

"We thought as much."

"What else did you think?"

"We thought you'd be happy to know that we've arranged a new friend for today's round of sightseeing, shopping and dining."

"How thoughtful."

"We knew you'd like it. Enjoy your hour."

The phone clicked dead in Sam's hand. The bitch of it was that he had intended to shower first thing, and the idea of a relaxing bath was also a good one. Human nature was easy to know, if hard to gauge. This was only one of countless things in the Committee's favor. But, what the hell? There was nothing Sam could do. He would enjoy himself.

Sam stood for a minute admiring the view across the harbor. Off to the right, one of the green and white Star ferries churned its way toward Kowloon, a name, Sam knew, that meant nine dragons. The early Chinese settlers of this area believed that dragons lived along mountain ridges, and they believed the surrounding mountain ridges to be home to dragons, a symbol of majesty to all Chinese. There were only eight ridges, and when the young Sung Dynasty emperor arrived in the thirteenth century, he remarked upon this discrepancy. He was told that he was the ninth dragon. The Chinese definitely had

flair, and Sam knew of many a place that couldn't hold a
candle to Hong Kong when it came to just about anything
he liked to do.

Sam walked across the room and into the bathroom,
shedding his blazer as he went and tossing it onto the big
bed. In the bathroom he quickly peeled off his trousers
and his shorts and hopped into the shower, which he first
made as hot as he could stand and then suddenly snapped
on to cold, again as extreme as he could stand. The icy
water braced him. He hadn't felt this good since his run
on Ibiza. That seemed a year ago or more. Time always
danced away from you. It played its magic on you when
you flew halfway around the world in huge jets, tripping
over time zones like so many little stones in a swift
brook. Today the Mediterranean, tomorrow the South
China Sea. Sam's was no job for anyone who hated
travel.

He stepped out of the shower and over to the tub. He
threw the stopper in and hit the hot spigot. The water
came steaming into the marble in a great rush. He sat on
the edge of the tub and draped his feet in the steaming
water. It felt good. He reached over and mixed a little
cold water in with the hot. When the mixture seemed just
right, hot enough to relax his muscles and cool enough to
leave the skin on his ass, he slid in and sat back. He lolled
his head back and let himself go. He went into a deep
meditation, and from there into sleep. He dreamed of
dragons.

The sound of his room buzzer being hit repeatedly
brought Sam awake and alert instantly. He was ready for
anything. Only, here he was in a tub full of tepid water in
a strange hotel room. He remembered the tailor and knew
instantly who was at his door. He got out of the tub and
called across the suite.

"I'll be with you in a minute. Please wait."

"As you wish, sir."

Sam hopped back into the shower and rinsed off. He

climbed back out and wrapped himself in one of the large Turkish towels hung on the chrome racks. He grabbed another of the towels and wrapped it around his waist. Then he walked out and crossed the bedroom and opened the door partway. In the corridor stood an elderly Chinaman in a tropical blue suit and two much younger Chinamen with hefty valises at their feet. The younger Chinamen were dressed in slacks and open-necked shirts with short sleeves; on their feet were openwork sandals. The elderly man bowed low.

"How do you do, Mr. Borne?"

"Fine. And you?"

"Splendid. Thank you. May we come in and outfit you now?"

"Give me a minute, please. I'll be right with you."

"As you wish."

The old man bowed low again. Sam nodded and closed the door. He went back into the room and grabbed some underwear from his parachute bag and went back into the bathroom. He rubbed himself down vigorously. When he was dry he went out and crossed to his bag again and took his razor and shaving cream out and recrossed to the bathroom. Once there he shaved quickly. Then he pulled on his underwear and replaced his white duck trousers and reopened the door.

"Please come in."

"Thank you very kindly," the older man said. He turned and gestured to the two younger men, and they grabbed the handles on the big valises and all three entered the bedroom. Sam closed the door after them and turned to face all three. The older man bowed again, then spoke.

"I am Mr. Chung, esteemed tailor, Kowloon. And these are my two sons." He swept his arm toward the two younger men, both of whom bowed to Sam. "We have come at the insistence of your benefactor, name to be unknown, to make for you a wardrobe the benefactor wishes you to have. Today we measure, tomorrow you wear. We very good, very quick. Everything fit like glove.''

"I hope not. I'll be arrested for indecent exposure."

All three men laughed, the sons much more heartily than the father. Sam smiled.

"We will begin now," the old man said.

"First tell me if you'd care for anything from room service."

"No. We are fine, thank you."

"Well, let's get to it, shall we?"

"Directly, Mr. Borne. Please step up onto platform," Mr. Chung said, indicating the platform with a gesture. The valises were open around it, and inside them were layer upon layer of fabric swatches. Mr. Chung had shed his suit coat and stood waiting with a yellow and black tape measure draped around his neck. Sam stepped up onto the platform without a word. He prayed silently for Oriental efficiency and a lightning-fast fitting, and he wasn't disappointed. All three Chungs set right to work.

Sam gazed off toward the harbor. Some junks rocked along amid sailboats and a launch or two. The sailboats had bright nylon sails of blue and orange and red and white, some solid, some striped, all combining to make a pleasing medley of primary colors. The junks had patched sails of old cloth, mostly sandy khaki and dull gray. He wanted to get this over with and get out across the water to Hong Kong Central and some excitement.

The Chungs, *père et fils,* worked with more efficiency than an Indy pit crew. They measured Sam across the shoulders, down the arms, across the chest, around the waist, along his inseams. They measured and calibrated his body, top, sides and bottom, front and back. They marked things down on a piece of paper and they smiled up at Sam constantly. They took swatches from the valises, took numbers off them and replaced them in the valises. Never did they ask Sam what he'd like, or which of two fabrics or cuts he preferred. They didn't ask him anything. They never made a false move; they never wasted a motion.

None of this displeased Sam. He loved good tailoring, and he knew when they were through with him tomorrow he'd look good. He also knew that, from the way the Committee dressed him, he'd have a strong clue as to what role he'd have to act out. Again Sam thanked his stars for his training at the Royal Academy of Dramatic Art. It wouldn't do for him, in his line of work, to assume that because he had the clothes he had the role down. He also had to know how to assume any identity, how to make himself believable in any guise. His ninja training didn't hurt with any of this, but he would surely look and act the horse's ass, and likely wind up dead, if all he had for background was a method actor's bag of tricks.

Before they left and after Sam had stepped down from the portable platform, the Chungs had one last measurement to make. Like a mad phrenologist, Mr. Chung took from one of the valises a set of rings and slipped them over Sam's head until he found the ring that fit perfectly. He marked something on his paper and smiled at Sam.

"We are finished, Mr. Borne."

"Good. Is everything in working order?"

Mr. Chung looked at Sam quizzically. His two sons did likewise. They didn't get Sam's brand of humor. Sam smiled, and they realized he had made a joke. Then all three smiled broadly.

"Tomorrow we return with complete wardrobe. Everything perfect."

"Fine," Sam said. "I'll look forward to it."

The Chung sons hefted the valises, and the father bowed and led the way to the door. Sam hurried over and opened the door for them and then extended his hand to each in turn. They all shook hands and left smiling. Sam closed the door and walked over to the window and looked out again. The harbor was still a hive of activity.

Shipping of every description, large and small, elaborate and simple, Oriental and Western, ancient and modern, plied the silvery waters.

Sam looked across the harbor to Hong Kong island. The skyscrapers soared in bland whiteness against the green backdrop of hills and mountains. Victoria Peak loomed above everything. Sam always thought of cities in terms of other cities. Hong Kong was the Manhattan of the Orient.

Sam walked back into the room and lay down across the broad bed. If I know the Committee, he thought, my "new friend" won't be long in calling. He closed his eyes and let his mind white out like a skier's vision in a blizzard.

Sam knew this: he would have to wear a hat for this assignment, and tomorrow he would know which one. I wear more hats, Sam thought, than a vaudeville clown; the difference is I play only tragedies.

The phone rang.

CHAPTER SEVEN:
DOWN AND DEAD

Sun Sun Compound
Central Highlands, Vietnam
August 17

The air was still. Across the compound nothing moved. No one came. No one went. The sun beat down steadily and all was quiet. Flies buzzed in the air. All around the basin the mountains reared up in their jungle-green majesty. Far away, off in the distance, figures moved to and fro on the mountainsides, but down in the compound all was still. It was late afternoon.

From one of the central cinder-block buildings, a contingent of Vietnamese bearing AK-47s emerged. They were fierce-looking men. There were five of them, all wearing discarded United States Army fatigues. Across their shoulders and around their chests were bandoliers full of ammunition. They looked ready to take on an army. Behind them came a group of four midgets, also armed to the teeth but carrying their AK-47s with the determination and the unwieldiness of normal men carrying ladders. They crossed the central opening of the compound, a parade ground roughly the size of a football field ringed by buildings. Many of the structures were thrown together from bamboo and palm fronds and hardly afforded any shelter against the elements, while others, in sharp contrast, were fashioned sturdily from cinder blocks and with pitched roofs made from good lumber and painted white.

The men marched, one group in front, the other behind, up to a particularly ragged building, nothing more than a hut really, and called out loudly in Vietnamese. The bamboo door to the hut was lifted from within and a Vietnamese dressed in fatigues came out, followed by the wasted figure of an American. Behind the American came another Vietnamese with a Kalashnikov assault rifle. The two men guarding the emaciated American said something fast and short in Vietnamese to the other men, and they all laughed. Then one guard turned and smashed the butt of his rifle into the shoulders of the American, and he pitched forward onto the ground.

After a brutally hard kick in the ass, the American managed to get himself onto all fours. He was dressed in flimsy black pants and a drab green T-shirt. His face was gaunt, his eyes sunken. He trembled on his arms and legs. It was all he could do not to collapse into the dust of the hot compound and stay there forever. The inside of his right forearm was stitched with a veritable railroad track of needle marks. Tears ran from his glassy eyes. A whitish snot ran from his nose, and mucus beaded in the corners of his mouth. Sweat stood out all over his ruined body, and when he rose to his feet again, he instinctively rubbed each upper arm and shoulder for warmth.

The Vietnamese laughed and prodded him with their rifles. Two of them, realizing the American was too weak to make it across the compound on his own, each grabbed an arm and half dragged, half carried him across the compound accompanied by his escort, with the midgets bringing up the rear. One of the midgets had a black medical bag slung over his shoulder. It swayed against his side as he walked along, balancing his AK-47 on his other shoulder. Another midget had a camera pack dangling from his shoulder. It jounced on his hip as he moved across the compound with the rest of the contingent. The American's feet left two runnels in the sandy dirt behind him.

They took the American to a hut at the edge of the compound. Beyond the ring of buildings were revetments of sandbags surrounding helicopter pads. A Huey slick sat on one and on another was a Cobra with its rocket and minigun pods bulging from its tiny wings. One of the Vietnamese in the lead looked at his watch. As if on cue, the whirring of a chopper's rotor could be heard. In a flash another Huey appeared over the ridge of one of the surrounding mountains. It set down, beating dust devils from the earth within the revetment. Out of the Huey jumped a band of sentries, and behind them, lumbering, came a big man with American dimensions but with mutilated eyes, an ogre with the face of a lizard. It was Doctor Sun Sun, the owner and sole proprietor of the compound.

Doctor Sun Sun was tricked out in a white linen tropical suit. From a distance he looked like Sidney Greenstreet in *Casablanca*. Up close he looked like a big iguana in a white suit with a job of plastic surgery done by an epileptic in seizure. In full flower, Doctor Sun Sun left the word "ugly" wilting on the vine; he was as far beyond ugly as rape was beyond woo. He was gross and obscene.

Like a debarking politician, Doctor Sun Sun waved to the contingent with the American as soon as he had cleared the spinning rotors of the Huey. The sentries trailed him as he walked off in the direction of the hut where the American kneeled outside in exhaustion and misery in the midst of his tormentors, who poked and prodded him for the sheer hell of it and because they knew each blow only increased his conviction that he had reached the very depths of the damned, an impression Doctor Sun Sun was determined soon to disabuse him of. The Doctor approached, trailed by his sentries and by a two-man crew carrying a minicam and a recorder with battery pack and microphone.

When Doctor Sun Sun and his entourage reached the

hut where the others waited, he greeted them all with a beaming smile.

"I'm right on time, I see," he said.

"Right on time, Doctor," one of the waiting sentries replied.

"Good, good, boys. After all, you can't operate without the good doctor, now can you?"

"No good operate without doctor," the sentries replied. They had obviously been rehearsed in this exchange. It had been used by them before, and they felt some sense of well-being and of duty fulfilled when they used it. They grinned at Sun Sun and he grinned back.

Sun Sun stepped into the circle around the American and snatched a handful of the man's matted hair and wrenched his head back violently. He peered down at the man and grinned.

"This man needs a doctor, gentlemen. I have never seen a worse case. You say he tried to get away from here, did he?"

The sentries and the midgets laughed. They didn't understand all the words, but they got the message.

"Why, this boy has been on some type of medication, it would seem, gentlemen, judging by the track marks running up and down his arms."

Sun Sun held up the man's right forearm so all could see the wide zipperwork of the needle tracks. Around the tracks the man's arm was stained purple and blue and yellow—many of his veins had collapsed long ago. Sun Sun reached out and squeezed the man's cheeks together and looked intently into his mouth. He had lost many teeth and the effectiveness of his smile long ago. Malnutrition had worked its evil in him to the fullest. Sun Sun flicked him forward and he toppled face first into the sandy dirt and lay there twitching.

"This boy, gentlemen, needs surgery." Sun Sun turned to the midget with the black medical bag and motioned for him to come to his side. He did. Sun Sun took the bag from him and looked at the Vietnamese sentry who'd spoken to him in English when he'd arrived.

"I want this patient taken into the hospital here and prepared for major surgery. I'll be ready directly, sir. And I want this done promptly." He nodded and the sentry nodded back.

The sentry turned and snapped an order in Vietnamese. The two sentries who'd dragged the American here now reached out and hauled him to a kneeling position. With his knees scraping the ground, they hauled him into the openwork hut. In the hut, rays of sunlight slanted in from the slits between the bamboo walls and between the fronds on the roof. The light lay in stripes across the green shirt and black pants of the wretched American. Without another word being said to them, the two sentries pitched the man down on the sandy dirt floor. Then one sentry stooped down and scooped him up in both hands and flipped him onto his back like a dying fish. From its resting place against one wall, the other sentry took a strange apparatus made of bamboo. It was a big cube with sides about seven feet long; as reinforcement two long poles crisscrossed it diagonally in back.

The sentry with the large bamboo rack dropped it onto the floor next to the American. It sent up a thick dust cloud that swirled in the striped sunlight. The two sentries then took him by the ankles and wrists and heaved him into the center of the rack. Next they took thick hemp from one corner of the hut and tied him to the four corners of the rack with it. When they had him firmly lashed down, they called out and the others entered, Doctor Sun Sun in the lead with his suit coat removed and with a large apron tied over an extra-large pair of black fisherman's waders. His sleeves were rolled up to his biceps. He looked down at the American and smiled at the two sentries who'd prepared him, and nodded. The sentries, grateful for his approval, nodded back. Then Sun Sun looked around, making sure the rest of his crew was in place.

The midget with the medical bag came up and stood beside Sun Sun. The midget with the camera, a black late-model Nikon, positioned himself off to one side and in front of Sun Sun. In the middle of the floor was a grate of bamboo the size of a mattress; from under it came a cacophony of cheeping and screeching. Sun Sun looked to the Vietnamese who understood English and spoke in a ham's voice: "Well, I can see that my services are once again called for, gentlemen. And I won't keep you folks waiting."

He reached over and opened the black medical bag held out to him by the midget. The man with the minicam came up and settled himself on one knee behind and off to the side of Sun Sun. He had fixed a light bar to his camera, and had attached the battery pack, which he held strapped over his shoulder and against his hip. His assistant fussed around him.

Sun Sun nodded to the sentries and they grabbed the rack and hauled it upright. Six of them braced themselves against it, two behind and four to the sides. They pushed and pulled against each other, making sure it was firm and that it didn't have much give. Sun Sun stepped up to the rack and feigned an examination, long and slow and deliberate. Then he turned to the midget with the medical bag and reached into it and extracted a surgical scalpel. The cameraman hit the switch on the minicam, and the bar of lights flooded the rack and Sun Sun with intense light. Sun Sun stepped up closer to the rack and slashed first this way and then that. The green T-shirt and the black pants fell away from the American and landed in pieces on the dirt floor. Despite the intense light flooding him from the minicam's bar, the American stared straight ahead like the sightless.

Sun Sun casually extended his hand with the scalpel and cut a tiny square in the skin over the man's breastbone. The incisions drew blood. The man made not a sound. Rivulets of blood started to course down his bony chest. Sun Sun frowned at his initial cuts, pretending to examine them, playing at the most serious profession on earth.

"This will have to come out, I'm afraid. Well, my little pets below can use an appetizer, I'm sure." With a twisting motion of thumb and forefinger, like a man peeling an apple, Sun Sun reached out and dug the scalpel under the square of flesh outlined on the man's chest. Blood spurted everywhere. The man cried out in pain, writhing back against the crisscrossed bars of bamboo. His body jerked in spasms as Sun Sun worked the scalpel patiently under the patch of skin. Blood ran down his hand, over his wrist, on down his forearm, dropped off his elbow and landed in the dry dirt of the floor. As Sun Sun tweezered the flesh off his chest, the man screamed, bucked and passed out.

Sun Sun held up the square of flesh. Blood spurted from the man's chest, a thick stream that ran down his torso and over his genitals before dropping off into the sandy dirt, where it formed dark stains. Sun Sun waved the dripping flesh before his audience.

"This will make a hell of a canape, gentlemen. My pets will get all worked up competing for this baby." He pivoted on his heels and walked to the center of the room. The sentries scrambled ahead of him and pushed back the bamboo grate over the opening. The cameraman followed close behind Sun Sun and came up and stationed himself beside him. Sun Sun let the tiny pelt of flesh quiver over the opening, dripping blood. The screeching and the cheeping grew louder, more frenzied. Sun Sun looked down, and the cameraman moved up beside him and flooded the opening with light. It was an oubliette, the French type of dungeon with an opening only at the top. On the floor of the dungeon, rats scrambled this way and that. Frenzied, they threw themselves against each

other, over each other, around each other, cheeping and
screeching in extreme hunger. Where the blood dripped
on them from the pelt Sun Sun held as if for a begging
dog, the rats scrambled over each other, standing on their
hind legs on each other's backs in a frantic contest to see
who would be king of the hill. No sooner would one rat
gain ascendancy than the others would knock it back and
another would rear on its hind legs like a prairie dog and
take its place.

Sun Sun dropped the flesh into the dungeon and the rats
went berserk. They lashed out at each other, biting and
snapping and tearing and pushing and charging. A tank of
piranhas could not have devoured the flesh sooner. Sun
Sun chuckled softly.

"Well, gentlemen, these little darlings are in a fine
mood today. I don't think they should be kept waiting too
much longer, do you?" He looked around at the sentries
and the midgets, all of whom grinned and nodded. Behind them the American on the rack groaned his way
back to consciousness. Beneath the cut in his chest, the
whiteness of his breastbone stood out against the bright
red of his oozing blood. His knees had buckled forward
and the weight of his body stretched his thin arms and
shoulders to the point where they were about ready to slip
their sockets.

Sun Sun stepped back from the oubliette, and the
crowd around him backpedaled quickly over to the rack.
Sun Sun hesitated slightly to allow the cameraman to re-
position himself before moving directly into position before the bleeding and helpless man. When the moment
was right, he reached out and grabbed the man's scrotum
and pulled it forward. The man groaned and tried to focus
on his torturer. Sweat had popped out on his face and
mixed there with the dirt and dust from the times he'd
been pushed into the ground.

"This part is nice and tender. The boys'll appreciate
this delicacy for sure." Sun Sun slashed with quick, short

strokes, and the man screamed an ungodly scream and ground his buttocks back into the crossmembers on the rack. When Sun Sun stepped back, he held in his hand the striated flesh of the man's scrotum. He looked back and saw the exposed twin testicles hanging bloody and quivering. Without a second's hesitation he snipped each cleanly off. The man passed out, his blood pooling blackly in the sandy dirt.

Sun Sun walked over to the oubliette and paused just long enough for the cameraman to get the right angle before he tossed the testicles in like two agates in an easy game of marbles. The rats swarmed, mad with energy, driven by hunger. When they were all bunched in two groups around the testicles, Sun Sun flipped the textured flesh of the scrotum as far away from the warring groups as possible. En masse the rats scrambled in the new direction.

"Damn, but I love effort. I love to see a scramble like this. It reminds you what life is all about, doesn't it, gentlemen?" The sentries and the midgets knew Sun Sun's question was rhetorical. They knew he rarely spoke in expectation of an answer. For Sun Sun, other people were adjuncts to his ego, mere props provided for the high drama of his own center-stage existence.

One of the sentries behind Sun Sun spoke up in Vietnamese. Without turning around, Sun Sun mumbled, "Dammit. I was hoping this boy would hold on through this operation, but I guess he's another one I'll lose halfway through." Sun Sun rubbed his jaw and turned in the direction of the rack. He snapped off an order in Vietnamese, and the sentries picked up the rack and carried it over to him. The cameraman followed the rack with the camera as it came toward him. The mutilated American flopped about with the jostling of the rack as the sentries walked it over.

Sun Sun looked quickly at the spread-eagled American and knew he would last only minutes longer. The man had completely lost consciousness. Without a word, Sun Sun stooped down and slashed the hemp pinning the man's ankles to the rack. He took a step back and the sentries hoisted the rack, three on a side, like pallbearers. The American swung out away from the rack, his body depending from it completely. The three sentries on each side passed the rack hand over hand across the oubliette to more sentries on the other side until the victim swung out over the opening.

No sooner did the American's legs fall into the oubliette than the rats swarmed and leaped up onto him. His last agonized groans played out in the silence as the rats gnawed into the flesh of his calves, leaping and swarming over each other. They were in a feeding frenzy that would have done sharks or hyenas justice. As soon as the rats had stripped the flesh from the bones of the lower legs and the feet, Sun Sun gave the signal and one of the sentries leaned over with a jungle knife and cut a single strand away from the knot around each of the dead man's wrists. His body slipped down another foot and a half into the dungeon.

The camera recorded the process of the rats stripping the man's thighs of flesh. Again they ripped and tore and fought. Chunks of flesh were gouged time after time. In a matter of minutes the man's bloody bones were exposed from his hips to his feet. At a final signal from Sun Sun, the sentry leaned out and slashed the knots with his jungle knife, and the head and torso of the American tumbled into the pit. Rats swarmed over the head and torso in waves. The cameraman recorded it all.

"Well, men," Sun Sun roared, "this will make a good instructional film for the rest of the American boys working with us. They won't be too eager to resign their commissions with us and leave the compound after they see what happened to Captain Fuller for trying just that. Have this film processed immediately and get the boys up at four tomorrow and show them this baby before their injections. Then get them working in the fields.''

Sun Sun stared down into the pit, a tremendous smile lighting his face.

CHAPTER EIGHT:
SHIPPING AND HANDLING

Hong Kong
August 17

Sam caught the phone before it rang twice.

"Mr. Borne? Hello, I am—"

"You're my friend for a day, right?"

"Right."

"And you're here to show me the sights and sounds of this wondrous city, right?"

"Right."

"And you're downstairs, right?"

"Right. And—"

"And just where are you downstairs?"

"Thank you for allowing me a more than one word answer."

"You're welcome and you're where?"

"I'm in the lobby." The friend had a lilting Chinese voice, very soft, very subtle, very patient.

"How will I know you?"

"I'm wearing a mint-green dress."

"I'll be right down." Sam hung up before his newest friend could say anything more. When the Committee was so clearly in control, Sam took the only defense he could and fought to control as much of the give and take between him and the Committee's emissaries as he possibly could.

It was an odd thing about the people the Committee

sent his way; they were always reliable conduits of the best information, but Sam was convinced, having seen some of them tortured to death before they could supply information the torturers wanted, that they rarely or never understood the real significance of what they were doing. Most of them, Sam realized, were being used as surely as he himself was. Like Sam, they probably had only a few things in common with the Committee: most likely its hatred of totalitarian abuse and its determination to put a stop to the mad schemes of people with plans to misrule the world. Whatever their role in the Committee's eyes, to Sam these emissaries were always people he had to control to some degree. So he controlled them.

Sam crossed to his suitcase and took out a fresh canary-yellow polo shirt and slipped it over his well-muscled torso. He tucked its flaps into his white ducks, slipped his feet into his moccasins and retrieved his blazer from its resting place on the foot of the bed. He went into the bathroom, doused his face in cold water, rubbed the Turkish towel over it and stood back and gave himself the onceover in the full-length mirror. He looked like any other casual tourist.

Sam left the bathroom, crossed the bedroom and snared his room key off the desk against the glass wall. He glanced out at the gorgeous harbor and knew he'd soon be out in the city and was glad. He left without a second thought. It always amused Sam when he read thrillers to see the tricks the spies used, like balancing a human hair on a suitcase latch. He had nothing to hide, nothing to steal. All of the information he carried he had carried since his days of training. Nobody could tap into it, nobody could steal it. Only Sam could use it, and by extension the Committee. Another thing the spies in thrillers were always doing was trying to see who was shadowing them, or whether a car was tailing them in traffic. They were always ducking into department stores and coming out different doors and hopping on and off crowded sub-

way cars. Stuff like that was what got all those CIA types
dead.

Sam hit the button, the elevator came and he got in. On
the way down he thought more about his so-called business. He supposed there were agents who were into intrigue; some of them probably snooped around trying to
filch secrets about the first computer with a personality
disorder or something. But as for him, it was all fuck or
be fucked. By the time an assignment landed on Sam's
agenda, all the tricks had been played. The CIA had
fucked up and the KGB had counter-fucked up, or vice
versa, or Interpol had triple fucked up. Or somebody else
had quadruple fucked up. At any rate, it was all fucked
up.

The elevator reached the lobby and Sam got out and
looked for a mint-green dress and found it immediately.
It was on a demure young beauty who looked like a Chinese equivalent of Marie Osmond: Miss Goody Fortune
Cookie. Sam crossed the lobby and went up to the brown
leather armchair in which Miss Goody Fortune Cookie
sat. She watched in silence as he came up to her and gave
him a small smile from under a conical straw planter's
hat.

"I'm Borne."

"I know."

"I know you know. But we have to start somewhere."

"Yes."

"And you're?"

"Wing."

"Wing?"

"Yes, Ling Wing."

"One of your parents a poet?"

"That is impolite."

"You're right. I apologize." Sam was famous for his
attitude. He always had this edge when he met Committee escorts. They were invariably so fucking dedicated it
was maddening. Dedicated to occupying Mr. Borne, to

informing Mr. Borne, even to instructing and chaperoning Mr. Borne.

"Are you hungry?" she asked.

"Somewhat."

"Would you like to have something to eat here in the Harbourside Restaurant with the view across the water?"

"It's the same view as my room. Would you like to go up and see it and order room service?"

"No. Are you going to be rude all day?"

"Not all day. More than half of it's gone."

"Where would you like to eat?"

"Anywhere."

"This is no help. I know Hong Kong. It is my city. I know many places to eat."

"Congratulations."

"I meant only I could take you where you'd enjoy." Ling Wing's tone was imploring and hurt. Sam felt like a schmuck. She was probably a terrific person. She probably didn't even know anything like the Committee existed. In all likelihood she was doing this task today because she believed in some big abstract concept of freedom that was worthy of the gods and with no more idea of what really went on than Mother Goose. It was time to lighten up.

"What I'd really like to do is leave here and ride the Star ferry, how's that sound to you?"

"Splendid. I love the Star ferry."

"Let's go." Sam stuck out his hand and Ling Wing took it and he helped her up from the chair. He smiled at her. It was time to make amends and to see what the day held and what Ling Wing could tell him that might just keep him alive on the far side of his date with Doctor Sun Sun.

"Is this your first visit to Hong Kong, Mr. Borne?"

"Sam, please. No, it's not."

"And still you like to ride the ferry, not take tunnel?"

"In New York I ride the Staten Island ferry for the hell

of it. In San Francisco I ride the Marin ferry. I ride ferries
all over, whenever I can.''

"Oh?"

"Oh."

"Why?"

"They always know where they're headed. They always come back to where they've been. They show a
sense of commitment I can relate to."

"I understand."

"Do you?"

"Yes. Consistency you admire."

"Something like that."

They passed out of the air-conditioned lobby and into
the heat and humidity outside. The air sat on their faces
like a fat lady's ass, but it was still exhilarating to be in
downtown Kowloon, and in minutes they would feel the
refreshing breeze as the ferry made its way across the harbor. They turned left and walked the three hundred odd
meters to the ferry terminal. Inside they put seventy cents
apiece into the turnstile and walked through for the upper
deck. The lower deck was twenty cents cheaper, and
faster if you were in a hurry, but they weren't in a hurry
and Sam preferred the view from the top. They didn't
have long to wait, as usual, A green and white ferry
pulled into the slip and unloaded its passengers for
Kowloon, and the gate went up and the mad rush was on
for those going to Central.

Sam and Ling went to the front of the upper deck and
stood looking off toward the peak as the bells rang below
and the ferry chugged out into the harbor. Gulls wheeled
about the ferry, dipping, squawking and landing on the
superstructure. The briny air was invigorating. It was always a marvel to Sam how the ferries in Hong Kong managed not to ram into the sailboats, tugs, barges, the
occasional police launch and all the other craft in the harbor, especially the special cruise junks set up for tourists.

What would have been chaotic disorder in the West was ordered chaos in the East. It was a marvel.

As they passed an authentic junk, Sam noted how like outsized fans the huge sails really were. The khaki mainsail on this particular junk hardly stirred in the harbor breeze; its wooden ribs spiraled out from the mast and wavered only slightly. The thought that these junks or ones just like them had sailed these waters for centuries made Sam humble. In the West they were always oohing and aahing over a three-hundred-year-old oaken door or escritoire, but to Sam more impressive by far was a mode of transportation thousands of years old that still got the job done. Hong Kong was a timeless town, as modern as tomorrow and as old as the four basic elements of earth, air, fire and water.

"We are coming to end of ferry ride. What next?" Ling asked. Sam looked down at her and saw a wide smile beneath her conical straw hat. He knew in the fullness of time she would get around to telling him what he needed to know. He had no definite plan to follow, but when in Hong Kong he did like to take the old tram to the peak and to look out at the whole panorama laid out below.

"What did you have in mind?" he asked.

"Not important. Only important what you want to do."

"In that case can you arrange for a private running of the ponies at Happy Valley, or better yet at Shatin?"

Ling frowned. She wasn't sure whether Sam was back to his streak of sarcasm or whether this was some special brand of American humor. It wouldn't do to keep her suspended.

"I'm only kidding," he said. "I know it's out of season for the horses now. It's just that I love to see thoroughbreds run with some of my money on their nose, and the silks and the crowds and the cheering and screaming here in Hong Kong are hard to beat. Understand?"

"No. Gambling no good."

"You must only be Chinese on the outside if you don't like gambling, especially on horses."

"No. No good." Sam had hit a nerve. He bet to himself that Ling Wing was the daughter or the granddaughter of a man who'd ruined himself with gambling. The Chinese were mad for it, and in Hong Kong it was practically the chief religion. Still, it wouldn't do to take this conversation farther with Ling Wing. She was dead set against it.

"I'd like to wander up to the peak eventually, if it's all the same to you. Other than that, I'm yours for the rest of the afternoon and evening."

"You like peak too, like ferry?"

"Yeah, I'm the world's foremost tourist."

"What you like about peak?"

"It knows where it stands." Sam smiled, Ling smiled. She got this one. The ferry bounced into the slip at Central, the bells sounded, the gate went up and the crowd scrambled off, the other gate holding back the passengers waiting to board. Even when they weren't in a hurry, the citizens of Hong Kong always rushed. During rush hour it was murder, millions rushing here, millions rushing there.

Sam and Ling let the crowd go and then followed. When they got out to the street, there were a few rickshaws lined up along the curb with the pullers crouched between their traces.

"I think we go to Hollywood Road and see some shops," Ling announced.

"Okay. That's not very far, is it?"

"No. Couple minutes. We take tram."

"Hold on a minute." Sam walked over to the first rickshaw puller in line and started to haggle with him for the fare to Hollywood Road. Ling came over to them, close enough to hear their exchange but far enough not to seem a party to their negotiations. Sam knew she'd probably never ridden in a rickshaw; after all, they were expensive as hell, the government wouldn't issue any new licenses for them and in a couple of years they'd be gone altogether from Hong Kong, all of which made it a better idea to Sam to get a ride in while you still could. They settled on a price. It was outrageous, but only half what the puller originally asked for.

Sam got in and looked back at Ling. She held her ground, glancing around as though trying to ascertain who the silly man in the rickshaw was waving to. Sam understood the level of her embarrassment, but he didn't give a damn; the only good snob was a reverse snob.

"C'mon, Ling, I haven't got all day."

"I know. Half the day is gone, remember?" She was all right after all; she could still get some of her own back.

Ling started forward, then hesitated. This was beyond her threshold of embarrassment, so Sam appealed to the thing that always got to his Committee emissaries.

"Remember how important today's work is. I think you should get in here quick." It worked every time. She came forward with a few mincing steps, then fairly bounded into the rickshaw and leaned back as far as she could go, hoping that the green canopy would shield her from the public. The puller bent down and hoisted the traces, and they took off at a trot, weaving in and out of the heavy Central district traffic. All around them skyscrapers of glass and steel soared. The feeling was exactly the same as in lower Manhattan, except for the rickshaws and the double-decker trams and the fact that most of the cars were small and there were scooters galore and too many bicycles for Manhattan.

In minutes they reached Hollywood Road. Ling leaped out of the red rickshaw and scurried into a shop. Sam paid the driver, who tried to convince him to have his picture snapped with an authentic rickshaw puller and his rig for an outrageous fee. Sam was not unaware that the pullers made more money posing for photos than they did transporting people, and he refused.

Sam entered the shop Ling had fled into and found her moving among the objects piled helter-skelter all over the place. An old lady with a kind face that was heavily wrinkled around a mouth creased into a permanent smile, trailed Ling as she tried to sell her everything in the shop, even though she couldn't have failed to note that Ling was hardly the typical tourist, replying as she did in Cantonese. The old lady turned when the bell above the door sounded as Sam entered. She was delighted to have another customer, and when Sam spoke familiarly to Ling in English, her heart leaped for joy. Sam looked like the monied American type, and the old lady was sure he'd married this lovely Chinese girl and would buy her whatever she desired. The old lady redoubled her efforts with Ling, singing up and down the scales of Cantonese like a lark.

While Ling danced away and the old lady followed doggedly, Sam took in the shop. It was loaded with heavy carved furniture of the kind favored by the Chinese middle class. There were lacquered panels and decorative lamps and bric-a-brac of every sort. After Ling had completed her round of the shop, she broke the old lady's heart by politely taking Sam by the arm and leaving empty-handed.

Back on the street, they strolled along and Sam was surprised how easily Ling took his arm and walked him proprietarially. It was out of character for her, he was sure, yet she did it. She must have thought that it made him more comfortable with her, or maybe she thought by doing it she could head off another outburst of sarcasm. No matter. Out of character for her or not, Sam liked it and liked her for it.

They visited other shops where Ling inspected the merchandise carefully, seeming to enjoy the very act of browsing as much as buying, the true sign of the serious shopper. After a quick inspection, Sam would most often leave the shop and stand in front and watch the busy street life flow past.

In one shop Ling asked him if he would like to buy a particularly beautiful jade statue of a horse and rider. Ling told him it was a good buy, but Sam had no special use for it. He did not believe, like the Chinese, that jade was the elixir of life, or that it held any magical powers. He did not believe in superstition at all. Luck to him was more a function of character than fate. The Chinese felt differently. They believed jade was the stone of heaven. There were even stories of wealthy Chinese being buried in jade suits, of one emperor who had worn jade sandals and of another who had given his favorite concubine a jade bed. The concubine must have been a hot number indeed if she could warm up a jade bed, Sam had thought when he'd heard the story. Sam offered to buy the statue for Ling, but she only blushed and declined the offer.

In the late afternoon they stopped in the Hing Wan tea shop for a rest before grabbing the peak tram. The shop was crowded and business was brisk. It was amazing to watch the efficiency with which the waiters replaced empty teapots. Customers would merely turn a pot's top upside down and a passing waiter would grab it and replace it with a full pot on his return trip. There was no need for a verbal exchange. It was like the sign language the merchants used in the jade market, where they silently inserted their hands inside each other's loose sleeves and with pressure from the fingers on the forearm let each other know how much they offered and how much they demanded until finally the twain met and the bargain was struck. This was a far cry, literally, from the uproar on the floor of the stock exchange in Wall Street.

In the Hing Wan, Sam and Ling had *yum cha* and the little savories, *dim sum*. To start, they had wonderful pan-fried dumplings and tangy Shanghai onion cake, followed by four-season dumplings, colorful pastries filled with pork and shrimp and topped with minced black mushroom, onion, carrot and cilantro. They accompanied this treat with mild jasmine tea. It was here Ling Wing chose to open up with Sam about Doctor Sun Sun. All she knew was that Sam was some kind of government investigator sent here by the United States Treasury Department to help the local authorities curb the growing drug problem among the Hong Kong youth. Ling Wing told Sam that she was a local social worker involved with many groups doing work among youthful Chinese addicts. She had been told confidentially by one of her superiors that a man in Vietnam planned to challenge the virtual heroin monopoly enjoyed by the *chiu chau* syndicates, the gangsters from Shanghai who after World War Two vanquished the notorious Green Gang for control of the Hong Kong drug trade. This man from Vietnam intended to compete with the present-day syndicates by flooding the streets and tenements of the Crown Colony with cheap heroin, thus making it readily available to any youngster who wanted to try it.

Of course, Sam was amused by this. Ling was being used. Sun Sun's target, as the Committee well knew, was not Hong Kong youth but American youth. And the role of the *chiu chau* syndicates was clear. Theirs was an act of self-preservation. Through the Committee and ultimately through Sam Borne, they would nail Sun Sun, thus protecting their gigantic share of the American market against being undercut by the Doctor's cheaper smack.

It wouldn't have surprised Sam to learn that the superior who had recruited Ling Wing for this assignment was in fact a member of the *chiu chau* syndicates. Hong Kong society was a complicated affair. The women rolling through the crowded streets from hilltop villas in pink Rolls-Royces were often the wives and mistresses of big gangsters with tight covers in legitimate businesses. Often these legitimate businesses were themselves profitable, if not so profitable as the money being made in gambling, prostitution and drugs, especially in drugs. Like their Western counterparts, Chinese gangsters wanted to be respectable. That was why the ladies in the pink Rollses were often headed to charitable functions, to community work and to other laudable enterprises.

Sam knew it was all a sham. Still, it was a fact that madmen like Sun Sun were not to be trifled with. They deemed world domination a game plan and not a delusion. They meant to win and to win big. If they had to wreck American society to do it, so be it. If they had to make freedom a historical artifact, like simony, that was that. Only when the globe was theirs would they be satisfied.

Later, over dinner at the restaurant atop the peak, Sam learned more about Sun Sun and his operation from Ling. They took the green tram, really a funicular, to the top and strolled around Lugard Road for an hour. The view overlooking the bustling harbor was spectacular, and off in the distance in the clear twilight they could see into China and Macao. They were lucky not to have cloud cover and to get such a clear evening. On their stroll, they made mostly small talk, but over dinner Ling opened up again about Doctor Sun Sun.

Ling told Sam that Sun Sun had not only gained control of the vice and crime in most of Vietnam, especially in Ho Chi Minh City, but that he had set up a vast network in the backcountry for growing and processing his own heroin. This involved a virtual fortress in the Central Highlands where he had a work force kept under guard by sentries and where he had a private cadre of very rough midgets overseeing administration and processing and even his personal needs. The midgets were a sort of Praetorian guard in reverse; they were fierce, ruthless and specially trained to guard and protect Sun Sun at all costs. Yet, instead of being giants they were midgets. There was a very practical reason for this.

Sun Sun had built his mountain redoubt in the Central Highlands over an old underground network left over from the heyday of the Vietcong. All of the key buildings of Sun Sun's compound were connected underground by passages and tunnels. The midgets had the run of the place. They were vastly more efficient than taller guards would have been at controlling the vast underground network. The entire compound was an unbelievable hive, constructed on several levels below the earth and making the place impregnable in many respects.

Sam did not tell Ling that he had seen a photo of the compound taken from the air by a spy plane. From the air it seemed innocent enough. Most of the buildings looked like nothing but native structures of bamboo and palm found in any Vietnamese mountain village. The square buildings of cinder block with white pitched roofs did not look native, but they weren't so unusual, considering some of the buildings the Americans had constructed during their years there and considering that the Communists were trying their feckless best to modernize the country. It wasn't so farfetched to think that Sun Sun's compound housed a large mountain cooperative set up by the Communists since their takeover.

What Ling did not know and what Sam understood was that the forced-labor contingent at the compound was made up of Americans listed as POWs and MIAs. Many of the forced laborers were former United States fliers. The thought of well-trained fliers being forced to toil out their existence in the earth, growing opium, was painful to Sam beyond description. These were men trained to operate at high levels of challenge and technological excellence, and here they were exploited, wasted and penalized by a madman. More than a few of the captured Americans had been chopper pilots during the police action. Choppers were the most dangerous craft to fly. When something went wrong in a chopper, there was no hope of a nice glide or a skilled emergency landing. A chopper failure was a chopper fatality. If the Jesus nut gave out on your rotor, it was next stop eternity and an interview with Jesus himself, since all you'd do was plunge straight down to earth. This was exactly the kind of injustice that set Sam's teeth on edge. What was worse, the Committee dossier detailed how the forced-labor contingent at Sun Sun's compound was deliberately addicted to heroin and worked fourteen straight hours in the sweltering fields. On top of this, Sun Sun subjected the American fliers to psychological torture and to brain-washing techniques, sometimes waking them in the mid-dle of the night or early in the morning to watch the pornographic movies he distributed worldwide or to show them torture films starring former buddies. It all put Sam in a cold rage.

"Would you like dessert?" Ling asked. The question snapped Sam back to the present. He would have plenty of time to work up his dander at Sun Sun and his cohorts, so it was just as well to enjoy the moment. Their table had a first-class view and with the lights winking on all over Hong Kong and Kowloon it wouldn't do to sit and brood over Sun Sun and his thugs.

"Not really. I'm not a big dessert man, but you have whatever you like," Sam answered.

"I will have some ice cream."

"Terrific."

"Then we must get you back to hotel. You need good night's sleep for tomorrow."

Sam had been prepared for this. It was the chaperone's duty to make sure he got back early. Still, Sam could have his fun.

"I thought you might join me there for a nightcap," he said, knowing his words were only a tease.

Ling blushed. This kind of talk flustered her more than Sam expected.

"No. I must go home now."

"You're sure you're not going to meet your steady man?"

"Oh, no." Ling could not bring herself to raise her head and meet his eyes. "Like you, I have big day planned tomorrow. I must be home soon."

"Well, then, we'll get you there."

"But first we get you to hotel." Here was the dedication to duty the Committee chaperons always showed; the Committee always picked their people for reliability. Even though these people were in the dark about what was really going on, they always had a kamikaze commitment to doing whatever they had been instructed to do. And if getting Sam Borne back to his hotel and out of harm's way was part of it, then he would end up back at his hotel and out of harm's way.

Sam paid the bill, and they took the tram back down the hill. As they descended through the dark forests toward the lights of the shimmering metropolis, the feeling of entering a light show was palpable. At the bottom Sam and Ling linked arms and walked to the Star ferry terminal, passing as they did the Supreme Court building and city hall. They were quickly on the ferry and crossing toward the lights of Tsimshatsui. On the Kowloon side, they walked back past the Space Museum and on into the lobby of the Regent. Their farewell was abrupt and formal. Sam thanked Ling for an enjoyable day's outing and told her honestly that he'd enjoyed every moment in her company and that he hoped to see her again someday. She seemed to be trying to contain a great well of emotion. She thanked him curtly and said she too had enjoyed herself.

"Be very careful, please."

"I will be," Sam replied. Before he could reach over and kiss her on the cheek, Ling Wing thrust out her hand, shook Sam's and was gone. At the lobby door, she turned and waved, but only for an instant.

Sam waved and walked across the marble lobby to the

reception desk. He asked for his messages and got two. One was a note from Mr. Chung saying he'd be at the hotel with Sam's wardrobe at eight o'clock in the morning. Sam smiled to himself and wondered again what he'd be wearing this time out. The other note was from the Committee and was accompanied by a packet. The packet held a ticket to Bangkok and one for a connecting flight to Hanoi.

Sam considered his options. He pretty much had to stay in the hotel. He could go up to his room, cool out, read a little and then hit the sack. He just might do that. If he went out, the Committee would be on his case for sure. Between assignments next time—provided there was a next time—he'd probably be sent to Greenland again if he bucked their orders. No, he had to stay in the hotel, but he didn't have to retreat to his room just yet. Sam decided it was better to have a drink.

Sam opted for a stool at the bar rather than a table. He thought vaguely that this would help him retreat to his room early. The view out across the harbor was exhilarating; it was more exciting by night than by day. The lights of Central blazed away across the water, casting bright channels out into the harbor; then above on the peak, lights winked at random. The effect was magical.

The room was crowded with tourists and businessmen sitting at tables arranged in clusters some distance from the bar. The bar itself was empty except for Sam and a man somewhat the worse for wear. He was no doubt a lonely businessman too long on the road, and looked soggy enough to pass out. It never surprised Sam how many traveling businessmen looked like they'd written a suicide note back in their rooms but just couldn't come up with the right complimentary close to act on it. The bartender came over to Sam.

"Good evening, sir. What would you like?"

"I'd like a Bushmills, neat please, with lots of ice."

"Of course." The bartender returned in seconds with a

high-necked bottle of Bushmills and an Old-Fashioned
glass brimful of ice. This was exactly the way Sam liked
it. As the bartender poured the whiskey into the glass,
Sam watched it spider the cubes with cracks. He let a
quick chill hit the whiskey before savoring his first sip.
For Sam there was nothing like the clean but smoky taste
of Irish whiskey, especially Bushmills. He sat back,
looking off toward the harbor, when a vision of beauty
passed him and he was suddenly in love.

She was tall, wispy and dazzlingly dressed. Her legs
would have won a gold medal at any sensual Olympics.
They disappeared into a magenta sheath that wrapped her
from knees to neck. She had nut-brown hair piled high
and coiled atop her head. Her face was fine and spare and
tricked out with delicate features, from a slender forehead
to high cheekbones on either side of a tiny nose above a
wide and sexy mouth. In each ear she wore a diamond
dewdrop, on her left wrist a single gold bracelet. But it
was the eyes that got you. They were large, mahogany
and set in her face like almonds, perfectly matched, perfectly spaced. Her lashes were long and exciting and her
brows were thin and sharp and arched in perfect parab-
olas. She slithered past Sam and perched on a stool
two down from his, placing her jet-black evening bag
on the bar and hitching her high-heeled feet in the struts of
the stool. The heels were pearl gray. As she waited for the
bartender she pumped her heels ever so slightly up and
down. Sam felt the salmon start upstream.

The bartender came over, flashing her a smile that
would have blinded Confucius. Leaning over farther than
necessary, he asked her in a voice an octave above a
whisper what her pleasure was. The French and the Chinese shared more than a passion for food; they both loved
a double entendre.

''I'd like a champagne cocktail, light on the bitters,
please.''

''Yes, ma'am.'' The bartender hurried away and came

back with his shaker and a split of champagne. He opened the split with more flourishes than Toscanini and poured the champagne into a chilled champagne glass into which he'd dropped a sugar cube splashed with bitters. The champagne fizzed to the top and settled. With a final flourish the bartender topped off the glass. He stepped back and indicated with a sidelong open palm that she should try this miracle of international mixology.

She took a sip, nodded, and the bartender managed to move down the bar from her more than half a meter, but just that and no more. She opened her bag, took from it a silver case and extracted a long filtered cigarette. The bartender stuck out a flash lighter and obliged her. She sat back with the cigarette and exhaled a flute of white smoke.

That was when the soggy executive got into the act. He slid off his stool and staggered down to hers. He tottered over her and she leaned away. The bartender wanted to say something but wasn't sure what. The soggy man smiled down idiotically at the lady. He was so far gone his leer was flabby. The lady took another long pull on her cigarette, then exhaled in a furling stream that climbed over the bartender's head. The drunk leaned his elbow against the bar and curled his face around in front of the lady's.

"I like the way you use your mouth," he said.

"I don't like the way you use yours," she snapped. She reached out and gathered up her bag and moved like a sylph onto the next stool, the one next to Sam. The bartender slid her drink down to her and turned to the drunk.

"Maybe time go bed now," the bartender said.

"Maybe time go fuck yourself," the executive replied.

"That language not allowed here," the bartender said. "You go now nice. No make trouble."

"Rotate on it, buddy."

"Not allowed here like that. No talk like that in Regent bar," the bartender said. He turned and walked to the

phone behind the bar and started to call. He would call
security, of course, and the menace would be quietly removed. Back in the home office of whatever conglomer-
ate had sent wonder boy to the mysterious East, they
would never know that this far from home junior had no
class.

But security would have to act fast. The drunk shoved
off from the bar like a ruptured duck, flew into a bar
stool, righted himself and crashed into the bar elbow first
next to the lady.

"How much for around the world, baby?" he asked
the lady, leaning down into her averted face. His knees
buckled but he caught himself with his forearm and
jacked himself back up.

"It's a lot more expensive than home again, home
again," she said. That set the drunk off. He reached out
and twirled the lady around by the shoulder. He never got
to give her the what-for he intended.

Sam came off his stool and around the lady's and had
the drunk suspended by his lapels and down the bar before he realized the source of his levitation. Sam carried
him to the last stool, propped him in it and held him upright by the chest like a cop stopping traffic for the minute
or so it took before the security men arrived, took the man
under the arms and led him away. All the while Sam held
him, the man flailed at him like an angry toddler. The
drunk had pummeled Sam's shoulder, knocking his
blazer askew. As Sam walked back to his stool, he
straightened himself. It was a cardinal rule for Sam never
to slap drunks around; fighting drunks was like striking
out the pitcher.

As he passed the lady, she looked up and said, "I guess
this is where I say thank you."

"And I guess this is where I reply you're welcome."
Sam resumed his seat on the stool next to hers. She
looked directly at him and flashed a devastating smile.

"My name is Cynthia Laws."

"And mine's Sam Borne, at your service."

"As I noticed."

"There's nothing like a little chivalry to stir the blood."

"Whose?"

"Why, mine, of course."

"It must be contagious."

"Glad to hear it. Your name's sort of forbidding." Sam noticed that the smile stayed on her face. There is nothing so pleasing as the feeling that one is making a hit with a beautiful woman. Cynthia Laws took a long pull on her cigarette and exhaled slowly. A blue and white plume of smoke swirled toward the ceiling.

"Are you going to tell me what brings you to Hong Kong, Mr. Borne, or am I going to have to guess?"

"I'm going to tell you right after you tell me what brings you?"

"Sort of I'll show you mine if you'll show me yours?"

"Exactly."

"I live here."

"Where?"

"On the peak."

"What brings you down here?"

"The view."

"The view from the peak isn't enough?"

"Haven't you ever wanted to look through a telescope from the other end?"

"You like the change?"

"That's it. Now tell me what brings you to Hong Kong."

"Business."

"And you're staying here at the Regent?"

"Yes."

"And can you say what kind of business?"

"I can, but I won't."

"It's that secret?"

"Sort of."

"Can you give me a hint?"

"After you tell me why you live here."

"My husband works here."

"In banking, right?"

"In banking, wrong."

"In the rag trade, right?"

"In apparel, correct. Why must Americans be so crude, and so deliciously appealing when they are?"

"It's our heritage."

"It's not your heritage to be secretive, so maybe you can give me a hint as to what business you're in?"

"Shipping and handling."

"In that instance, were I to ship myself to your room do you suppose you could handle me?"

"With care."

"Then let's try, shall we?"

"By all means."

CHAPTER NINE:
POST TIME

Hong Kong—Bangkok—Hanoi
August 18

During the night, somewhere toward dawn, Sam Borne and Cynthia Laws exhausted each other and drifted off to sleep. When the rising sun cleared the peak of the island across the harbor and splashed into their suite, Sam awakened instantly. His eyes were especially sensitive to light, and he hated to let a day get much of a jump on him. He elected not to wake Cynthia and slipped instead into his white ducks and polo shirt and took himself for an early morning constitutional. He left the sleepy hotel and strolled through the hotel district of downtown Tsimshatsui.

You don't know a city till you see it come awake. In Kowloon just after dawn the traffic was light, with only scattered red and silver taxis, bicycles and the odd pedicab. A scooter or motorbike whined by Sam every now and again, but the young riders who wound thousands of these machines each night as tight as they could go were home now sleeping off their energy in rooms with laundry dangling outside. Even out in the harbor, when Sam looked back as he left the hotel, the water traffic was light, with only a police launch scooting along and a lone green and white ferry making its way toward Central. Scavenging gulls swept back and forth across the harbor, giving Sam an even more soaring feeling about the morning.

He walked up Nathan Road through the hotels of the Golden Mile, then ducked into the green tranquility of Kowloon Park. Dew wet the grass, and the early morning air, light and fresh, was filled with the cheeping of birds. Sam shucked off his moccasins and walked diagonally across the park to Canton Road, came out, put his moccasins back on and went along up to the typhoon shelter. In the shelter the sampans and junks were bedecked with gaily colored laundry and women moved about, shifting things for the day, beginning to prepare the simple breakfasts most of these people fed their children. On an impulse Sam waved to one barefooted young woman cradling an infant, and she waved back.

He turned and started back along Canton Road. Behind and to the left the green mountains of the New Territories hunched in the sunshine. On the right the piers jutted out into the harbor. Hong Kong had the world's third busiest harbor, but you wouldn't know it at this time of the morning. As he watched the limited activity of merchant seamen on one of the long piers, he wondered if Cynthia would still be there when he got back to the hotel.

Sam headed off around the end of the peninsula. When he passed the Marco Polo Hotel, he couldn't help but think with admiration that there was a traveler, Marco Polo. At the ocean terminal ahead, two cruise ships were moored. For sure none of their passengers were up yet. These were the people, the happy tourists, that Sam indirectly worked for. It was for them that he put it on the line, under orders from the Committee. Even though he sometimes wanted out of his crazy existence, even though he resented the total and absolute control the Committee exercised over him, even though he especially bridled when the Committee used blackmail to keep him in line, with threats to reveal him as the murderer in any number of crucial political assassinations he'd performed over the years, even then Sam knew that he liked to think he was making the world safe for the gentle kinds of people who took cruises, mowed their lawns on Saturdays, bought their grandchildren candy and contributed to the fight against cancer. These people deserved to spend their lives as they saw fit and not to have some dictator or madman telling them what they could and could not do, what they could and could not think, where they could and could not go. No, freedom was all, and Sam was all for freedom.

As he rounded the end of the peninsula, Sam saw that the Star ferries were picking up business and that the early commuters were already aboard for their seven-minute trip across. Hong Kong was on the move and Sam knew in his bones that he would soon be too. He could feel the assignment on him now like a second skin, and it felt good. He looked up and saw on the side of the bus terminus the red neon outline of the rooster that glowed so prominently from the peak at night. He felt like a rooster himself, one about to crow, and it quickened his step on the short walk back to the Regent.

When he got to his room, Cynthia was there. She was stretched like a lioness on the sheets, and Sam had never seen a better sight. He wanted to wake her and play, but he well realized that most people didn't have his endless supply of energy and that she might need her rest. Instead he went to the desk by the glass wall and took out a Gauloise. He would enjoy a quiet smoke and contemplate the delights that would await him if only Mr. Chung and his noble sons would delay their morning visit long enough.

This dream was immediately shattered. The phone rang once and Sam speared it.

"Borne here."

"Good morning, Mr. Borne, so sorry to disturb you. There is a man here who insists he has an appointment with you now. I have tried to encourage him to come back later, but he is insistent."

"What is his name?"

There was a pause on the other end. Then the desk man came back on the line. "His name is Mr. Chung. He has identified himself as your tailor."

"He is."

"Oh, I see."

"Could you put Mr. Chung on the line, please?"

"Yes, of course, Mr. Borne."

There was another slight pause and then Mr. Chung came on the line. "Good morning, Mr. Borne."

"Good morning, Mr. Chung, how are you and the two younger Chungs this fine morning?"

"We are fine, Mr. Borne."

"Delighted. What can I do for you?"

"We are here with your wardrobe, all finish. We would like to come up and fit you and make any adjustment necessary."

"Fine, but tell me, Mr. Chung, do you suppose I might have ten minutes or so before you arrive?" Sam noticed that as always with people who weren't native English speakers he was slipping into their speech pattern, with a heavy British overlay. He was a natural and compulsive mimic, a talent his years at RADA had honed to perfection.

"Of course."

"Good. Then I'll see you here in ten minutes in my room, agreed?"

"Agreed. Ten minutes."

"Fine. See you then." Sam hung up and was across the room before Cynthia had time to shift herself awake. At times like this, the best way to end it was the shortest. He would have to be gruff, maybe even rude.

Even before he reached the bed he clapped loudly. Cynthia stirred. Sam reached out and shook her by the shoulder. She opened one eye and looked up at him invitingly. No mermaid singing to sailor ever worked more magic than that one big inviting fish-eye did to Sam. He tried to ignore it.

"Rise and shine," he chirped, trying to take the edge off the inevitable separation.

Cynthia propped herself on an elbow, smiled and said, "What's good for the gander is not always good for the goose. Come back to bed and let's ease into the day."

"Sorry, that's not possible." In his mind Sam damned the Committee.

"Why not?"

"It's just not. I can't explain."

"Secretive again. You Americans love intrigue."

"I am truly sorry, but you'll have to get dressed and leave immediately. My business associates are in the lobby. This is an emergency." Sam turned his hands palms up and shrugged, hoping to defuse any understandable anger on Cynthia's part. "Please get dressed," he said, handing Cynthia her magenta sheath; its silky touch was another temptation in a series of agonizing temptations. He gathered up her gray heels, her sexy lingerie and her purse and placed them gently, almost imploringly, on the bed beside her. He stood over her. She looked up, the smile gone, shock radiating from every pore.

"I've heard of the bum's rush, but this is ridiculous."

"It is, you're right. I'm sorry, it can't be helped. Please don't make a dreadful situation worse."

"I mean, really." Cynthia stood up beside the bed and pulled on her dress. Her lingerie she stuffed into her purse. She slipped her feet into her shoes and without a word walked to the door, opened it and was gone. Looking after her, Sam frowned and rubbed his temple. His was a life that would get to Job at times. Before she closed the door, Cynthia stuck her head back into the room.

"Thanks for the memories," she said.

"You're more than welcome."

Cynthia slammed the door so hard Sam was sure she'd wake every guest on the floor. Next came a ruckus from the corridor. Sam couldn't get to his door too soon. In the corridor Mr. Chung was sprawled on the floor amid his valises, which his sons had dropped to assist him. Cynthia stalked off beyond them to the elevator. Mr. Chung was mumbling, "Excuse me, madam," over and over again. The Marx Brothers touch was all Sam needed to cap the scene he'd just played.

Sam left his doorway and walked over and helped the brothers Chung raise father Chung. The old man was deeply shaken and seemed somehow convinced that he wasn't blameless. When he turned to pursue Cynthia to the elevator to apologize, Sam took him firmly under the arm and led him off toward the room, assuring him it was unnecessary to apologize further and tossing off over his shoulder that the two sons should follow them into his room. Once he got Mr. Chung into the room, it wasn't long before Sam succeeded in calming him down. Instead Mr. Chung apologized to Sam.

"I am sorry, Mr. Borne, to come at this early hour."

"I'm sure you are."

"It is only, you see, Mr. Borne, that your benefactor said you must hurry to a plane, so we come this early."

"I understand, I understand," Sam reassured him. Sam realized that Mr. Chung was still jumpy. The old man's brief encounter with Cynthia Laws had unhinged him more than it would have a younger and less formal man. Mr. Chung's whole image of himself as an exemplary gentleman had been called into question by the contretemps.

"How would you like a nice cup of tea, Mr. Chung?" Sam asked.

"I mustn't while working, Mr. Borne."

"Not a bit of it. That's exactly what you need. I'll call down for it." Sam turned to the two sons. "And how about you gentlemen? Would you care for anything?" Both sons looked at their father. Mr. Chung nodded.

"We'd like tea also, Mr. Borne," one of the sons said.

"And how about something to eat?" Sam asked.

"No, no," Mr. Chung blurted out. "Just tea, Mr. Borne, please."

"All settled. Tea for three it is then. I'll order a little coffee for myself and a croissant and we'll be all set." Sam called down the order. When he turned back, the Chungs were ready to go, the valises open on the floor and clothes spread on the bed and chairs.

Mr. Chung bowed. "You will be pleased, I believe, Mr. Borne, with this excellent wardrobe. Please step over here." Mr. Chung indicated the space at the back of the bed and Sam strode over to it. On the way he started to pull off his polo shirt. He slipped off his pants and stood in his jockey shorts and bare feet. Mr. Chung barked out instructions to his sons, and they handed Sam the trousers to a beautiful white linen suit. Sam slipped into them. Next the one son handed Sam the suit coat that went with it. It was double-breasted. The coat and pants fit perfectly. There was no basting up in this operation; there was no time. Sam knew the Committee kept his pattern up to date, so he wasn't surprised that a good tailor had been able to work this seeming miracle. The Committee could dress him for any occasion at the snip of a thread.

"How does it feel, Mr. Borne?" Mr. Chung asked.

"Perfect."

"Very good. Please slip that off now and try on another."

Mr. Chung made a gesture like a man twirling a lasso, and one of his sons handed Sam a pair of beautifully cut dark blue linen trousers. Sam took off the white trousers to the suit and slipped into the blue slacks. They fit as well as the white ones had. The other son held out to Sam a gorgeously woven linen suit coat with a beige background under a subtle blue pattern. It fell beautifully across his shoulders and draped elegantly from his chest.

"This too looks good, Mr. Borne," Mr. Chung volunteered.

"It feels great. You're top-notch, Mr. Chung."

"Thank you so much. Now we will try the others."
Mr. Chung again signaled his sons and they brought Sam
a succession of outfits, one a double-breasted blue blazer
with white linen trousers and the other a navy-blue
summer wool suit, again double-breasted. They then
crowned each outfit by handing Sam two stunning straw
hats; each made Sam more rakish than the other, even
lending Sam a sinister air. Then came the shoes. These
were guaranteed to make sure Sam wasn't mistaken for a
banker. They were two-toned, one white on brown, the
other white on black. Sam realized he was all tricked out
to dazzle people from tip to toe; he could impersonate
anything from a dandyish college professor with flair to a
flashy drug dealer with class. When they laid the shirts
and ties on him, they too were on target.

Mr. Chung stood back virtually applauding his work.
He shot smiles around the room like sunbeams. His sons
joined him. They were a happy group. And proud.

"Your benefactor, Mr. Borne, will be very pleased
with you. You look perfect," Mr. Chung said.

"My benefactor usually sees to that."

"Well, this time there can be no question."

There was a knock at the door.

"Come in," Sam said. It was room service. The waiter
wheeled a trolley in. Sam signed the chit, and the waiter
left. Sam assumed the role of host and handed the Chungs
their tea. He then poured himself a cup of coffee and took
up his croissant. The Chungs let silence hang in the air
like smoke. It was up to Sam to carry the conversation,
but his mind was spinning more along the lines of what to
do with Sun Sun when he met up with him than with
small talk. Then he had an inspiration.

"Tell me, Mr. Chung, do you ever play the ponies?"
Sam asked.

The two sons grinned broadly and the father hesitated.

"I have on occasion gone to the racing course."

"Just at old Happy Valley or also out to Shatin?"

"Ah, I have seen both, Mr. Borne."

"Yeah, they say Shatin is something. I was hoping to see it. It's too bad I'm here out of season."

"Yes, regrettable. Perhaps another time."

"Let's hope so. I'd like to see what these new electronic tracks are like. I've been to the ball parks in America and seen the screens. They're fun."

"Yes." Mr. Chung was less than forthcoming. Sam decided to have some fun.

"What's the most you ever hauled in on a horse's nose?" he asked.

Mr. Chung shifted uncomfortably from one foot to the other. He hesitated. He dipped his head, almost like a horse, then he cleared his throat. His sons were enjoying this conversation even more than Sam.

"You see, Mr. Borne, I am by nature a very cautious man. I am wondering why you want to know, please?"

"Just making conversation. The most I ever won on one horse's nose was a little over seven thousand dollars, U.S. It still gives me a thrill to think about it. This was at Santa Anita. Horse was a filly too, named Lady Tango."

"This was very fortunate, Mr. Borne."

"I'll say it was. But even when you lose, it's fun if you go to see the critters run. They're beautiful, don't you think?"

"Yes, very beautiful."

"The whole damn thing is beautiful. Why, there's more poetry in the names of thoroughbreds than you find in most anthologies."

"Yes, very beautiful."

"So you're going to keep your own counsel and not tell me your biggest bonanza at the track, is that it?" Sam prodded. Mr. Chung fidgeted. The two sons grinned. "Well," Sam went on, "can you at least tell me the name of the noble beast? You must remember that, right?"

Suddenly Mr. Chung flowered. "Yes, his name was Count Con. He had never won a race in his life before. I bet him because I like the silly name."

"And you won big?"

"Very big, Mr. Borne, very big indeed." Mr. Chung was all smiles, and his sons gave in to chuckling. Sam figured there must be an interesting story back of this big strike, but he wasn't sure how much farther he could push his teasing curiosity. Just when he'd decided to push it a little more, the phone rang. He walked across the room and picked it up on the third ring.

"Borne here."

"Mr. Borne, your car and driver are here. Shall I have them wait?"

"Yes. Have them wait."

"When shall I send the bellboy, Mr. Borne?"

Sam was starting a slow burn, but what was the use of getting angry? The Committee was making sure he was under control and on his way. He wouldn't have missed the plane under any circumstance, but they always kept the governor on for as long as they could. They had this bad habit of leaving him alone only when the crunch came. Sam looked at his watch. There was plenty of time for him to get a quick shower, hop into his new duds and still make the plane with time to spare.

"I'll call down when I'm ready for the bellboy," he said.

"Very well, Mr. Borne, I shall inform your driver to wait."

"Thank you." Sam hung up. He looked at the Chungs, but they needed no word. While he had been on the phone the two sons had taken the new outfits and packed them neatly into a wardrobe carryall bag; even his shoes were packed in. All he had to do was throw his toiletries and underwear into the parachute bag and take off. The Chungs even had a neat little leather case for carrying his

extra hat that didn't make him look like Auntie Mame's
houseboy. He was all set.

Mr. Chung put his cup of tea on the trolley and extended his hand to Sam. "It has been our pleasure to
serve you, Mr. Borne, and may you wear your clothes for
many hours of joy and comfort. We hope to see you
again."

"I hope you see me again too—more than you know."

"Very well, we shall be gone." Mr. Chung bowed.
The two sons bowed. Then all three were at the door, and
even before Sam could reach out and hold the door for
them they were through it and heading down the corridor
for the elevator, each son carting one of the huge valises.
Sam stood at the door and waved to them, then went back
inside. I'll get a quick shower, he thought, and hit the
road. What the hell, it's post time no matter how you look
at it.

Less than half an hour later Sam checked out, went out
to the driveway and met his driver. The driver was short
and slight and looked like he might be a college student.
He was not grizzled, he was not a regular, and he was not
on his normal beat. No doubt, like Ling Wing, he was
committed to eradicating evil in our time. He bowed gra-
ciously when Sam went up to him, and he immediately
helped the bellboy put the bags into the trunk of the Rolls-
Royce. While these two were thus engaged, Sam got in
the shotgun seat in the front of the car. As the driver slid
into his seat, he was disconcerted to see that Sam wasn't
riding in back. He stared at Sam, unsure of himself.

"Take that cap off and relax," Sam said. "I like riding
in the front. In fact, maybe I should drive."

"Please, Mr. Borne, don't do that. I must drive."

"And who are you?"

"I am Tommie Hung."

"Great name."

Tommie Hung was thrown off by this, but recovered
quickly.

"If you say so, Mr. Borne."

"Are you a friend of Ling Wing's?"

"This lady is not known to me."

"Damn shame. You'd make a great couple."

"If you say so, Mr. Borne."

"I say so." Sam fell silent. This was going to be a long ride, even allowing Tommie Hung time to swallow his lump and divulge the information the Committee had placed him in this car to impart. All Sam had to do was keep up the banter and the ride would seem longer than the siege of Troy. They pulled out of the driveway and fell into the heavy traffic of downtown Kowloon. Once they got free of the district of shops, bars and hotels, they'd be at the airport in no time. Sam wondered if there were enough watches on sale in Hong Kong to outfit the wrist of every man, woman and child on the globe, or if it only seemed that way.

When they'd cleared the downtown traffic, Tommie started to sing his little tune. The gist of it was that Sam would act like a tourist. He would stop in Hanoi and tour for an afternoon, then spend the night in a central hotel. The next day he would move on to Ho Chi Minh City. There he would play the tourist by day, then at night work his way around, hitting night spots, letting it be known, very discreetly, that what he needed was an inexhaustible supply of number-four heroin for the American market at a reasonable price, since the Hong Kong syndicates had gone crazy with greed and were squeezing him dry. It wouldn't be easy. This last piece of advice came by way of homily. Sam should be careful, also by way of homily. Sam said that he realized it wouldn't be easy and that he'd be careful.

They got to the airport and wove their way through the traffic to the main entrance. Sam got out quickly and handled his own luggage before Tommie Hung could add any more advice. In a panic to be of service, Tommie offered to wait with Sam and to carry his luggage and to do any little thing that might come up, but Sam waved him off with the help of an impatient cab dispatcher and was soon through the doors and gone.

Sam found his airline desk and checked in to Bangkok. He paid the irritating airport tax of one hundred Hong Kong dollars. There was something wrong when you had to fly from Hong Kong to Bangkok to fly to Hanoi, but nothing in the way of Communist inefficiency could surprise Sam anymore. As soon as the Communists got control of a country, they dismantled its transportation system, closed it off from the free flow of trade, not to mention ideas, and then wallowed for decades in a stagnant economy, and yet they seemed never to connect the isolation and the wrecked transportation with this economic collapse. To hell with it, Sam thought, and went into the large, functionally raw restaurant to wait for his flight, which like all flights from Kai Tak would not be called but would instead merely be registered on the computerized departure boards.

Sam's wait seemed interminable amid all the squawking, the bustle and the clutter of the airport restaurant. Glad to see his flight number finally roll up on the board, he made for his gate immediately. From there it wasn't long before they were down the runway and gone. The flight itself was uneventful. During it, Sam planned what strategy he'd need in the initial stages of his ruse to contact Doctor Sun Sun. He would approach things systematically, as the ninja masters had drilled into him to do. He would wait, he would bide his time, he would roam the late night streets letting things develop; he would spend time in what night spots the Communists hadn't closed, and he would, he felt sure, come to the attention of the scum who ran these spots for Doctor Sun Sun. His drug business in Ho Chi Minh City he would eventually let slip, discreetly, gradually. There would be the contact and then would come the time to play his cards right, to move Sun Sun to the point of commitment, to have Sun

Sun enter negotiations and to see how, through the application of systematized intelligence and superior training and skill, learned and relearned and practiced and repracticed long ago among the mountain redoubts of the ninja masters and on the military bases of the United States armed forces, he would pull Sun Sun down and with him his mad schemes.

When they reached Bangkok, Sam had a short layover and then it was on to Hanoi via Air Vietnam. The service was terrible, but the flight was short. The whole way Sam thought about Sun Sun. His anticipation was high. It was time to go in for the kill.

When they announced their descent into Hanoi airport, Sam looked out his window. The small jet was skimming bomb craters that had become circular rice paddies. The plane's shadow rolled over the terrain below, and then Sam experienced the good feeling he always got when the shadow came up to merge with the plane itself. They touched down.

He was in Hanoi.

CHAPTER TEN:
SECOND CITY

Hanoi
August 18

Hanoi was dull. No longer the charming colonial city of tree-lined boulevards and carefree strollers it had been under tne French, Hanoi was gray and lifeless. Even though many of the scars of war had been removed, enough of them remained to cast a pall over the entire city. Upon arrival, Sam felt immediate discomfort. The passport-control booth at Noi Bai airport was manned by armed guards, and as he approached it he had a moment's anxiety wondering whether he would be treated with greater disrespect because his passport and visa were American. But nothing out of the ordinary happened. The guards looked at Sam, looked at the passport, looked at the visa and waved him through after a quick stamping. Sam had been to this country before, so he knew that they distrusted all foreigners, not just Americans. They had been at war with foreigners for centuries. Only recently they had fought with the Pol Pot in Cambodia and with the Chinese along the northern border. In fact, there were still reports of skirmishes with the Chinese, so there was no real reason for the Vietnamese to single out the Americans, even if Americans had played a large role in their recent history.

On the way in from the airport, traffic was heavy. Bicycles were everywhere, with only a few cars, mostly

Russian Volgas and Zhigulis. In among the bicycles and cars were carts drawn by water buffalo, and every now and again they would come across a scooter or a motorbike, but these were surprisingly few. One of the things Sam noticed in traveling in Communist countries was how somber they were. There were no high-winding scooter engines or motorcycles or sports cars. The traffic was quieter, as though even it was depressed by the drabness of the collective way of life.

When they reached the Red River, they encountered the usual bottleneck at the bridge the French had called the Paul Doumer Bridge and the Communists now called the Long Bien Bridge, a rail-and-road span whose iron black girders had been cast in Paris between 1899 and 1902. It was this very bridge that had become a symbol of persistence to the Vietnamese during the many bombings that rocked the North during the police action. It was this bridge that had been the conduit for the supplies rolling down from China all during those years. Now it was the Chinese who were at undeclared war with the Vietnamese. Who won that particular war was now of no concern to Sam.

What was of concern to Sam was whether or not the bridge held up until he safely crossed it. Like all Vietnamese, Sam's taxi driver was not supposed to speak to foreigners, but he grinned broadly when Sam snorted upon seeing the angle at which the bridge listed. Sam noticed that for a long stretch trucks of all kinds were pulled up along the side of the road leading to the bridge. Surprising him, his driver broke into bad French and explained to Sam that the trucks were permitted to use the bridge only at night, when traffic was lighter. From the angle at which the bridge tilted, Sam thought this was good civil defense, if not good civil engineering. After a long wait, they got onto the bridge and made their way across.

On the other side, in the city itself, life was listless.

They passed stucco building after stucco building, all low and yellow. It was as if time had stood still since the French had made the city prosper in the 1950s. There were reports of Russians and Cubans coming here and building projects, but none were in evidence to Sam. The old trams still followed their narrow-gauge tracks amid the cyclists; black iron girders the French had built still supported what electrical wires there were; and the narrow streets were just as sleepy as they had always been beneath the lacy green canopies formed by the leaves of the tamarind trees. The city seemed frozen in time since 1954. And these same narrow streets were filled with carts drawn by water buffalo like those in the stream of traffic that bottlenecked at the bridge.

They turned left after crossing the bridge and in minutes drew up in front of the Thong Nhat Hotel. Sam had opted for the older Thong Nhat because it was more convenient to the city, and since he was supposed to be a mere tourist, he preferred to stay where he could walk to the sights. Besides, the modern hotel in the suburbs, the Thang Loi, had reportedly been built by the Cubans, and Sam didn't feel like being their guest unless he had to. Everything about Cuba vexed him. There was no doubt in his mind that next to the unwinnable police action in Vietnam, where the military had been told to fight but not to win, the Cuban debacle was the worst foreign policy mistake the Americans had made since the end of World War Two and the wholesale sellout of Eastern Europe to the Russians.

The taxi driver leaped out and helped Sam get his luggage into the hands of the bellhop. At the airport Sam had not bothered to change any money, so he had no dong on him. He quickly handed over two American dollars and the driver was gone before Sam could gesture for him to keep it all. The situation here with currency was not news to Sam. He had read that the average civil servant or teacher made two hundred dong a month, and this didn't go very far in an economy where a tin cooking pot cost three hundred and fifty dong or where a single pack of American cigarettes cost a hundred dong or where a pair of hideous plastic sandals would run nearly two hundred. It was hard to imagine what kind of staggering mismanagement lay behind an economy where a pack of cigarettes could cost someone, anyone, half a month's income, but the Communists had managed this and more, and hunger, the real bottom line for an economy and the single most important factor in any government, was a serious problem here in the unified Vietnam of Communist dreams.

The taxi screeched off and Sam turned and entered the lobby of the Thong Nhat. It was tatty, as might have been expected, but it wasn't offensive; everything was clean, if worn. Sam got himself a room for one night for twenty-odd American dollars, and followed the bellboy into the elevator and up a few floors. The room itself was dingy. None of the furniture had been replaced for years, but again it was relatively clean and by no means a dive. It had a small Russian air conditioner in the window and, on a bedside table, a Chinese thermos bottle beside a functional office-style black phone. Grim was probably the best word to describe the accommodations. It was a hell of a sight from the Regent in Hong Kong, and unlike his Regent room, this one had no view to speak of. Sam handed the bellboy an American dollar, which he then squirreled away like it was a pure gold ingot. He bowed and left.

Sam walked over and unpacked a few things from his garment bag and hung them in an old-fashioned teak wardrobe that stood along one wall. Then he took a few toilet articles from his suitcase and put them out in the bathroom. He brushed his teeth and contemplated a shower but decided against it. It was late in the afternoon and he wanted to have a look around before everything closed for the day. He would take a walk and then double back and shower and maybe lie down briefly before taking a look at Hanoi by night. The prospects on any front didn't please him. He rinsed his face with cold water and went back down in the elevator.

At the desk he learned that he could just catch the exchange department for foreign money at the state bank of Vietnam if he hurried. He went out and along the street a few steps and into the bank. The foreign exchange was in an annex. He went to this section and found he was the only customer. While he waited for five hundred American dollars to be converted into dong, he noted how many people were becoming involved in this rather simple exchange. By the time the transaction was completed, sixteen people had been engaged in it in one capacity or another. They had filled out forms, written down serial numbers, checked and double-checked both Sam's visa and his passport. They had looked up more than three times to make sure he was the person depicted in his photo. They had counted and recounted both the dong and the dollars. Finally they were satisified and they handed Sam his cache of dong. Sam quickly calculated the conversion rate at approximately ten to one; dollars would get you doughnuts this rate was a fraction of what Sam could have gotten outside on the black market. He smiled all around and left.

Back on the street Sam decided to walk to the little lake in the center of the city known accurately enough in French as the Petit Lac. It didn't take him long to get there. He felt conspicuous on the streets, where most of the natives were lightly dressed in the pajamalike outfits they favored, with only an occasional woman in a dress. There were a few Russians, sweating in their clumsily cut and badly styled synthetic suits. It pleased Sam to think that he was so much better dressed than these Russian advisers.

When he reached the little lake, Sam walked around it taking in its charms. Like almost everything French, it had class. There were graceful willow trees tracing their leafy green patterns all around the edge of the lake itself, and in the center, on a tiny island, stood the Turtle Pagoda, marking the spot where legend had it that a turtle rose from the water bearing a sword used by an ancient Vietnamese warrior to drive out Chinese invaders. The relationship between the Vietnamese and the Chinese was like the relationship between the Hatfields and the McCoys. These two tribes were always at it, so it wasn't surprising to Sam that they were still scrimmaging with each other along their border. It wouldn't have surprised Sam if the Chinese had launched a full-scale invasion of the Vietnamese.

After a good long look, Sam left the Petit Lac and headed over to the Ho Chi Minh mausoleum. On the way, he stopped and looked briefly at the Chau Mot Cot, or One-Pillar Pagoda. Like the Turtle Pagoda, it too stood on a small island in the middle of a lake. It had been erected in the shape of a lotus to commemorate the birth to an emperor of an heir. Sam preferred the Turtle Pagoda. He crossed over and entered the line for the mausoleum. From the little open square in front of the mausoleum, Sam noticed how dull it was, like its prototype in Moscow for Lenin. The mausoleum showed the same starkness and lack of imagination as Lenin's tomb did; it was reared up on the same square columns as the original, and it was every bit as inelegant. Although simple, it had none of the Bauhaus élan well-designed simplicity could convey. It just stood there, dull and massive. It had no distinctive Vietnamese features, and it made Sam wonder if the whole idea of Vietnamese independence and freedom was really a sham.

The line moved slowly, but finally Sam entered. There were armed guards at the entrance. He filed past the embalmed remains of Ho with interest but without reverence. One of the most ironical features of Communism, that most contradictory and unworkable of philosophies, was that it preached against the importance of the individual yet exalted the cult of personality. The Russians had Lenin, the Chinese had Mao, and now the Vietnamese had Uncle Ho. It amused Sam to see that Ho still sported, even in death, the little goatee that had symbolized him in life. He wondered how much comfort Ho would derive from knowing he was the only former Paris dishwasher with his own mausoleum.

Outside the air was light, and Sam was grateful. The slight breeze on his face was refreshing after the morbidity of the mausoleum. In the little open square in front of the mausoleum some Vietnamese tourists snapped photos while soldiers looked on. Sam headed across the square toward the river. It was restorative to see green trees, grass and life again. And it was relaxing to know he'd done his duty as a tourist. There would be one more stop for him, at the crowded market, and then he would walk back to the hotel along the river.

As he made his way to the market, Sam noticed how staid life was here in the north. In Saigon, when he'd been there on his first assignment years ago, there had been an abundance of life. The entire city throbbed with discos, bars and street life galore. But here in the north he passed only endless drab shops and stores, with the odd stall perched against a building, and people cast only glancing looks his way, probably figuring him for another well-off tourist and letting it go at that.

When Sam reached the market it was bustling, but most of the activity was devoted to closing up for the day. The first soft hours of the long summer twilight had begun, and the merchants and stall owners were packing up their fish and vegetables and making ready to leave for the day. Shutters went up, hasps were clasped, stalls were wheeled into sheds. Seeing the food made Sam hungry. Some of the merchants were packing their wares onto carts drawn by water buffalo. Sam exchanged smiles and nods as he wove his way among the merchants.

Food, Sam knew, was rationed; rice was at a premium. If you were an office worker, you would likely get half the allotment given a laborer, a miner or a stevedore. Somehow you would have to come up with food. Sam would bet his eyeteeth that the black market was in full swing, even as the legitimate market shuttered itself away for the night.

Sam left the market and walked over to the river. The traffic was still jammed on the long bridge. The bridge still tilted at its perilous angle. As Sam strolled along slowly, he realized that someone was shadowing him on the other side of the road. When he stopped under a tree and glanced across the swift river to the other side, the man approached him. Sam was mildly surprised. He had thought the shadow was a policeman, someone whose duty was to shadow a capitalist tourist and make sure he behaved himself here in the workers' paradise. But this man was no policeman.

"Bonsoir, monsieur," the man said. Sam turned to face him. The man was dressed casually in an open silk shirt, Western trousers and sandals with leather straps. He was about the same age as Sam, thirty-three or -four, Sam guessed. He was tall for a Vietnamese, about five foot six. He smiled. Sam waited.

"Voulez-vous une femme pour ce soir, monsieur?" he asked. Of all things, Sam thought. He was a pimp. The man smiled and encouraged Sam with a nod.

"Non, merci," Sam answered. He hoped that would end it. He started to walk away, but the man followed again. After Sam had gone about half a block, the man hustled up beside him.

"Pardonnez moi, monsieur, voulez-vouz un garçon pour cet soir?" As he asked this, the man stepped up his trotting pace, leaned his face into Sam's and grinned. Sam looked down at him, at his bobbing face, so eager to please, and at his grin, so wide and hopeful. There was no way Sam could look down on this guy. He was a hus-

tler in a land that placed no real premium on hustle. Sam was not partial to pimps, but he was partial to people who tried to inject some life into a lifeless system.

"*Non,*" Sam said.

"*Voulez-vous changer un peu d'argent?*"

"*Non,*" Sam answered, then got curious. "*À quel prix, monsieur?*"

The man answered. Sam was astounded. The man had offered a rate slightly under a twentieth the official rate. That meant with a little pressure Sam could close the deal at twenty to one or better. Of course, Sam wasn't about to do this. He wasn't idiotic enough to jeopardize a whole mission for a petty infraction, and he had no way of knowing whether the man was a plant, though he seriously doubted it. The man had opened up with him as a flesh peddler, and Sam would not have risked slaking even his curiosity if he had thought for even a minute that the man was into entrapment.

Sam turned to the man and said in rapid and fluent French that he was not interested in anything but being left alone immediately or he would call the police. The man blanched and stood riveted to the spot as Sam marched off down the street. Sam heard him shout something in Vietnamese, an imprecation no doubt, and then it was quiet again.

Sam was tired. He decided to drop the idea of seeing some of Hanoi's nightlife later on. He would go back to the hotel, take a nap, then slip out and have a quiet little unrationed dinner somewhere. After that, he would come back, stretch out in bed and read for a while.

Tomorrow it would be Ho Chi Minh City. How was that for a cult of personality? A city with a name so beautiful and poetic as Saigon had been renamed by the Communists Ho Chi Minh City. This was what always happened when the people in the second city, the people in cities like Hanoi, the people with the complexes about being second best, got hold of a country. The little people had won here, and now the whole country was being changed into a huge second city, drab, dull and inferior. What had they done to Saigon, Sam wondered? What had they done to the little Paris of the Orient?

Tomorrow he'd find out.

CHAPTER ELEVEN:
PEARL OF THE ORIENT

Ho Chi Minh City
August 19

Saigon was no stranger to drugs and to drug dealing. The history of drug abuse in the Orient was staggering, and Vietnam was right up there with such user nations as India and China when it came to opium abuse. In the days of the colonial Opium Monopoly, as late as the 1930s and '40s, almost three thousand opium dens and retail shops operated in Indochina, and the addict population was estimated at more than 100,000. By 1944 Indochina produced more than sixty tons of opium a year. As late as 1938, opium revenues accounted for fifteen percent of all colonial tax revenues for the French in Vietnam, the highest percentage in all of Southeast Asia. Saigon and drugs went together like Amsterdam and diamonds.

And Ho Chi Minh City would be no different. Like almost every form of pleasure under a puritanical regime, vice under the Communists suffered only the debilitating effects of inflation, not the fatal effects of extinction. Saigon had been wide open and democratic where pleasure was concerned, with almost every citizen able to afford its glittering prizes, but Ho Chi Minh City was closed tight, with almost no one able to afford its drab offerings. Only the privileged Communist elite, the rulers and shakers, were able to wheel and deal at the highest levels. Where Saigon had been overt and ebullient, Ho

Chi Minh City was clandestine and stealthy. No longer could a citizen drop into the largest whorehouse in Asia, the Hall of Mirrors, presided over at its dedication years ago by a government minister; or into the two legendary casinos, the Grande Monde in Cholon or the Cloche d'Or in Saigon proper. No longer could an average Joe or Ho boogie the night away in any of the countless downtown discos. No, now it was all undercover.

But of course it was all still there, and always would be. And Sam Borne would have to work his way into it, would have to work his way beneath the surface and contact the scum who could put him in touch directly with the great traitor himself, the irrepressible Doctor Sun Sun, high lord of the Vietnamese underworld.

These were some of Sam Borne's thoughts as he arrived in Ho Chi Minh City in the midmorning heat. At Ton Son Nhut airport, the inspection process was so repressive it was almost like reentering the country. Sam had to present his passport and visa and wait patiently while two guards checked and rechecked them, looking Sam up and down, before restamping them and handing them back. This official hokum was about as enjoyable as the rocky flight down from Hanoi on the Soviet Antonov turboprop.

Outside, Sam caught a cab and headed into the city. It was an easy drive, the roads much better than they had been in the north. Sam encountered nothing like the mad bottleneck at the bridge in Hanoi. The taxi was a rickety old Peugeot, but it got the job done. Sam had heard that the only way the old French taxis were kept in service was through the auspices of the Cholon Chinese, on whom the government was still dependent to make things run here in the south, but given the rate at which Chinese families were fleeing the country, it wouldn't be long before even a decent cab ride would be raised to the level of a miracle.

The first thing Sam noticed when the cab entered the

city was that traffic was lighter than it had been when he'd last been here in the late sixties to take out a rogue CIA agent who'd taken the Phoenix Program as a license to run around blowing away anyone he wanted to. Sam's memories of that trip were still vivid. He had been very young then, a late teenager eager to prove himself, which he'd done by eliminating not only the agent but the sub-agents and henchmen he'd collected around himself as a phalanx. Sam had penetrated a suburban villa on that trip, circumventing an up-to-the-minute surveillance system by picking his spot carefully and going in when he knew the sentries would be occupied with a group of whores Sam had recruited especially to keep the boys occupied while he got into the inner sanctum. Sam had merely nodded his way past the distracted sentries, entered the drawing room of the villa, set aside his bag of golf clubs and waited for the agent to look up. The agent was a tremendous golf enthusiast, and it was not unusual for Saigon pimps, touts and high rollers to pick him up and take him out for a good workout on the links. Only, Sam dipped into his bag and extracted an iron not ordinarily used by golfers, a Vietnamese K-50M submachine gun that lanced out seven hundred rounds a minute in one short burst as the agent glanced up from the wispy French antique desk he had been sitting placidly behind, counting up his latest profits from drug running with some Vietnamese air force officers he'd thrown in with. Sam could still see pieces of the beautiful fruitwood desk flying through the air amid hunks of flesh and bone. Sam then spun around and took out the henchmen as they poured through the double doors, aware they'd fucked up but unaware it would be their last opportunity to do so. Stepping calmly to the door over the piled bodies of the henchmen, Sam checked out the corridor. The whores had absconded at the first sound of gunfire. Sam went back and tossed the smoking K-50M onto the hardwood floor, walked out into the garden, riotous with bougainvillaea and frangipani, strolled calmly to the stucco wall, scaled its red-tile top and dropped down onto the sidewalk beyond. He had walked away at a leisurely pace. The next day, before he departed to cool out in Hawaii, he had read in the papers that the multiple murders were the work of a lone Vietcong terrorist equipped typically with a K-50M. You could fool them every time if you plotted your strategy carefully.

The importance of plotting strategy carefully had been drilled into Sam time and again in a four-hundred-year-old Japanese farmhouse in the mountains of Nabari. The tenets of the ancient Japanese art of ninjitsu had been hammered into Sam deeper than the marrow in his very bones. He had spent years in the mountains absorbing the philosophy and strategy of the ninja. It had been the same basic exercises over and over. He had mastered the sword, the dirk and the dagger; he had learned the precise use of the caltrop. He had learned to conceal himself and to protect himself. He had been schooled in the art of hand-to-hand combat. He memorized, reviewed and memorized some more the importance of surprise; he had embraced the philosophy of gaining the upper hand through superior preparedness and superior planning; he had learned that the art of spying and the profession of killing called for the casual only in appearance, that the real game, like an iceberg, was ninety percent submerged. Then, after hard days of ninja training, in the long evenings there had been the comfort of Zen, and he had learned to meditate and to think, and to be sufficient unto himself.

The taxi moved into the downtown traffic. Amid the older cars and trucks, there were lots of pedicabs, scooters and motorbikes. Sam noticed with delight that many of the young residents of Ho Chi Minh City clung to styles adapted from the West; they wore lettered T-shirts and jeans, jewelry and snappy shoes. Young girls lounged against the walls, dressed in miniskirts, clogs and fuck-me heels, obviously still plying their trade despite official restrictions against prostitution. Vendors sold black market American cigarettes from wooden suitcases perched on easels. Sam wondered whether the cigarettes were still supplied by Sun Sun's network; he'd bet they were. These youthful vendors were the last links in a chain of contraband that would inevitably lead back to Doctor Sun Sun. Sam was pleased that some commercial vitality still lingered in this city, that people could still get somewhere through hustle. He was delighted that some of the take from these street vendors was sure to land in their own pockets. No doubt Sun Sun got a big bite from the black market, but it was inevitable that even he was chiseled somewhat by the street people, and this pleased Sam.

When the taxi drew up in front of the Cuu Long, Sam climbed out quickly. He gave his luggage to the bellboy and settled with the driver. If it weren't for the necessity of not drawing attention to himself, Sam would have laid a whopping tip on this driver, who had answered Sam's few questions on the drive in with a polite thoroughness despite the injunction against talking to foreigners, but Sam couldn't risk making a splash. Ho Chi Minh City was in some real senses an occupied city; the northern Communists had come in and taken over, and the occupying forces kept a close watch here. It would mean police surveillance and periodic sweeps to clean up the black market. It would mean Sam would have to be careful. He would have to seem a tourist while being cagey enough to radiate an ulterior motive: an ulterior motive, that is, that wouldn't bring the apparatchiks down around his head. He would have to play a subtle game, and he was good at subtle games.

Sam entered the hotel. The lobby was somewhat worn, but still elegant. Though the Cuu Long, like all hotels in Vietnam, was now owned by the state, the walls still sported faded old Pan American World Airways posters speckled with fly droppings. These posters had a glossy 1960s look and managed to inject a liveliness into the surroundings that wasn't carried off once you took a good look around.

Sam crossed to the desk and ordered a single room with a river view. The clerk stalled a bit before handing Sam a card to fill out. Without being asked, Sam surrendered his passport and visa. The clerk inspected these as if they were a contract for the Vietnamese's life. He fumbled and vetted, vetted and fumbled. Sam waited.

"You would like a room with a river view?" the clerk finally asked without looking up.

"Yes."

"Ah, this may not be possible."

"I see," Sam said. He palmed some dong and without exposing it, extended it toward the clerk. The clerk took it without a word.

"Please check again," Sam said, for the sake of propriety. The clerk went over his ledger, then turned to the board of pigeonholes behind him and extracted a key. He looked up at Sam for the first time.

"Ah, yes," he said, "here is a room with a nice view of the river. High up, very nice."

"Glad it turned up." The clerk held out a pen. Sam took it and signed the appropriate forms.

"Can you tell me," the clerk asked, "just how many days you'll be staying?"

"I'll be here three or four days, a week at the outside."

"I see. I shall put down a week in that case, just to be safe."

"Thank you," Sam said, and wondered who would spend a week in Ho Chi Minh City. If the time started to stretch, his interest as a tourist would have to be bolstered with some free-lance scholarship into Vietnamese architecture or some other pose. If such a ruse became necessary, he would be ready. Sam could hold his own in almost any discussion, despite having no degrees. He was always qualified, never certified; it was built into his education. The Committee had regaled him with the best education money could buy. He had had tutorials with some of the most learned men in fields too diverse to mention, but he had never been allowed to matriculate at any university or to enroll for any degree. He had spent nearly four years at the Defense Language Institute Foreign Language Center at the Presidio in Monterey, California, where he'd astounded everyone by getting the nearly impossible three-plus grade in all six languages he mastered, but he'd never been officially matriculated even there, though it was run by the government. And he had spent three years at the Royal Academy of Dramatic Art in London as an unmatriculated student. He'd toured up and down the spine of England and Scotland playing everything from Hamlet to Algernon Moncrieff to Lear in dusty school auditoriums and drafty airplane hangars, honing his skills as an actor. When he sometimes fantasized about the retirement job in the American Middle West teaching English, raising a great shortstop and going to Pizza Hut every now and again, he questioned where his curriculum vitae would come from, but he never seriously doubted the Committee's ability to provide this. After all, the Committee could put him in or out of any country in the world, with any and every kind of identity imaginable.

The clerk rang a small bell on the counter and a bellhop came forward. The clerk gave the bellhop a key on a large holder and he picked up Sam's bags and started for the elevator, Sam following. In the elevator they rode silently. On the top floor Sam followed the bellhop down a corridor until he stopped in front of a door and quickly opened it. He motioned Sam past him into the room. Sam entered. The room wasn't bad, but it wasn't good either. Like the furnishings in the lobby, the furnishings here were getting shabby. The wallpaper had not yet begun to peel, but it was buckled in places. The counterpane on

the bed was faded from a bright gold to a tawny yellow.
The desk on the window side of the room was scratched
and heavily scuffed up around its lower edges, as though
a careless maid had rammed it many times with a vac-
uum. The upholstery on the armchair in front of the desk
was worn, though not yet threadbare. The rug, once a
deep blue, was faded and stained. Near the window the
rug was much lighter from the strong sunlight beating on
it. While the bellhop settled the luggage, Sam walked
over and spread the curtains on the window. On the river
there were a few small boats, one a police launch and another a runabout that looked like it was now used as a sort
of river taxi, though it had probably once been the play-
thing of a rich merchant's son. There were two or three
sampans and a raft of some kind. Sam turned back into
the room. The bellhop stood waiting patiently. Sam
handed him a tip. The man smiled. He had only two or
three teeth left in the front of his mouth, giving him the
smile of a jack-o'-lantern. He bowed and left, closing the
door softly behind him.

Sam crossed back to the window and parted the curtains again. Across the river on the quay a lot of bicyclists
passed to and fro. Some of the bicycles had large baskets
attached to them, and in some of the baskets Sam could
see vegetables and fruits. In a few there were briefcases;
people would be heading back from the office for a lun-
cheon break at home. At the edge of the quay were food
vendors with their stalls on wheels. Some had umbrellas
fixed to the stalls for shade. As Sam watched, a woman
walked along the quay under a parasol. She was dressed
in a beautiful long dress of native design. The dress was
scarlet, the parasol powder blue; the effect was smart and
soothing.

Sam smiled to himself and turned away from the window. He walked over and sat on the edge of the bed.
Moving his weight up and down, he tested the mattress; it
seemed good, firm but not stiff. He would look forward

to getting a good night's sleep or two here before the fur started to fly. Once he contacted Doctor Sun Sun, he couldn't be sure what would be in store for him, but it was a good idea to be well rested.

He reached down, untied his shoes and slipped them off, then settled himself on the bed with both pillows propped under his head. In a little while he'd go down for lunch. For now he'd relax. He closed his eyes. In the afternoon, after a good salad and a cold beer or two, he would drift through the city, stopping from time to time to admire a sight, but not indulging in any serious touring just yet. He would have to ration his sightseeing, stretching it out slowly. With luck he'd contact Doctor Sun Sun's network within two or three days; without luck it might take a week.

Tomorrow night was Saturday. He would attend the officially sanctioned dance for foreigners at the Rex Hotel. Maybe he could work his way through the taxi girls there and find one with an inside track to Sun Sun's underworld.

Time, Sam reflected, brought many changes and not a few surprises. Time had certainly changed Saigon. It no longer seemed worthy of its designation as the Little Paris of Asia, nor of its title as the Pearl of the Orient. Wondering what surprises time spent here would hold for him, Sam drifted off to sleep.

CHAPTER TWELVE:
LADIES' CHOICE

Ho Chi Minh City
August 20

The colored lights revolved, bouncing beams of red and
green, of blue and yellow off the faces of the Vietnamese
taxi girls and the foreign visitors. The singer on the stage
slithered around, leading what passed at one moment for
the world's most inept rock band and at another for the
world's most inept swing combo. They were mixing rock
standards like "Satisfaction" with stuff Glenn Miller
cranked out with verve half a century ago, songs like
"Moonlight Serenade," "Chattanooga Choo Choo" and
"Little Brown Jug."

Sam Borne stood at the bar. This room, and this dance
constituted the Communist regime's elaborate official attempt to provide entertainment for foreign friends. Visitors to Ho Chi Minh City found that this was what had
replaced a nightlife rivaled in Asia only by Tokyo,
Bangkok and Hong Kong.

It was clear to Sam that he would need luck to get to the
heart of the Sun Sun organization by working the Saturday night dance at the Rex Hotel. This very room had
once been the U.S. officers' club during the police action. On his one former trip into what was then Saigon,
when he'd blown away the renegade CIA officer and his
cohorts, Sam had dined here pleasantly with a friend in
the United States Army, a Ranger officer. After a nice

dinner, they had taken in a few clubs along the downtown strip. Sam associated that era with the music of the Doors, the Airplane and the Stones, and it was nostalgic and eerie at the same time to hear some of the same rock under these radically altered circumstances. The Big Band stuff was even weirder, like something from *The Twilight Zone*, something that belonged in science fiction.

On that night some fifteen years ago, Sam had sat in this room and remarked upon its efficiency and class. It had been expensively decorated in those days; the silver, the linen, the service, everything had been up to snuff. The place had exuded class. Now it was different. What furniture there was consisted of a few chairs and tables scattered around the dance floor. The paint on the walls was smudged and scored, the bar was run-down and the selection of drinks was limited. It wasn't like the days of the officers' club, when you could get the best hootch on earth. Now it was cheap Scotch and vodka or Coca-Cola. There was wine, but it looked vile.

One of the girls approached Sam. She was tall for a Vietnamese, maybe five foot three or four, with the grace all Oriental women seemed to convey so easily. She was wearing tight stretch jeans and a hot-pink shell top. Her feet sported expensive sandals, probably French, with leather straps that wrapped her ankles before climbing sexily up her legs to the base of her calves. In each ear she flashed a shiny silver loop. Her face was angular, with high cheekbones, a wide forehead and eyes like filberts, only coal black instead of deep brown. Her breasts rode high and full, especially for a Vietnamese girl. Sam was glad to see her.

"Would you like to dance with me?" she asked. Her smile was full on a wide mouth framing beautifully aligned teeth, white and even.

"Sure."

"Costs only five dollars American. You American?"

"Yes."

"Five dollars."

"What does that get me?"

"We dance."

"You mean I pay you five dollars and we dance and then that's it?"

"Yes." She stood looking at Sam. He thought for a minute. The idea of paying for a dance didn't thrill him.

"That's dear," Sam said. She looked at him puzzled. *"Très cher,"* he said.

"Okay." She started to walk away as though she understood Sam's feelings, as though she thought she'd embarrassed him because he didn't have the money. Sam put his drink on the bar and followed her. When she stopped at the edge of the dance floor, he came up behind her, put his hand under her elbow and led her out onto the floor. She looked up at him. He handed her the equivalent of ten dollars. She smiled and started to boogie. Sam did too. The rock, though atrocious by Western standards, was suddenly more bearable.

"You get two dances," she said, laughing. It seemed to make her happy that she'd sold Sam on dancing with her. She spun away from him, then danced back to him provocatively. Sam felt his blood start to thicken. They moved together, their arms wheeling about their heads, their bodies shaking and rolling. They turned, they shimmied, they slipped and they slid. It felt terrific. Then the music stopped.

Sam knew he had another dance coming and only hoped it wouldn't be some slow tune from the Big Band days. He looked off toward the bandstand and was delighted to see that the musicians were taking a break. Many of them were mopping their brows with handkerchiefs, some had put aside their instruments and were heading for the bar, still others just stood and stretched. The lead singer, a woman in her late forties or early fifties in a tight and slithery black satin dress, pranced off toward the bar escorted by two musicians. If his luck held, Sam would be able to share the break with this angel.

Sam looked at his partner. "I'm entitled to another dance, right?"

"Correct."

"And the band's on a break, correct?"

"Correct."

"Can I assume I'm entitled to the break, or do you have to report to the commissar?"

For a minute Sam's new friend looked at him forbiddingly. It was clear that she understood what he'd said, and it didn't seem to sit well with her.

"That's a joke," he said. "It wasn't meant as an insult."

"I know."

Sam waited for her to say something else, to explain how she felt, but she only stared at him. Her face showed many changes, sorting through a lot of emotions.

"Let's go to the bar," he suggested, reaching out and taking her arm. Suddenly she gave a very large smile. Things were all right. When they got to the bar, there was a crowd. Two bartenders scurried around filling orders placed mostly in fluent Vietnamese, broken English and copybook French. Sam went to the spot where he'd left his Scotch and noticed it was gone. It didn't matter. He led his new friend farther down the bar, then leaned down and asked her what she'd like.

"Coca-Cola, please," she answered. Sam always noticed the way foreigners gave the great American soft drink its formal name. To them it was always Coca-Cola, never Coke. He smiled a big smile and she smiled back.

Sam turned to the bar. He was taller by a head than the Vietnamese at the bar. Only the Russians were as tall. They congregated together at one end of the bar, screaming for vodka. Sam caught the bartender's eye and ordered a Coke and a Scotch on the rocks.

"Sorry," the bartender said. "We have no more ice. Ice machine no good now."

Sam would have to settle for a cold Coke from the cooler or for hot Scotch. It was already hot enough in the room, despite the feeble attempts by the air conditioning to make it bearable. Sam wanted to be refreshed, so he ordered two Cokes. The bartender brought the drinks, putting two paper cups on top of the cans. Sam put down a few dong and the bartender gave him change, which he left on the bar as a tip. He handed one Coke to his new friend, poured the other into his cup and took a big drink.

"What is your name?" he asked.

"Amy."

"Amy is a strange name for a Vietnamese girl."

"Not really. My father was an English professor at the university."

"I see. My name's Sam, Sam Borne."

"Nice to know you, Mr. Borne."

"Sam."

"Nice to know you, Sam."

Sam was suddenly stuck for something to say. He didn't want to be rude, but he wanted to know how Amy had come to be a taxi girl on Saturday nights at the Rex Hotel. He wanted to get to know her, yet he knew that the taxi girls were discouraged from fraternizing with the foreigners once the dance officially ended. So Amy would leave at midnight and he'd never see her again. Now was his chance to guard against that. For sure this would be the band's last break. It was nearly eleven-thirty; they would play only a few more numbers and that would be it.

"It's nice to know you too, Amy. In fact, I'd like to get to know you a lot better. Do you think maybe we could meet somewhere sometime?"

She looked down at her sandals. Sam looked too. Her nails were painted a fire-engine red. Someone once said that feet were not sexy, but that someone hadn't seen Amy in her sandals with her nails painted.

"This is not permitted," she answered. "We are not permitted to see visitors after the dance, ever."

"Rules are for fools."

Amy looked at him. For a minute Sam wasn't sure she'd understood him. He started to think how to re-phrase his message, how to get her to meet him, when suddenly she said, "I will meet you at the Number Fifteen Bar tomorrow night. Please never mention it to anyone."

"Never."

"Good."

"What time?"

"Between ten-thirty and eleven."

"That's a date."

Sam felt a glow steal over him. He felt exhilarated by Amy. There was a vitality to her you didn't often encoun-ter. Just then, a tap came on his shoulder. He looked around to find himself face to face with a tall Russian who motioned for Sam to move along. Sam did not. The Russian glowered and spat out something in his native language that even a deaf-mute could understand. Sam knew Russian. The man wasn't polite. In Russian Sam told the man that he'd paid for two dances and that he had one left.

Jabbing his index finger into Sam's shoulder for em-phasis, the Russian told him to shove off. Sam pushed his hand away and stood toe to toe with him. Just then a heavy ox-blood nightstick thrust itself between them. A Vietnamese bouncer, not half the size of Sam or the Rus-sian, stood off to the side, from where he pressed the stick first into Sam's chest and then into the Russian's. They stepped back. A uniformed policeman pushed through the gathering crowd and exchanged a nod with the bouncer. The policeman was armed. The bouncer shoved the nightstick hard into the Russian's midriff, indicating for him to withdraw. The Russian grumbled and hissed that Sam's time would come. With a last hard stare at Sam, he turned and rejoined his two friends, who'd come closer along the bar in case he needed help.

Sam nodded his thanks to the bouncer, took his Coke off the bar and finished it. Amy smiled. The music had restarted, a soft old tune from the days when slow dancing was king. Sam led Amy through the crowd and onto the dance floor. He took her hand in his and started to lead her in a rhythmic glide. The combo threw into the room the sibilant swing of Glenn Miller's "Moonlight Serenade," only slightly off key. Sam could feel the swell of Amy's breasts against his chest, and as they moved their thighs would kiss ever so subtly in the dips and reverses. When the number came to an end, Sam walked Amy over to the edge of the dance floor, hoping they'd be able to chat a little more. This hope was shattered when the band segued into "Light My Fire" and the Russian stumbled over with a fistful of dong and every intention of getting a dance with Amy.

Amy took the money and the Russian commandeered her, glowering at Sam over her shoulder. On the dance floor the Russian hurled himself into the number, gyrating wildly, his arms flailing around his head, shaking his outsized ass and generally making a fool of himself. Opposite him Amy slithered halfheartedly, a study in understated sensuality. When the number ended, the sweaty Russian clamped a thick hand on Amy's shoulder and propelled her over to where one of his friends waited, money out and ready. The next Russian started to move to the hard beat of "Wooly Bully," underplayed and off key, but still as potent as ever.

When the number ended, Sam had to watch as the third Russian paid for a dance with Amy and led her out onto the floor. This one started to dance much more wildly than the first two had. Amy pretended not to notice. Suddenly he grabbed her by the arm and reeled her toward him. He twirled her around and started to grind himself against her. She was obviously not going to be a party to this, but when she tried to disengage herself, the Russian clamped her tighter. His two friends started to shout encouragement to him in Russian. They used very rude language. Amy tried to free herself again, but the Russian pinned her hard. Sam took a step onto the dance floor, but the bouncers reached Amy and her partner before he did and disengaged them. Sam was standing to the side, minding his own business, when a thunderous sucker punch caught him on the jaw and dropped him to the floor. His head spinning, he immediately attempted to stand, but as he reached all fours, a kick caught him in the solar plexus and toppled him backward. Shouts and cries ringing in his ears, he fought to get off the floor. Before he did, another wrenching kick landed against his ribs. It knocked the wind out of him. In a blur above him, Sam saw people pushing and shoving. Next thing he knew, a policeman and a bouncer were helping him to his feet. A short distance away the big Russian who'd first threatened Sam was being escorted from the dance floor by a group of bouncers and policemen. Another policeman held his revolver on the other two. All three Russians were then herded from the room. In a medley of languages, the bouncers determined that Sam was all right, with no broken bones. He would have a sore jaw and stiff ribs, but no permanent damage had been done. He thanked the bouncers and policemen as they led him to the edge of the dance floor. People went back to dancing. The band had not missed a beat through the entire incident.

Amy came over and stood beside him as he collected himself. They chatted briefly until "Ninety-Six Tears" ended and the overhead lights came on full force. Till now the wall sconces had kept the place subdued. In the harsh light it was apparent how bleak this once gala room had really become. The furniture, what there was of it, was scuffed and scratched, scored and ugly. The walls were smudged, stained and soiled. The drapes were frayed, dirty and shapeless, with smears from spilled food and drink drawing patterns on them like moiré silk; and the fixtures, like the wall sconces, were crooked, dull and in disrepair. Even the brass on the bar didn't shine. Like a comment on Sam's sadness, the band broke into a halting "Goodnight, Sweetheart." Sam quickly pulled some dong from his pocket and handed them to Amy. What the hell, he thought, he might as well make the best of the situation. He led her onto the dance floor.

Sam took Amy in his arms and propelled her around the dance floor, now bright, harsh and sad beyond sadness. She smiled at Sam throughout the number, and when he whispered in her ear that he'd give two years off his life for one night with her, she only giggled and slapped him affectionately on the back. As the music wound down, they leaned into each other with conviction, but it didn't amount to anything but a crime against real passion. As soon as the dance ended, Amy stepped back from Sam and shot out her hand. They shook hands and she was gone, strolling across the floor and out through a separate, special exit. He and the other foreign friends were all herded by the bouncers toward the main exit.

Sam fell into step with the others. He glanced back in the direction Amy had disappeared and saw the musicians leaving through the same door the taxi girls had used. They all carried cases for their instruments. Their silver stands stood like lonely sentinels, set to guard the empty bandstand till next Saturday's hoedown, by which time, Sam hoped as he looked at them, I'll be cooling out somewhere and Sun Sun will be on ice, his schemes kaput.

Sam waited in the corridor for the next elevator down and out. A few other foreigners waited as well. From the conversation of one pair, Sam gathered that they were representatives of an East German tool-and-die firm here to close a deal. From another conversation, between two badly dressed men, one of whom was hideously over-weight, Sam realized they were Czech engineers here to monitor the locomotives they'd sold the government for the run from Hanoi to Ho Chi Minh City. The train was off limits to foreigners, and this piece of information made Sam shudder for those forced to use this means of transportation. It must have been grim beyond imagining to have been declared off limits. Sam had once been told that it was on a train trip from Hanoi to Saigon that Noël Coward had written "Mad Dogs and Englishmen." Sam thought that this country could have done a lot worse than Englishmen, as it was learning under the mad dogs now in charge.

The elevator came and Sam filed silently in. The East Germans and the Czechs filled the ride down with gut-tural chatter. When they hit the lobby, Sam was glad to get out. He was the first off the elevator and didn't mince a step in getting back on the street, which was nearly empty and badly lighted. Traffic was scarce. It would be good to walk off his disappointment by taking his time getting back to his room. There he could turn in early and ponder what brunch would be like in the morning. He planned to take himself to the terrace of the Palace Hotel and see if anything remained of its former elegance.

Sam hadn't walked far when he noticed that someone behind him was taunting him. He was being impugned in slurred Russian. As he got it, he was not a man but rather only a certain part of a woman's anatomy. In the second barrage of insults, he was not interested in that part of a woman's anatomy but rather in its analogous part in male anatomy.

Sam glanced back and confirmed what he already knew: it was the three Russians from the dance. He had no more than turned back when a bottle whizzed past his

head and smashed off the pavement in front of him. His
three assailants laughed. He had had enough.

Sam quickened his step and noticed a small side street
ahead off to the left. There were times when Sam didn't
understand himself completely. He could easily hail a
pedicab and let the whole thing ride, but he wouldn't.
Somehow, it just didn't work for him, that kind of civi-
lized behavior. He glanced back, making sure as he did
so that the Russians saw him. They did. They impugned
his mother, someone Sam never knew. It didn't matter.
He was keyed into some personal instinct. He was going
to reel in a little line and see what was on the other end.
He had once seen an interview in which Federico Fellini
said that an artist always pulled on a little tail and sometimes on the other end was a big elephant. Sam was going
to pull on this tail. He was on automatic.

At the opening to the side street, Sam turned in. Before
he'd gone in two steps, he had taken in the lay of the
street, top to bottom, side to side. The Russians were
about half a block behind him. Twenty yards in front of
him was a building with a drainpipe fastened to its side.
From the second story up, this building had little balco-
nies on each floor, one on either side of the entrance. Sam
scurried to the drainpipe and climbed up it. He scaled the
railing to the first balcony and crouched down against the
building. In the nimbus of gray light cast by a street
lamp, he saw a red clay pot the size of a huge basketball.
He heard the Russians wheel around the corner, then he
heard them exclaim quickly. They thought Sam had taken
flight. They started to run down the street. Sam came out
of his crouch and hefted the pot up onto the railing. When
the Russians were right under him, he dropped it. The pot
shattered against the head of the trailing Russian, taking
him down like a pile driver.

The man screamed before his skull cracked like a
shelled walnut. He lay on the sidewalk, absolutely still.
His companions stopped, spun and came running back.

They were looking up and down, then up again, running as they came. Sam had slipped back into the shadows against the building. When the Russians disappeared from his angle of vision, he leaped forward onto the railing, poising himself like a man about to snatch and jerk barbells from the floor. He scanned below and timed his leap perfectly.

He landed as he'd intended, on the head of the Russian who'd first insulted him and tried to take Amy from him. Right before he landed, he kicked out at a forty-five-degree angle and caught the man directly under the chin, his heels striking exactly, snapping the man's head back, toppling him over in a spinning sprawl. He roared in pain. Sam landed on his hands and somersaulted immediately. The third Russian hurled himself at the spot where a normal man would have fallen after delivering so powerful a kick. But Sam looped himself upright out of the somersault and stood ready, hands spread, arms out, on the balls of his feet. The Russian spun around on him, astonished and frightened. His one friend was dead, his head splattered on the sidewalk like a run-over Pekinese. His other friend was moaning loudly and trying unsuccessfully to regain his feet. He hesitated, then yelled and charged Sam. That was exactly what Sam knew he would do.

Sam sidestepped and reeled him in, grasping his forearm and cartwheeling him headlong against the building. He hit the stucco wall with a solid thud, but staggered to his feet, dazed. While he got to his feet, Sam glanced quickly back at the other Russian, then walked over and took the dazed man against the wall firmly in his hands, which he locked on either side of his neck. He thrust his knee up and in. The man took the blow in his groin and his knees buckled. Holding him firmly in his hands, like a man about to give another a hearty embrace, Sam firmly pressed in with both thumbs, checking the other Russian over his shoulder as he did so. The man in his hands kicked madly. Sam anticipated this and stepped to the side. When Sam looked back, the man's eyes were bulging in terror. Sam waited half a second to allow Sergei or Dmitri to square himself with the ghost of God or with the soul of Lenin before he snapped his thumbs forward like a man putting a hubcap in place. The windpipe collapsed with a swooshing pop. Sam released him and he crumpled to the ground, shapeless as a mannequin.

That left the big guy. Sam turned and stood looking at him as he stumbled to his feet in the street. He held up his hand like a man stopping traffic. His other hand was grasping desperately at his throat. No sound issued from his mouth, though he worked it vigorously. Sam stood looking, arms akimbo, hands on hips; he might have been a clothing salesman sizing up a customer for a suit. He waited. The Russian stumbled toward him, his hand outstretched in a gesture of friendship, in an effort at reconciliation. Sam took his arm and whipped it around behind him, up against his back, the man's hand resting backward against his own nape. Sam increased the pressure so that he started to kneel. He kneeled in the gutter in the grainy light from the street lamp, just beyond the cone the light cast. Sam said to him clearly and slowly in patient Russian that he was not sorry. He then raised his knee against the man's nape, hitched his joined hands under the man's chin and snapped sharply. The sound of the neck breaking was like the crunching sound a boot makes on impacted snow. Sam released his grip and the body toppled forward.

Sam looked around. The street was empty. No one had noticed. Bending down, he quickly stripped all three corpses of their wallets, then strolled off down the dark side street. As he walked, he extracted the dong from the wallets. Then he took out his handkerchief and wiped all three wallets of prints. After wiping each one, he tossed it against the wall. The police were sure to find the wallets in the morning; this would reassure them that the crime was one of motive, namely, of robbery rather than of passion, which in truth it was.

Sam entered the next wide street he came to and walked like any citizen intent on returning to his hotel. The dong he'd taken, he figured, would just about cover the price of brunch on the terrace at the Palace.

CHAPTER THIRTEEN:
NUMBER 15 BAR

Ho Chi Minh City
August 21

The Number 15 Bar was crowded. Men and women stood three deep at the bar and spilled over into the area of tables and booths. This was the one spot in Ho Chi Minh City that could pass for an officially sanctioned hot spot. The trouble was that once the spot got good and hot, the authorities were likely to come charging in and close the place down. This was something Sam had seen done often enough in other places; it wasn't at all uncommon for the Communist authorities. You could see it anywhere, in Hungary, in Czechoslovakia, in East Germany. When fun got too good it got ousted.

But for now the Number 15 Bar was in full swing. Waiters and waitresses worked the tables and booths quickly, weaving in and out with loaded trays. From the old jukebox in the back the hits of the Stones, the Airplane and the Doors rocked on. It really was as though music had stopped here in the early seventies. But the crowd didn't mind. It was what they had, so they made the most of it. It was clearly better than nothing.

Sam wriggled past the crowded entrance and picked his way down the bar, swiveling in and out, keeping his eyes open for Amy the whole time. Finally he spotted her at a crowded table in the back. She sat surrounded by men; not one other woman sat at this table or stood near it. This struck Sam as odd.

Amy looked up, saw Sam and waved. He waved back. It took him a few minutes to wend his way to the table. When he got there, to his surprise one of the men rose and insisted that Sam take his seat. After a few protests, Sam relented and sat down. He was next to Amy. That didn't seem accidental. Sam began to feel that there was more on the line than met the eye. Amy smiled a big smile at him and he smiled back. Then in the din she introduced her friends, tipping her hand at each as she introduced him. They nodded in turn, the ones near Sam extending a hand in greeting. Amy's friends were all about her age, mostly in their mid- to late twenties. They were dressed in flashy clothes for Vietnamese, clothes with a lot of Western flair, jeans and printed T-shirts and bright La Coste shirts. If it weren't for something being slightly off, they could have been young people out for a good time in Paris or Rome.

Amy leaned over and whispered in Sam's ear, "I am happy to see you."

Instinct told Sam to answer her in an audible voice. "I'm happy to see you too," he said, loud enough to be heard above the music and the noise all around them.

All of the faces around the table were turned toward Sam.

"What would you like to drink?" Amy asked.

"Do you think it's possible to place an order?" Sam joked, nodding toward the crowd swelling against the tables and around the booths.

"It's easy. We're used to crowds in Ho Chi Minh City."

"In that case, I'll have a gin and tonic."

One of Amy's friends across the table raised his arm. He was a handsome man, dressed well in one of the La Coste shirts. He had an easy air of authority about him. In a twinkling a waitress pushed her way to his side. He ordered in Vietnamese. Sam noted that the man had not asked anyone else if they wanted anything. The man who'd placed the order looked across the table at Sam and stared at him hard. In an interrogator, it would be the stare of intimidation. Sam stared back.

One of the other friends at the table said something in Vietnamese to the staring man. He answered back and everyone laughed. Amy laughed too. Sam gave her a quizzical look.

"They think you are overly formal," Amy announced. She shook Sam's arm in a teasing gesture, one meant to relax him. He was dressed in his linen sports coat with the beige base under the woven blue pattern. Under this he had on a yellow polo shirt above the blue slacks. He didn't think he was that formal, although most of the young customers in the Number 15 Bar were more casually attired. Sam speculated for a moment that the staring man had said something entirely different that made the others laugh. But he would hold his fire. He would speculate all he wanted, but he would not tip his mitt at all. He would not react other than how a foreigner would react. He would be the dumb tourist, if that was what was called for.

The gin and tonic came. The waitress brought it to the staring man. He signed for it, Sam noticed. That was strange in a boite like this, where everything was normally on a cash-and-carry basis. The staring man took the drink and made a show of handing it across the table to Sam. Sam reached out, took the glass, tipped it toward the staring man and took a drink. It was hard to fuck up a gin and tonic, but the Number 15 Bar had succeeded. The drink was watery and dull, even the lime only a sliver and that sitting on the bottom of the glass like wispy algae.

"What did you do today in our fair city, Mr. Borne?"

The staring man had spoken. His question was not half as casual as it could have been. This was a man of purpose who wanted that fact clear to everyone.

"Call me Sam."

"By all means. Now, what did you do today?"

"I took in some sights."

"What sights?"

"I had a look at the basilica—"

"An undistinguished and decadent pile of stone."

"My sentiments exactly."

"Then why did you come all this way to see it?"

"I wasn't aware that I'd said I'd come all this way to see an undistinguished and decadent pile of stone."

The staring man ignored this. "What else did you do today?"

"I went to the zoo."

"Are you a zoologist?"

"Is every gardener a botanist?"

"You are sarcastic, Mr. Borne. Why? There is no need of sarcasm in a simple tourist."

"Nor is there a restriction against it, to my knowledge."

"You like zoos, is that it?"

"I wanted to see the tiger that pissed on Ambassador Lodge way back when. Is that a good enough reason to visit the zoo?"

"A good enough reason, if sarcastic."

There was a ruckus toward the front of the bar. People surged back against each other, forcing everyone to crowd into the back, between the tables and booths. A waitress dropped a tray with a loud clatter. Some people started to push each other and to trade insults. One of Amy's friends said something to her in Vietnamese. She said something back. Then the staring man announced something above the din. Everyone at the table expressed disappointment and anger. Some spat out what were obviously curses in Vietnamese.

Amy leaned in to Sam. "The police are here. They are closing the bar for the rest of the night on account of unseemly and decadent behavior in the capitalist mode. We must go when the crowd clears."

This did not disturb Sam. He was enjoying the Number 15 Bar about as much as a prostate examination. Before he could ask Amy where they might go, the staring man said something to her in Vietnamese. She responded. Then the staring man and his friends got up and prepared to leave. They pushed money, cigarettes and lighters into their pockets while hastily finishing off their drinks. As they filed out, they waved and gestured to Amy. When they were gone she turned to Sam.

"I should leave you here, but I'll take the risk if you'd like to come back to my place for a bit."

Sam would like to.

"That sounds just great," he said. He rose and Amy did too. Standing, she looked spectacular. She was dressed in jeans and black T-shirt with the sleeves and neck cut away in the latest *Flashdance* fashion. Sam wondered how she knew to do this. He doubted that *Flashdance* had played in Ho Chi Minh City. It was more likely that the fad had come in through the French tourists who occasionally visited, or through a few Vietnamese who got to visit the West each year. Then again, he thought, there might be a black market in American movie magazines controlled by Sun Sun. It was more than possible. At any rate, she looked dynamite.

The crowd had mostly dispersed. Sam followed Amy as they wended their way through angry stragglers to the front of the bar. Policemen lined the bar, jostling night-sticks in their hands as the customers left.

On the street Sam wondered if they shouldn't hail a taxi. Amy just smiled. "You are welcome to ride the back saddle on my scooter, if that's not too much for you."

"It's not too much."

Amy led the way down the line of scooters and motor-bikes parked diagonally in front of the bar. They made the small street even smaller. When they got to a gray scooter, Amy hopped aboard and gunned the motor to life. Sam stood beside her. After revving the engine a few times, she flicked her head and Sam climbed on behind her. They backed out of the space, into the middle of the street, Amy expertly seesawing the scooter back and forth from one foot to the other before straightening it out and roaring off down the center of the street.

Sam gripped her about her waist. They whipped out into the traffic on one of the large boulevards. So far as Sam could tell, they were headed west, southwest, toward Cholon. It wasn't long before Sam's surmise proved right. The streets got narrower and much more crowded as they streaked into the old Chinese section of the city. The light here, unlike the harsh yet murky light of center city Ho Chi Minh City, was weaker, the darkness more pronounced, the shadows more plentiful and threatening.

At a stoplight, Sam leaned forward and shouted into Amy's ear, "This is Cholon, right?"

"Correct."

"You live here?"

"*Oui.*" Amy's answer floated behind her as the light changed and she gunned the scooter forward. They wound around this corner and then that, entering a maze Sam was sure he couldn't find his way out of. He was on his own now. The thought crossed his mind that maybe Amy was making one or two turns too many, that maybe she was making sure he wouldn't be able to find his way out. There were few taxis in this part of town, Sam noticed; the traffic was nearly all bicycles. Even pedicabs didn't seem to come this deep into Cholon. They crossed a canal and Sam made a note of it, but then they crossed two more small bridges over canals and Sam decided it was hopeless. He'd have to depend on Amy to get him back to his hotel. Cholon was definitely sinister, if not by day, then surely by night.

Suddenly Amy slowed the scooter to a crawl and guided it over a curb in front of a shuttered shop with its woodwork lacquered red. They were on a quiet corner. Down one side street was an old wrought-iron street lamp; curled and scrolled, it was the type once popular in Paris. It threw a cone of light onto the ground, delineating in a circle the uneven stonework of the old street. Down another side street all was darkness except for one feeble light caged in an iron basket above the entrance of what looked like an old warehouse.

Amy coaxed the scooter across the narrow sidewalk and killed the engine. It felt odd to Sam to have the vibration so suddenly stilled. Amy swung off the seat, reached out and took a chain from its resting place against the wall. The chain was fastened to the wall through an eyebolt. She yoked the chain over the handlebars of the scooter and through the ring of the eyebolt. Then she clasped it shut with a heavy lock. Sam sat through this whole procedure. When Amy looked up from the lock, Sam smiled.

"Are you going to sit there all night or are you coming up?" she asked.

"I'm coming up."

Sam swung his leg over the seat and stood beside Amy as she inserted a key into the door beside the shuttered shop. It opened and she stepped back and motioned Sam in ahead of her. He stepped into the small entryway and waited while she relocked the door. The light was poor in the entryway. All he could see was a narrow staircase straight ahead with an old railing and steps with deep runnels in them. In the dim light Sam could make out a simple flowered pattern in the black and white tiles of the floor and the walls of the entryway. When Amy had relocked the door, she motioned Sam ahead of her, but he declined. Amy went ahead. They followed the old staircase up three flights to the top. There they went to the door at the front of the landing. There was another door at the back which Sam assumed led to another apartment. Amy slipped her key into the door and opened it. She stepped into the room and Sam followed her.

As soon as Sam peered into the darkness of the apartment, his eye picked out the red eye of a glowing cigarette. His senses snapped immediately onto red alert. He did not panic, but he entered no farther. He waited in the doorway, his eyes adjusting to the darkness, until Amy walked into the room and lit a small lamp on a table between two rattan armchairs.

In one armchair sat the staring man from the Number 15 Bar. He was calmly smoking a cigarette. Dangling from his right hand was a standard 7.62mm pistol, the kind used in the Chinese army. A type 51 or 54, it had probably been around since the days of the police action, when Chinese weapons flowed down the Ho Chi Minh City trail like rain in a monsoon. Sam could have been just a memory. The staring man was letting him know that. Sam stood his ground.

"How do you do, Mr. Borne? It's a pleasure to see you again," the staring man said.

"Likewise, I'm sure," Sam answered.

"You remember Bui, Sam," Amy said.

"Yes." Sam would have liked to have added, And what the hell is he doing here, but he restrained himself.

"Bui is my brother," Amy said softly. "He comes here often."

"How come he has a Vietnamese name?" Sam asked.

"My imperialist name was Byron, Mr. Borne. I've long since renounced it."

"Do you always dangle a Chinese army pistol when you visit?"

"Mr. Borne," Bui spoke up. "I have come here to put some questions to you. You can cooperate or you can meet another fate."

Sam looked at Amy. "He talks tough too."

"This is no time for games, Mr. Borne," Bui stated in

a flat voice, one he hoped would be as menacing as anything in a B-movie. "We are not playing cowboys and Indians here, you see. I want you to understand your options."

"And my options are that you will put certain questions to me and I will give answers or be shot to death, is that it?"

"You have a talent for précis, Mr. Borne."

"I also have a first name, which I told you at the bar you're entitled to use."

"I prefer the formal to the lax, Mr. Borne."

"I see."

"My sister Amy will come here and sit beside me. You will remain where you are. I will not take longer than necessary." Bui extinguished the cigarette in his left hand in a large beaten-brass ashtray on a tiny bamboo table between the rattan armchairs. Then he extended his left hand and Amy followed his outthrust finger to the chair beside him. She sat and crossed her legs. She did not appear to be enjoying any of this. On the contrary, she looked annoyed. Sam stood waiting. Bui let a long silence hang. He had a second-degree idiot's grasp of the techniques of a disciplinarian. Sam knew the type: everybody in his classroom writes right-handed, everybody parts his hair on the left, everybody keeps quiet till spoken to.

"Why have you come to Ho Chi Minh City, Mr. Borne?"

"Why do you ask?"

"We will play no games, Mr. Borne. I will ask the questions, you will answer them. A simple arrangement."

"Under what authority?" Sam asked.

"Under the authority vested in me by the eight slugs in this pistol, Mr. Borne. Are they persuasion enough?"

"They'll do."

"I repeat, Mr. Borne, why have you come to Ho Chi Minh City?"

"I have come to familiarize myself with Asian culture, especially with Asian architecture, which I happen to teach in a college in the United States."

"Where?"

"Harvard. Have you heard of it?"

"Such sarcasm will get you dead, Mr. Borne, be warned."

"I'm warned."

"So you have come to Asia to study its culture, Mr. Borne, and you are now swinging through Ho Chi Minh City to see it close up, Vietnamese style, is that it?"

"Close enough."

"And where has your itinerary taken you and where will it take you?"

"I started in Hong Kong and had a look around and now I'm here and I thought I'd swing through Cambodia and then into Thailand, then home. I have to start teaching in a few weeks."

"I see. Now, what especially do you want to see in Cambodia, say?"

"Angkor Wat, Angkor Thom chiefly."

"Yes, one would want to see them in Cambodia."

"They're marvelous."

"So you have seen them before, yet you come again?"

"Is one look at the *Mona Lisa* ever enough?"

"It was more than enough for me, Mr. Borne. My one obligatory visit to the Louvre during my student sojourn in Paris was more than enough. The trappings of the West hold no charm for me."

"Well put."

"Your sarcasm quickens my temper, Mr. Borne. And I am stroking a trigger, you realize."

"I realize."

"Now, Angkor Wat I understand, and Angkor Thom I understand. You teach their superior beauty to dull-witted American college students more interested in football and fucking than great architecture; this too I understand. But why Vietnam, this I don't understand. Explain please?"

"Easy. To know the whole range of Asian culture you have to know it in all its aspects, even in the Vietnamese hybrid, inferior as it is in its amalgam of influences—Chinese, French, what have you."

"And you thought to see the basilica, a rubbish heap."

"And the Xa Loi Pagoda, another rubbish heap."

"I would say you are wasting your time in Vietnam, Mr. Borne."

Sam wanted to reply that everybody in Vietnam was wasting their time, but he thought better of it. "I wanted to see Asia in all its aspects. It's reasonable. And in the interests of academic freedom, more than acceptable."

"And so you are sure this is why you have come to Vietnam, Mr. Borne. To see Asian culture, to experience its architecture. I see."

"Good."

"And tell me, Mr. Borne, how much longer do you expect to be in Ho Chi Minh City?"

"I had hoped to get some permits to travel upcountry using Ho Chi Minh City as a home base, but this may not prove possible. I would expect I'll be here a few more days, to answer your question."

"But there is nothing more to see."

"There is if you have the eyes to look."

"Clever, Mr. Borne. I shall remember that."

"Please do."

"So that is your story. You teach a course in Asian studies at Harvard and you are having a look firsthand at

Hong Kong and Vietnam and then it's on to Cambodia and maybe Thailand.''

"That's right. I take it as it comes. I like to drift in Asia. It's the best way to get the feel for the place.''

"I believe many would agree.''

"At least Marco Polo would.''

"Your sarcasm again, Mr. Borne. I believe it will eventually inhibit your understanding of Asia and Asians.''

"We shall see.''

"I hope that we do see, Mr. Borne. For I shall leave you now with my sister, who is less discriminating than I, but I think we shall meet again, especially since you share my interest in things Vietnamese.''

Bui rose from the chair and waved the pistol at Sam, motioning him to the side. Sam stepped over against the wall. Bui strode to the door. He turned and with the pistol waved Sam into the chair he'd vacated. Sam walked over and sat down.

Bui opened the door and leaned against it. He was clearly going to make a big statement. "I am sure we will meet again, Mr. Borne. I can only hope that the circumstances of such future meetings will be more pleasant.''

Sam let Bui's words hang in the room, to reassure the Vietnamese that they had sunk in and that Sam would mind his Ps and Qs. In many assignments Sam undertook, he had to play the fool, and this was one such situation. The wheels would roll now. Like a sap, Bui would check Sam's cover, which was easily fabricated and easy to expose. In a matter of hours the skids would be greased. Bui and whoever he worked for would know that Sam was a drug dealer scouring Asia for a better connection. When the *chiu chau* heavies from Hong Kong got into the act, they would appear to mark Sam for death for trying to find a cheaper supply of heroin than they offered. They would appear to sell Sam down the river. Of course, Bui and his boys would take the bait hook, line and sinker.

And if Sam was right, he'd be on his way to a head to head with the biggest boy of all, Doctor Sun Sun.

"See you around, Bui," Sam said.

Bui nodded, went out the door and closed it behind him.

Sam was alone with Amy.

"Would you like some tea, Sam?" she asked.

"Among other things."

CHAPTER FOURTEEN:
ALL THINGS COME

Ho Chi Minh City
August 22

Time hung heavy. Sam Borne sat in a wicker café chair in front of a small wicker table on the veranda of the Dong Khoi Hotel, formerly the Continental Palace Hotel. This was about as near as you could come these days in Ho Chi Minh City to sitting in a café watching life parade by. Sam had carefully arranged to be here to pass the time in this early evening hour. He watched the light change in the plaza directly in front of the National Assembly. He had liked the National Assembly much better years earlier when it had been the National Theater. On that first visit years ago, he had seen a fairly well-mounted production of Molière's *Tartuffe* in this very theater, but nothing that lighthearted was likely to be staged here again. It wouldn't do for the Communists to show life as playful; no, now everything had to appear grim.

Grim was exactly how Sam was feeling. It was only a matter of time before he heard back from Bui and who-ever controlled him. Bui's presence the previous evening at his sister Amy's apartment was no accident. He was sure to be back. In fact, Sam was annoyed that things had developed as slowly as they had. He was certain he had done all the groundwork necessary when he'd fed Bui the story about his being a professor at Harvard. A phone call or two would dispel that fabrication. Bui should have been here already, especially since Sam had specifically told Amy that he'd be on the veranda at the Dong Khoi from seven to eight in the evening.

Out in the plaza some kids kicked a soccer ball around in an impromptu game, their shouts filling the air. Watching them carried Sam back to the days of his own boyhood, when he'd been an urchin, a street fighter, a hustler. He had led a band of roving thieves the same age as the kids playing soccer. In Tokyo, Sam and his band had roamed the downtown streets where the GIs went to get liquored and laid. As the leader, Sam would wait for the right moment, then fling himself into action, spearheading attack after attack that resulted in some drunken GI losing his wallet, his watch and rings, and sometimes a tooth or two. There were even cases where Sam's victims had to have their jaws wired and then had to eat baby food through a rubber grill in the front of their mouths while their broken jaws healed. Eventually, after so many of these attacks, the American MPs succeeded in running Sam and his gang to ground.

Sam had been marked out immediately and referred to high-ranking intelligence officers who'd quickly discovered that he'd been left in a hand basket on the United States air base at Mount Susshima on the second day of November in 1951. They further learned that his father had been one of the paratroopers with the Eleventh Airborne, nicknamed "The Angels," who had been killed in action at the drop at Munsan-Ni on March 23, 1951. Sam's mother was a Japanese boat woman, a river prostitute who had sailed out of his life moments after he was born. Abandoned, Sam had been adopted by the paratroopers at the air base—they were called *"rakkasans"* by the Japanese, or literally, "falling-down umbrellas." He'd been given the name Sam Borne—Sam slapped on for Uncle Sam and Borne because his father had been in the airborne division. Sam had eventually ended up in the streets when the base was closed and the unit transferred out of the country in the late fifties.

The intelligence officers had then given Sam a battery of mental and physical tests, all of which he'd passed with flying colors. Then, in cooperation with the Japanese, a group of ninja masters devised what they considered the supreme test. They had Sam, without a word of instruction, taken into the central mountains and let loose, blindfolded and bound, without a single weapon. Miraculously, he had shown up a week later back in his old haunts, mugging drunken soldiers and sailors, at the head of his gang, as ruthless, fierce and feral as ever, completely unscathed by his survivalist ordeal. The American and Japanese authorities had then taken over Sam's training, honing and polishing his skills. The wheelworks set in motion back then now resulted in Sam's sitting on the veranda of the Dong Khoi, waiting to be grabbed by Bui, waiting to take the first step on the path that he hoped would lead him to Doctor Sun Sun.

For now it was all waiting, and at times Sam was not a good waiter. But since he had to, he would wait, but reluctantly. He had learned in his ninja training that waiting was often part of a good strategy, that it was often necessary, frequently unavoidable. Still, he hated it. Even his training in meditation, in Zen, had been of little help when the surge was fully on him, as it was now. He was ready to get to Sun Sun, to let the chips fall where they might.

The evening air was taking on the bluish tinge that told you night was not far off. Sam requested his bill and paid it. He picked up his hat, snapped it into place, shuffled out of his chair and left the veranda. He had waited long enough.

Sam walked away from the hotel a few blocks before realizing his feet were tired from traipsing around all day photographing buildings he knew to be second or third rate. But it was important to keep up appearances for however long it took, so he would. He hailed a pedicab and climbed in. As they slipped out into traffic, Sam sat back, his mind drifting with the soothing rhythms of the carriage. Sam's driver, pedaling away on his bicycle, was no match for the scooters and motorbikes screaming by, nor for the old Peugeot and Renault taxis bobbing and weaving past them with empty back seats. The drivers of Ho Chi Minh City were no different from what the drivers of Saigon had been; they had picked up the European habit from the French of driving with maximum disregard for safety, even when empty and merely cruising for fares.

A consummate actor, Sam was a consummate liar. He could dissemble at will, deliver any line straight, convincingly; he could project what he had to project. Yet he could never kid himself, and he couldn't kid himself now. He was disappointed. That Bui hadn't shown up was one thing; that Amy hadn't was another. Sam had thought she would show if her brother didn't. Last night they had been fantastic together. When Sam had told her, as she lay against his chest, that he'd be on the veranda at seven, and had invited her to join him, he thought for sure that she surely would, if Bui didn't show up first.

Sam mulled over his disappointment as the pedicab pulled up before the Cuu Long. He paid the cabbie, entered the lobby and crossed to the reception desk. The clerk smiled and nodded.

"Good evening," Sam said. "Borne is the name. Are there any messages?"

The clerk turned and checked the pigeonholes behind him. The one for Sam's room was empty. He turned back to Sam and extended both palms upward. "Sorry, Mr. Borne, there are no messages for you."

"Thank you." Sam spun around and crossed to the elevator. There was no point in dwelling on his disappointment. If wait he must, it would have been nice to take Amy to dinner at Madame Dai's. Her restaurant was reputed to be one of the best in Ho Chi Minh City. Although small, Madame Dai's was famous for its excellent French cuisine and for Madame Dai herself, a charming and provocative woman. She was strong willed, well-known for going against the grain, and had even gone so far as to employ as a waitress a princess from the former royal family of Amman. Now he would go there alone and see what the legendary Madame Dai had to offer.

The elevator came and Sam got in. He rode up thinking about all the things that could have occurred and hadn't. Something told him something wasn't right. All of his instincts told him that Bui should have contacted him by now. If by tomorrow morning he had not been contacted, he would have to take more chances to penetrate the underworld and contact someone who could take him to Doctor Sun Sun. As Sam walked down the corridor to his room, he was convinced more than ever of this.

He turned the key in his door and entered his room. It was close, fetid and as shabby as when he'd left it that midmorning. The watery rays of the dying sun shone through the big windows. Sam tossed his camera onto the bed and walked over and unhitched the brass latch on the big windows. He pushed them back and looked out. The river was nearly empty, as was the quay across the way. The vendors had long since closed their stalls and departed for the night. Only a few strollers and cyclists coursed up and down the quay.

Sam decided he could use a Gauloise. He went back into the room and over to his suitcase. From his shaving kit he took a crumpled pack and shook one out. He lit it and took the first rush into his lungs, savoring it. A Gauloise made no compromises. Smoking one wasn't smart, but it was definite, it was pure.

He walked back to the window and looked out. The sun cast a bronze channel on the river. In the channel a sampan bobbed like a cameo inset. As Sam watched, a young girl came out and sat on the edge of the sampan.

She let her arm hang over the gunwale, resting on the top of an old tire lashed to the side as a bumper for docking. From downriver a blue and white runabout sliced toward the sampan. Soon it entered the bronze channel and passed the sampan. In the runabout's wake the sampan bobbed violently. The young girl waved to the man straddling the controls in the runabout, but he ignored her. If she looks up, Sam decided, I'll wave to her. Sam waited. She didn't look up.

Sam's attention was drawn back across the river. Two Vietnamese soldiers had come out onto the quay. Dressed head to toe in khaki and wearing pith helmets, they carried type 56 assault rifles slung over their shoulders. This was a bit much, Sam thought, for urban soldiers. From the right cover and in the hands of a man who knew how to use it, a type 56 would suffice to hold off a company. You had to give the devil his due; the type 56 was a fabulous weapon.

It was time for that shower. Sam snubbed out his Gauloise against the window jamb and flicked the butt out into the wind. It would tumble and swirl to the street below where a street sweeper would whisk it away with one of the curved straw brooms that looked like they belonged to a race of giant witches.

Sam strode back across the room, pulling his polo shirt over his head as he went. He threw it on the bed. He would have to have some laundry done tomorrow. In the bathroom, with its tiles starting to lose their grouting, Sam slipped out of his slacks and hung them over the towel rack. In seconds he was under the stream of the shower, soaped and letting the hot water work its way into his muscles. As he offered his face to the refreshing stream of water, its needles pricking and reviving him, he thought back to his amusement that morning at seeing photos of the three dead Russians in the newspapers. He didn't have to be able to read Vietnamese to know that his little encounter had provided the papers with a story they could chew on. No doubt the press would blame this apparent robbery and murder on the river pirates, the renegades the Communists could not subdue, the dreaded desperadoes of old Saigon who operated from the hamlet of Binh Xuyen, just south of Cholon and within easy reach of the dense Rung Sat Swamp. In the impenetrable jungle amid the labyrinth of mangrove swamps, they were invulnerable. Rung Sat translated as Forest of the Assassins, and it lay at the mouth of the Saigon River where it debouched into the South China Sea. The river pirates would be there, Sam would wager, till the Communists declared Christmas the birthday of Lenin. Yes, the river pirates were in for the duration, and being blamed for the murder of three Russians, whom they would surely have killed for the hell of it, would not faze them at all. Sam smiled at the thought of them taking the rap.

Sam turned away from the nozzle and let the water drill into his shoulders. He hunched over like a pitcher awaiting his sign from the catcher. The water bounced off his shoulders and streamed down his back. Then he stood up, turned the hot faucet back, the cold faucet forward and leaned his chest into the cold flow. It revived him. He felt ready for anything. He cut the faucets and came alert like a cougar. As the faucets squeaked closed, Sam thought he heard movement in the bedroom. He listened carefully. There was no sound. He listened some more. There was silence. He could have sworn he'd heard something.

He stepped over the edge of the tub and snatched a towel from the facing rack. He quietly began to dab himself dry, listening all the while for the slightest sound. None came. He started to relax, yet something told him he wasn't alone. He finished drying himself, leaned over and opened the small window beside the sink. The fresh evening breeze wafted into the room, clearing the steam from the mirror above the sink. He picked up a can of shaving cream and looked at it carefully, still listening. It was Old Spice, the kind with the white frigate stenciled on the red can. Sam stared at it, waiting, listening, concentrating. Finally he decided to proceed. He snapped off the red plastic cap and depressed the nozzle. On his left fingertips a cone of cream accumulated. He dabbed this over his beard, took his blue Gillette Good News razor in his right hand and, starting with his right sideburn, scraped down the length of his cheek.

From the bedroom there came a clear and definite click.

Sam stood motionless. Then he walked lightly to the door and stood listening. A man with a faceful of shaving cream, a terry-cloth towel around his waist, a blue plastic razor in his hand has not a lot of dignity to protect.

"You can come out now, Mr. Borne, or should I say Professor Borne." It was Bui's voice. There was no question. It was gratifying to Sam that Bui had come through. Sam's instincts, as ever, were right. Leave it to Bui to be so catty about the title of professor.

Sam opened the door and took two steps into the bedroom. Bui sat with his hands on his knees at the worn chair in front of the desk. Standing on either side of him were Vietnamese men of about Bui's age. Both held AK-47s pointed directly at Sam, who pretended not to notice them. He looked right at Bui.

"You look a bit like Santa Claus with your white whiskers, Professor Borne. I hope you have some presents for me."

"That will depend on whether you're a good boy."

"This is no time for sarcasm, Professor Borne. I simply hope for your sake that your sack is not empty so far as we are concerned."

"Who's we?"

"You will find out directly, Professor Borne. For now, go back and finish shaving, then we will take you for a little ride, as they say in the American gangster movies."

"Where to?"

"For now, you shave. And we will ask the questions."

"As they say in the American gangster movies."

"That is correct, Professor. Now shave—with the door open."

Sam walked back into the bathroom and started to shave, showing not an ounce of pleasure at being discovered. He was impassive yet elated. The wheels had turned, the fix was in. He was almost certainly in contact with the Munchkins who would lead him down the yellow brick road to his rendezvous with the wizard of the Vietnamese underworld.

And Sam knew what he wanted: the wizard's life.

CHAPTER FIFTEEN:
CLIFFHANGER

Ho Chi Minh City
August 22

Sam rode in the back between the two goons with the AK-47s. Bui sat magisterially in the shotgun seat. The driver drove impassively, in silence; the goons were silent. Every now and again Sam and Bui exchanged a cutting remark or two. Bui would never deign to turn around in his seat and address Sam directly. Instead he stared forward and treated Sam disdainfully, making his answers as short as possible and keeping Sam totally in the dark. Outside the evening traffic was light. They made good time and after a short haul arrived at a tall apartment building with a short semicircular drive. At one time this was no doubt a good address to have in old Saigon.

The black Citroen pulled into the driveway and the goons hopped out on either side. While the one on the side nearer the building held the back door open, Sam got out under the surveillance of the other goon, who'd come around the back of the car and stood, indifferent to the stare of the doorman and other onlookers, with his rifle trained directly on Sam. Sam slid across the seat and got out. Bui walked into the lobby. With a nod from one of the goons, Sam followed. The two goons flanked him from behind on either side. They marched through a glass and marble lobby of no particular charm and over to the bank of elevators. Two older Vietnamese women perched on a tattered velvet couch on one side of the lobby followed Sam and his escort with their eyes, but neither said a word. Citizens of Ho Chi Minh City were long accustomed to the bizarre and militant, and these old ladies seemed to accept as normal a man being marched across their lobby with two assault rifles trained on his back.

Bui held the elevator door and the goons entered right on Sam's heels. In the elevator Sam braced himself against the back wall, the two goons ahead of him, facing him, their rifles pointed at him. Bui stood to the side in front of the control panel and didn't look around the entire ride up. Bui had selected the top floor, the penthouse floor. When the elevator stopped on a lower floor, Bui quickly said something in Vietnamese and the middle-aged Vietnamese couple waiting to board the elevator merely smiled and stepped back into the corridor. The doors closed again, and they continued up to the penthouse floor without interruption.

In the penthouse corridor, there were only two doors. They were on either side of the elevator bank. Sam thought that the Communists would have broken up these luxurious suites into smaller units, but that was not the case. Bui turned to the door on the right and rang a small bell in the center under a brass nameplate. The nameplate was empty. The door was opened from behind, seemingly by itself, and Bui entered. Sam followed, the goons bringing up the rear. As Sam passed the door, he looked to the side and saw that an elegantly dressed Vietnamese woman of about fifty stood behind it, holding it open very deferentially. Bui had not greeted her and neither did the goons. Bui strode down a short corridor with old Impressionist prints on the walls and entered a large living room with leather Scandinavian furniture, couches, love seats and loungers and with a wall of glass running along its length. The drapes along the wall were parted slightly and Sam could see that beyond lay a narrow balcony with a black wrought-iron railing around it. Bui snapped out an order in Vietnamese and the goons stopped on either side of the archway from the small corridor. Sam stood just within the living room.

Bui turned in the middle of the room and indicated with an outstretched hand that Sam should have a seat on the long sectional couch against the right wall. Sam walked over and sat. Bui took a seat to Sam's right in a lounger. He sat back and waited just long enough to be dramatic. Sam could wait as long as Bui wanted him to.

"Now comes the moment of truth, Professor Borne," Bui started. He let that statement hang in the air for dramatic effect. "You will tell me," he continued, "in the interests of making things easier on both yourself and me why not twenty-four hours past you fed me such an easily disprovable line about yourself and your life's work."

Bui waited. Sam waited.

"Do you wish to be difficult, Professor, or are you merely taking your time in concocting your next bit of fiction so it will not be so easily disproved?"

Sam decided to act officious, the way any self-respecting tourist would have. He must play this for appearances, no matter how certain he was that things were falling just the way he wanted them to. So he would be officious and invoke his rights.

"I'd like to know by whose authority you've abducted me at gunpoint and brought me here for interrogation?"

"Never mind that. Answer the question."

"Not until you identify yourself."

"Professor Borne, dear man, the question under discussion is not who I am but who you are. You are surely not a professor from Harvard University, so who are you?"

"A tourist, like another."

"Try again."

"Try what again?"

"I will ask you once more politely: tell me who you are."

"By whose leave?"

Bui turned to the goons and flicked his index finger toward one of the closed doors at the far end of the living room. One of the goons left his station at the arch, walked across the room and tapped on the door nearest the windowed wall. A voice answered from the other side in Vietnamese. The goon opened the door and entered. He left the door open behind him. In a matter of seconds he emerged with a small Vietnamese man dressed only in sandals and khaki pants. Behind the little man came another armed goon, this one with a 9mm MAT-49 submachine gun left over from the French days. In complete silence the goons led the small man in wrinkled khaki pants to the windowed wall. Bui had signaled the goon left in the doorway and he crossed the room and stood with his rifle trained on Sam while Bui went to the glass wall and drew back the drapes. A double glass door separated the balcony from the living room. Bui opened it. The two goons on either side of the small man led him out onto the balcony.

Bui crooked his index finger and the goon over Sam swung his rifle barrel toward the balcony. Sam hesitated.

"Professor Borne, please don't keep us waiting," Bui said from the balcony doorway. Sam slowly rose and took his time about crossing the room. When he got to the balcony, Bui indicated with a nod that Sam was to walk to one end. He did. The goon escorting Sam followed him and leaned up against the glass wall with his weapon still trained on Sam.

Bui stepped up in front of the man in khaki and asked him something in Vietnamese. The man made no answer. Bui waited. Then he asked another question. The man in khaki made no answer. Bui nodded to the goons on either side of the small man. The goon with the 9mm MAT-49 handed it to Bui. Bui held the machine gun on the small man. The other goon put down his AK-47, and at the same time as the other goon he took hold of the small man by the upper arm and then reached down and hooked his arm under the man's thigh. Together they hoisted the small man up to waist level, then rested his back on the black railing. Bui spoke to the man again, softly. The man declined to answer. Without so much as a raised eyebrow from Bui, the two goons slid the man over the railing and let their hands slide down to his ankles. The man dangled over the railing. Sam looked down. It was a long way down, about forty stories, Sam estimated. At the bottom the building abutted a canal. The water was dark and still. Bui waited. The man dangled. He did not squirm, he did not buck. Sam had to crane his head over the railing to see the man's expressionless face. Bui cleared his throat loudly. Then, with long pauses punctuating the space between each word, Bui asked the man a question. There was silence. With the motion of a man flicking a cigarette from him, Bui flexed the fingers of one hand. The goons released the man's ankles. A loud scream followed, receding, and then a loud splash.

Bui turned and in the yellowish illumination from the lights in the room behind them, he addressed Sam. "This man was disinclined to cooperate with us, Professor Borne, and now he has no choice. Would you like to join him?" Bui had put all the contempt into the title "Professor" that one voice could convey. He was getting himself all revved up.

Sam made no answer.

"Shall we go back inside, Professor Borne, and have a nice chat, or are you going to be obstinate and say so and save us time trying to convince you to cooperate?"

Sam said nothing.

"I feel we can save time and trouble by using a little persuasion on you immediately," Bui said. He turned to the two goons who'd dropped the little man and nodded to them. They started down the balcony to Sam. Instinctively Sam stepped back and braced himself, alert and ready. But this was only for effect. Sam knew above all else that now was a time to be convincing. His performance now was the hinge that would swing open the door to Doctor Sun Sun. So it was all natural and good to seem combative. He let it happen effortlessly, the true sign of the professional. When the third goon, the one against the glass wall fronting the living room, poked Sam forward with the rifle's muzzle in the small of his back, Sam jerked forward into the grip of the other two goons. He bucked and fought, making a show of pushing and shoving, putting up a resistance that was more than convincing. The thought that with a dip and a flick he could catapult both these assholes off the balcony was delicious to Sam, but there was a time to be subdued. So when the third goon put the muzzle of the AK-47 to the nape of his neck, he stopped.

"You will do well to contain yourself physically, Professor, and to express yourself linguistically instead," Bui said. He made a show of coming down the balcony toward Sam as slowly as possible. Sam waited, each arm twisted behind him up against his shoulder blades. Bui stopped when he was close enough to thrust his face right before Sam's. He looked Sam dead in the eye for a long couple of seconds, then smiled.

"Now then," Bui began, "who are you and what are you doing in Ho Chi Minh City?"

Sam remained still. He made no reply. He lowered his eyes and kept them steadfastly on the four pairs of shoes on the concrete floor. His sense of timing now would be no ordinary matter of good and bad reviews. His life literally hung on knowing when and how to deliver his next lines. Silence roared in his ears.

"I can see that you are not a man easily persuaded to help out," Bui said. Then he snapped out some orders in Vietnamese. The two goons without guns grabbed Sam under the arms. The muzzle stabbed into the back of Sam's neck. He felt himself twirled around like a top and hauled off his feet. There were arms around his legs, arms around his arms. He looked up and saw the stars winking from a jet backdrop; there was no moon. Sam's ass rode the railing. He felt a hand push down on the front of each pectoral. All he had to do now was resist and it would cost him his life. Overplay this role, overreact, lash out, and with the luck of an orphan he'd buck himself free of the two galoots holding him and get the fast trip down and away.

"What will it be, Professor Borne, the short course in aerodynamics or a little cooperation? Your move." Bui had a way with threats, Sam had to admit. What the hell, a gamble was just a chance with a lot of elastic in it. He would hold the line one more time, risking that he'd get the same treatment as the small man in khaki had gotten.

The hands on his pectorals fell away. The arms around his arms let go. As he rushed three feet over the rail, Sam saw all the lights of the Ho Chi Minh City skyline climb. It was exactly as if all the buildings had suddenly jumped, all together, in perfect synchronicity. Then they bobbed and jerked and were suddenly still, swinging now closer, now farther as Sam swayed toward the balcony and then away.

Here came Bui's big scene. Sam was sure of it. Not for nothing did Sam exercise in the gym religiously when the Committee slammed him back onto a military base every now and again. For a plug nickel or the life of a cat, Sam would catapult himself erect in one huge sit-up and slam a fist into the faces of each of the goons holding him, but what the hell, he'd never beat the trigger finger of the third goon, and Bui wouldn't get to feel like Torquemada.

"Dear Professor, who are you?"

It came all in a rush; convincing, authentic.

"Sam Borne, drug dealer."

"This shows intelligence I can admire."

"How about admiring it face to face?"

"Not so quick, Mr. Borne. We have much more to discuss."

"Let's discuss it over a drink."

"What makes you think vermin like you are welcome in Vietnam?"

"Nothing but hope."

"Hope is a foolish emotion."

"I couldn't agree more."

"Where do you deal drugs, Mr. Borne?"

"Harvard."

The skyline jumped again and wheeled around to the side. Sam swung upside down by one leg. He could feel four hands on it, and was grateful. A drowning man is said in a flash to review his entire life. Sam merely recalled someone telling him once, in California he thought, that hanging upside down was good for the spine.

"You have a fatal sense of humor, Mr. Borne."

"Not humor. I have a network keyed into drug dealing on American college campuses. Like a lot of great men, I almost perished for truth."

"Perhaps you will yet."

"You're the one with the fatal sense of humor."

"Revolutionists are without humor, Mr. Borne. I am no exception."

"Spare me. I'm just a happy-go-lucky capitalist, awaiting the triumph of the Communists and the dissolution of the state."

"Where are you headquartered, Mr. Borne?"

"All over."

"This is not an answer I appreciate. Surely you are one place more than another, you have a central office."

"I move around constantly. I live in different places different times of the year, mostly in hotels or in apartments."

"Where are these apartments located?"

"I'm trying to tell you it changes. I have no permanent address. I want it that way."

"How do people contact you? How do the people who run your organization get in touch with you when they need to?"

"I get in touch with them. I have it set up so they know I'm always there, so to say."

"But you rent apartments?"

"I have women rent them for me, under their names."

"I see."

"Can I be brought up now?"

"Do you intend to cooperate and to answer all questions truthfully and immediately?"

"I've answered your questions."

"I have more."

"I have more answers."

The skyline dipped and Sam got a quick glimpse of the stars before a fist jolted into his chest. He was balanced upright on the railing with Bui's fist locked on his shirt and his eyes locked on Sam's. Over Bui's shoulder the goon with the AK-47 still held it at the ready. The other two goons held Sam with one hand each locked on his wrists and the other hand clamped on his upper arms where they joined his shoulders. Bui gave Sam a long and dramatic look.

"We have many questions for you, Mister Borne, and we will require your unstinting cooperation. You will remember always that the balcony is here and that there will be no dangling, no persuasion, no games." Bui jammed the knuckles of his fist against Sam's chest and shook him out over the railing, forcing him farther and farther out against the tension of the goons holding him on either side. "Do you understand, Mr. Borne?"

Sam craned his neck to look Bui in the eye as well as he could while forced to lean back at such an acute angle. There was something in Sam, something deep and energetic, something reckless and ineradicable, something that made defiance of wanton authority a matter of pride and dignity, a matter of honor and courage, a code really, a way of life. As an actor he was peerless; he could play a craven wimp with the best of them. Still, whenever an authority junkie went too far, Sam recoiled. He would give Bui what he wanted, what he needed, but he'd give it just barely. He would throw the game, but not before he'd forced it to the brink of overtime.

"Let me see if I have it right," Sam started, and paused. Bui ground his knuckles into Sam's sternum, leaning out as far as his arm would allow. With effort Sam strained to keep his head upright. "It's like this: answers you live, silence you die. That's right?"

"Wrong. Answers you live longer, silence you die immediately. Do you understand, Mr. Borne?"

Sam swallowed.

"I understand."

"Good."

Sam believed in rematches. He believed in settling scores. Bui was on the list.

CHAPTER SIXTEEN:
ROLLING THE BONES

Cholon
August 23

The house was old. They had got there by winding down alleys, around curves and through gangways. It was twilight. The Citroen was again driven by the impassive wheelman from Sam's trip to the high rise. Again Bui sat up front with Sam positioned in the back between the two armed goons. The third goon had been left behind at the high rise; Sam could only assume that there were other guests spending time at Bui's big penthouse aerie. At any rate they had bundled Sam off in the Citroen and brought him by many a turn and curve to this imposing old mansion in the ancient Chinese twin city to bygone Saigon, the ever-mysterious Cholon. Sam had got a good look at the mansion when they pulled up. It was four stories high and imposing in every way, with big floor-to-ceiling windows on each floor and an elaborate and well-maintained orange-tile roof overhanging its cream-colored stucco walls. Beyond a doubt, this had once been the grand home of a Chinese merchant, one wise enough, Sam hoped, to have cleared out of this bollixed country by now. As Sam passed through the front door, he wondered if the old Chinese merchant had built a floor each to house each wife and her offspring, as was the ancient Chinese custom. Four floors meant four wives. Sam was sure it beat monogamy.

Within the foyer, all was in darkness. Sam was reminded how tired he was. The previous night Bui had pressed him for information into the small hours of the morning and beyond. They had sat in the living room of the penthouse on the Scandinavian sofas and Bui had got the full rundown from him, the one Sam had worked out in advance, the one that the Committee had rigged with the Hong Kong boys to hold water. Sam was ideal for Sun Sun and his mad scheme to infiltrate America and convert its youth to a nation of junkies. Sam knew this. But he couldn't let Bui know he knew it. He had to appear to have been trapped in a real way and to be at the mercy of Bui and whoever he worked for. Bui claimed loudly and more than once to be a revolutionary; Sam was therefore not just whistling in the dark in hoping that Bui was the straight liaison between the dour Communist authorities and the expedient and vengeful Doctor Sun Sun.

All through the night, Bui had grilled Sam. He had not tortured him outright, but he had reminded Sam when he was slow with an answer that the balcony was only steps away. The three goons had held up the walls, weapons in hand and pointed in Sam's direction. In the hours of full dawn, Sam had been sent to the room from which the little man in khaki had been led to his death. There on a cot he had lain with one goon slouched against the far wall and tried to sleep, unsuccessfully at first. He had lain with his eyes closed and listened intently. He thought he heard Bui on the phone, talking at length. Then he'd smelled the good strong aroma of coffee and he'd drifted off. Not long after that, he was roused and forced to sit up in a ratty leather armchair in one corner of the room. Twice during the day Bui had come in, and Sam was permitted to lie on the cot each time, but each time he was roused again shortly. Bui had some knowledge of the techniques of brainwashing and interrogation; he knew that a tired and worn subject was more easily broken and manipulated.

Sam knew the game. He knew two could play. Each
time he'd been allowed on the cot, he'd dropped as
deeply and firmly into a full meditation as it was possible
to get. And each time he'd slipped from meditation into
sound and rejuvenating sleep. When they'd had him in
the ratty leather armchair, he had coasted into a medium-
range meditation, one that allowed him to remain in tune
with his surroundings and sensitive to any changes in
them, but which still permitted him to lower his heartbeat
and to put his body and mind into semistorage, conserving his energy for the encounters that would surely follow.

Despite this strategy to preserve his strength, Sam was
still tired, and the darkness of the mansion's foyer, so inviting, reminded him how lovely it would be to lie down
and tap out eight hours of sleep. The foyer itself, as Sam
could just make out in the blue light of dusk when the
street door swung open behind him, was a nice sized
room with a door at its end opposite the street door. The
inside door was dark, mahogany it appeared, and in
its center was a geometrically patterned, multicolored
stained-glass window. Underfoot were octagonal ruby
tiles. The street door closed again and Sam stood in darkness. Bui went ahead and opened the interior door. Soft
light briefly crept up to Sam's feet but was quickly gone.

In the darkness the goons passed some comment.
They laughed. Sam yawned. It would be delightful, he
thought, to find that he had a whole floor of the capacious
old mansion to himself with nothing but a sunken tub, a
large canopied bed and a naked Amy to sail the night
away with. Something, everything told him this would
not be the case. He wondered where Amy was at this very
moment.

The foyer door opened again and the soft light crept
back to his feet. Backlit and framed in the doorway was
Bui. He nodded and a goon prodded Sam in the back with
the muzzle of his rifle. Sam walked ahead, trailing the

goons. Bui stepped aside and held the foyer door for Sam.
Sam passed into a large old living room full of heavy
carved furniture. Vases stood in corners, woven runners
lined inlaid wooden floors, porcelain hounds guarded
either side of a carved wooden fireplace and lacquer panels decorated the walls. In one corner of the room stood a
black wire mesh bird cage the size of a cabana. In the
cage was a large green parrot with a brilliant red comb.

Bui indicated two facing settees perpendicular to the
fireplace, with a heavy low coffee table between them.
Sam walked over and sat down on the settee with a view
of the bird cage. For some reason, Sam wanted to see the
parrot. The parrot was perched on a jutting branch of a
gray forked tree trunk in the middle of the cage. The
parrot reminded Sam of one owned by a professional
fishing guide in the Bahamas named Finnegan who'd
trained it to ask for a piece of ass. Finnegan and his parrot
had flustered many an uptight woman along with her
wealthy husband on a marlin run.

The soft light in the room was supplied by table lamps
of black enamel with red pin-striping that sat on end
tables at the ends of the settees away from the fireplace;
the lamps had large square shades the color of sand. Sam
noticed that the goons had not entered the room with him.
Bui sat down across from him.

"Where are my bodyguards?" Sam asked.

"No jokes, Mr. Borne."

They sat in silence. The only sound in the room was
the scraping and occasional chirping of the parrot. After
about five minutes, Bui checked his watch. Shortly there-
after the sound of a car pulling up outside was distinct.
Then the sound of another car pulling up could be heard.
The click of the outside door being opened followed.
Then the foyer door swung back and a midget entered and
held the door back.

Doctor Sun Sun entered.

Excitement pumped through Sam. He was no longer

tired. He was looking right at his target. He was in contact with Doctor Sun Sun and this was it, the beginning of the end. There was always a charge at first sight of the quarry.

Sun Sun shot a glance at Bui and Sam and said something in greeting in Vietnamese to Bui, who answered. Sun Sun strode across the room and stood at the parrot's cage, purring and cooing in resonant undertones. The parrot reversed itself on the branch and faced the wall. Sun Sun cooed some more. The parrot walked down one fork of the branch, crossed the trunk and walked up the other branch, the one farther from Sun Sun. The parrot kept his back to Sun Sun. Sam watched all of this without comment. The tips of his fingers tingled. So absorbed was he in Sun Sun's attempt to bill and coo with the parrot that Sam did not notice at first that a beautiful Vietnamese woman had followed Sun Sun into the room and now stood motionless within the area defined by the swing of the inwardly opened door. The midget was partially visible behind the door, with his wrist hitched on the knob like a straphanger, one leg crossed over the other with the foot of the crossed leg on pointe.

Sun Sun suddenly abandoned his courtship of the parrot and turned back toward the others, mumbling over and over in English, ''This bird loves me, I know it.'' He kept mumbling as he passed the woman and the midget and came to the end of the sitting area bracketed by the two settees. Bui rose. Sun Sun took Bui's outstretched hand and flipped it away from him like a man discarding a candy wrapper. If Bui took umbrage, he didn't show it. He simply backstepped and resumed his seat across from Sam. Sun Sun stepped right past him and stationed himself in front of Sam. Sam looked up at Sun Sun; Sun Sun looked down at Sam. Sun Sun reached out and chucked Sam under the chin and said, ''A real live goddamn pusher. What do you know.'' He laughed loudly. Then he clapped Sam's cheeks between his hamlike hands and, bracing Sam with the left hand, smacked him several loud smacks with his right hand. Sam's left cheek smarted from the smacks.

"Well, I'll be goddamned. A real live fucking heroin pimp right here now. Goddammit, what do ya know?" Sun Sun clapped his hands and stood back. "Stand up, fuckface, let's have a look at ya."

Sam stood. He was a good four or five inches shorter than Sun Sun. Sun Sun's girth kept them from being close. His gut overhung his trousers by an easy half foot. Sun Sun was wearing a garish green, yellow and blue flowered Hawaiian shirt outside a pair of lime-green chinos above open sandals with leather stirrups for the big toes and straps across the insteps.

"So you're Mr. Sam Borne. May I ask, Mr. Borne, whether or not you are acquainted with me?"

"No."

"I expect not. Yes, I expect not. Well, I am Doctor Sun Sun. How does that grab you for a name, son?"

"It'll do like another."

"It'll have to. It's the only one I got." Sun Sun roared at this; like a fool, he enjoyed his own wit. Sam noticed how poor a liar old Laidlaw was, or how insane. Sam wasn't sure which, though it could be both—they weren't mutually exclusive. Sun Sun wheeled around suddenly.

"Honey, get your ass over here and meet Mr. Sam Borne, heroin jockey. Yes indeed, get right over here." The woman standing just within the door started across the room. She stepped lightly into the sitting area, came up to Sam and Sun Sun and stood just to the side of them. "Honey, meet Sam. Sam, meet Honey."

Never had Sam had a more penetrating look from a woman. In a trice all sexual longing volleyed from Honey to Sam and back. Sam prided himself on being able to return any woman's sexual serve, but this one had a lot of top spin on it and he barely got it back over the net. He

was sure that, under the right circumstances and with
enough time, he could inflame Honey's libido to the
point where he could weld with it. Sweet dreams are
made of this, he thought.

"Delighted to make your acquaintance, Mr. Borne,"
she said, ever so softly. Her hair, raven black and
shiny, slanted over one eye. She was dressed head to toe
in an emerald-green silk dress with white fleurs-de-lis
appliquéd in a random pattern over its entirety. A
stand-up collar braced the longest, loveliest, sexiest neck
Sam had ever seen on so petite a woman; she couldn't
have stood a pin's width over five foot five. Her breasts
were full and pushed enticingly against her silk bodice.
As Sam took her hand, he noticed that her shoes were
fawn colored with cutouts for the toes. Her toenails were
lacquered bright red. So were her fingernails. On her extended hand was a monstrous diamond in the shape of a
teardrop. Sun Sun saw with satisfaction that Sam had noticed the ring.

"How do you like that rock, Mr. Borne? It's probably
worth more than your entire half-ass operation, wouldn't
you say?"

"I'd say."

"Tell our guest, Honey, just what that little mountain
signifies."

"This is my engagement ring, Mr. Borne," Honey
said. "I am to marry Doctor Sun Sun next month."

"Congratulations. He's a lucky man."

"Luck has nothing to do with it, Borne. My fortune is
the result of design. My future's rosy because I plant the
seeds that make it that way."

"Congratulations. You're a self-made man."

Sun Sun stared hard at Sam. He was clearly not used to
people around him speaking to him frankly. He looked
from Sam to the seated Bui.

"I told you he was sarcastic," Bui said.

"Yes. You did," Sun Sun replied, then turned back to

Sam. "You know, Borne, they say a word to the wise is sufficient. Here's a word. Sarcasm with me could get you dead."

"That's sufficient."

"Good."

Sun Sun flashed Sam the pure grin of mania, then turned and flashed it on Honey, to underscore his power. Honey tweaked her nose. Sun Sun pivoted back on Sam and drove his right index finger hard into Sam's chest. "Sit down, Borne," he commanded.

Sam sat down. Sun Sun stood over him. "What I'm going to do now, Borne, is sketch your fate for you. And I'll tell you why. You see, Bui here has briefed me extensively on who and what you are. I've got the whole picture. At least the picture you want me to have. But I'm no man's fool, Borne, and I've checked you out, see, and you check out with my sources. But something's bothering me about you. Maybe it's you're too good to be true. I'm not sure what, but something about you is too pretty, like Honey Pot here, only Honey here's been for the test drive more than once, and she passes good."

Sun Sun paused to let what he'd said sink in. He flashed his maniac's grin down at Sam full force. Sam looked up at Sun Sun, betraying no emotion but the one he wanted Sun Sun to perceive: deep apprehension.

"So what I'm going to do, Borne," Sun Sun resumed, "is test-drive you. I'm a great admirer of Oriental culture, a convert, you might say. So I'm going to put you to an Oriental test." Sun Sun paused again. "Yes, what I'm going to do is very Oriental. You see, there's an old Chinese saying that if you want to find out what kind of man you're dealing with, you invite him for a game of mah-jongg. Do you play mah-jongg, Borne, old boy?"

"Yes."

"That's good, son. You just saved your life. I never explain, you see. You either play or you die."

"Saves time."

"That's sarcasm, baby, but I'll file it under gallow's humor, the only kind of sarcasm I tolerate. All old soldiers admire gallow's humor, Borne, and I'm an old soldier."

"Maybe *I'm* the lucky man."

"We'll see. Because we're going to play a friendly game of mah-jongg now. Me, you, Honey and Bui. If you don't go out first, mister, if you don't win, you're dead."

"It'll hold my interest."

"Three to one. How do you like those odds?"

"They'll do."

"You got pluck. I admire that. It'd be a shame to lose you. I half hope you win."

"My hope is twice that."

"That's understandable."

Sun Sun clapped his hands and barked, "Let's go," as though he were commanding a charge up San Juan Hill. He walked over beside the fireplace and touched the mantelpiece where it joined the wall. A panel in the wall revolved outward. Bui stood up and gestured for Sam to follow Sun Sun. Sam walked over and entered the room beyond the panel.

The room was small. It held a small table the size of a card table in its center. The table was of black lacquer, as were the four armchairs arranged around it. The walls were covered in red damask. The floor was a single piece of gray slate. The black cushions of the chairs were embroidered with fiery suns, gold ringed with red. Sam turned and waited while Bui, Honey and finally Sun Sun entered. Sun Sun told everyone where to sit. They followed instructions. When Sun Sun had seated himself, he pulled out a drawer under the edge of the table and took from it a velvet-lined carved teak box the size of a cigar box.

Neatly lined in the box were the tiles for the game

along with the three dice necessary to begin. Sun Sun spilled them onto the table.

"Aren't they magnificent, Borne? These tiles are pure ivory, over three hundred years old, all hand carved, all hand engraved. Simply magnificent, no?"

"Yes." In truth the set was magnificent. All the tiles were the traditional inch long and brick shaped, but otherwise they were unique. The Chinese characters were engraved beautifully in bright blue and red and green patterns. It was indeed lucky for Sam that one time between assignments while cooling out in Greece he'd chanced upon an unspeakably beautiful Jewish girl from Forest Hills who had been addicted from an early age by her mother with the habit of playing mah-jongg. She had taught Sam to play mah-jongg and he had taught her to play, period. Sam would have done anything to get to her, but he never realized that all his faked ardor about mah-jongg would someday be so crucial to him. The Committee, like the Lord, worked in mysterious ways.

"We will play this under sudden-death rules," Sun Sun announced, "with only one go-round. I will be the leader." He stopped and grinned his maniac's grin. Sam didn't need a millisecond to figure that he was seated to Sun Sun's left, in the last position to draw; he was in the three-o'clock position, and of course they'd go in the traditional counterclockwise sequence.

"I wonder what the real odds are?" Sam asked, looking right at Sun Sun.

"You have a chance, Mr. Borne, and chance is the willing mistress of fate, is it not?" He laughed a deep laugh, a maniac's laugh, a laugh to make Mephistopheles jealous. "We will play in the time-honored Chinese way," Sun Sun continued. "We will go like hell, no dilly-dallying, no stalling. Destiny will pass through this room like a breeze. One go-round. If our distinguished guest,

E. B. Cross

the heroin whore Mr. Sam Borne, goes out first, he lives. If not . . . well, if not, what can I say?'' He laughed the deep laugh again.

Mah-jongg, Sam knew, was an ancient Chinese gambling game developed in the twelfth century B.C. and derived from dominoes. The Chinese played it avidly in the time of Confucius. Up until the nineteenth century, the game was restricted to nobles, men exclusively, but since then it had been taken up widely by all classes and both sexes, and not only by the Chinese, for in the late nineteenth and early twentieth centuries the game spread worldwide. The Chinese, in celebrating their New Year, still play mah-jongg for three days and three nights straight, despite official attempts by the government to stamp it out in favor of more physical recreation. Mah-jongg also falls afoul of the Chinese government in its campaign to eradicate gambling, which is the equivalent of trying to withdraw tea from the English. Oddly enough, the name ''mah-jongg'' was not given the game by the Chinese but rather by an American, Joseph P. Babcock, long a resident of Shanghai. The name means simply ''the sparrows'' and may have been pure whimsy on the part of Babcock, who introduced the mah-jongg craze to the United States in 1920.

Like rummy, mah-jongg is a simple game of skill and chance in which the players vie to form ''hands.'' In order to achieve mah-jongg, the winning player must form a hand of four sets of three matching tiles, for a total of twelve tiles, then match the last, or thirteenth, tile with the free-floating, all-important fourteenth tile. The player who gets the four sets of three first and matches the thirteenth with the fourteenth tile achieves mah-jongg and gins out, just like in rummy. There are variations of the game in which sets of three, four and five are allowed, but this is the basic scheme as the game has been played classically by the Chinese for more than three thousand years. The game starts with a dice roll and proceeds swiftly, usually taking only five to fifteen minutes.

"Let's roll the bones, shall we?" Sun Sun said with gusto, shaking the dice beside his right ear. He spun the dice out. They fell, tumbled and were still.

Everything that followed happened in a blur. The tiles were positioned, the game begun. Sam compartmentalized his mind. While riveted on the game, he still devised a plan he could instantly fall back on if he lost. He would not panic. He would await his chance. There could be no doubt that the house was surrounded by armed guards, that his chances were slim. But he would wait, he would watch, he would devise a way, if at all humanly possible, to cheat fate of what it held in store for him if he lost.

Before Sam knew it, his dance with fate began turning into a waltz. He had lined up before the others the four sets of three tiles; three were three of a kind and the fourth was a three-tile straight. Then, incredibly, he couldn't get the fourteenth tile to match up with the thirteenth. Sun Sun completed his four sets of three in the meanwhile. Then Honey completed hers. Sam would lose if he did not nail a match on his next draw, provided he survived long enough to get a next draw.

Sun Sun drew and failed to go out. Bui drew next and completed his four sets. Then it passed to Honey. She failed.

It was Sam's turn. It would be his last. He drew, it matched.

He'd won.

He sat perfectly still. The air was suddenly lighter. The clacking of the tiles ceased. The slamming and pounding of ivory on wood no longer resounded like gunshots in the tiny room. Sam's fingertips caressed the edge of the table, lined masterfully with beveled nickel. He looked at Honey. He thought she started to smile.

Then he looked at Sun Sun.

"We have a deal to cut, Mr. Borne."

CHAPTER SEVENTEEN:
THE BEWITCHING HOURS

Cholon
August 24

On his back, his arms cradled under his head, Sam lay in an old canopied bed obviously imported years ago by the Chinese merchant to lend his house that *je ne sais quoi* without which a snappy house in Cholon had no snap. Occasionally a sound would drift up from the street below. Once there was a clatter, the result, most likely, of a stray cat or dog rooting in a garbage can. Otherwise all was deathly quiet.

Sam's room faced the front of the house and overlooked the street. Through the chintz curtains hung on the twin windows the tawny light from a single street lamp cast a webwork of shadows into the room. Sam could not sleep, only think. There was much to review, much to calculate. Sun Sun had been emphatic with Sam after he'd won the round at mah-jongg. He had plans for Sam, which Sam would carry out. Together they would do business, Sam never forgetting that they were not partners, that he worked for, and was controlled by, Sun Sun. Sam had not so much participated in a discussion as attended a briefing. During the session, Bui had functioned as audience, laughing or smiling at remarks of Sun Sun's while Honey functioned as hostess, overseeing the service of tea and *dim sum*. Throughout the session they had sat in the big living room, on the carved settees in front of the big fireplace. The parrot had clattered and hopped around in his cage, but when Sun Sun had taken a break and billed and cooed with it, the bird had again played hard to get.

The results had been clear-cut. Not only would Sam function from here on out as an employee of Sun Sun's, but he would go with him tomorrow to the opium farm and refinery he kept in the country. Sam knew from his Committee dossier that this would be the compound in the Central Highlands. There Sun Sun expected Sam to lay out for him the workings of Sam's operation. This did not disturb Sam. The dossier from the Committee, surely structured with certifiable accuracy by the Hong Kong gangs, had included information he should lay out in such a contingency. He knew what names to name, what cities and campuses each name controlled. Sam was not disturbed on that score.

He was disturbed because Sun Sun seemed to gloat. He seemed to feel that he was more in control of the situation than his simple madman's ego would account for. He seemed to act like a man who wasn't just one up on the opposition, but two or three. Sam felt more than ever like a pawn. Not that he didn't always feel like a pawn on assignments for the Committee, but this time was different. There was something so cocksure about Sun Sun that it kept Sam awake. It kept him thinking.

Suddenly Sam came alert. He had heard the softest swishing sound from the corridor beyond his bedroom door. He heard the sound again and again, approaching. He rolled over and propped himself on an elbow, staring at the door and the thin horizontal line of light from the corridor beneath it. The corridor was lined with a mat runner, and the sound was the light tread of someone approaching down its length.

Quickly he lay back, eyes closed, feigning sleep. The sound grew perceptibly louder, then stopped outside his door. Sam opened his eyes only enough to detect changing light in the room. The door clicked open. A trapezoid of light spread from the edge of the door. The light spread along the wall, then receded; the door clicked shut. Sam was not alone.

Footsteps padded softly across the room in his direction, then stopped at the foot of the bed. He could hear the shallow breathing of his visitor. He opened his eyes in time to see Honey step out of low-heeled straw bedroom slippers with red flowers blooming on the insteps. In the tawny light from the street lamp she let a white silk peignoir lined with gold satin slip from her shoulders and off her outstretched arms. The robe gathered at her feet like surf. Her ebony hair cascaded over her shoulders and down to the crests of her perfect breasts. She had the most beautiful breasts on an Oriental girl Sam had ever seen.

Their eyes met. Honey gave him a tentative smile. He rose on one elbow and winked at her. She smiled with assurance and started to walk to the bed and his outstretched arm, her breasts jiggling enticingly. When she came within reach, he let his hand play over her shoulders and stroke her hair, winding it sensually in his palm, then releasing it. He caressed her shoulder, then slid his hand over her breast, slowly. Honey sighed, then whispered, "Good evening, Mr. Borne."

"It's night."

"Whatever."

"You're far from the master bedroom."

"On the contrary. Tonight I can choose my master." She moved closer to the bed, right up against him. He leaned over and kissed her on the mouth, a long, hard kiss, a probing kiss. He felt Honey shudder. With his fingertips, he soothed her cheek. He took his lips from hers and kissed her down the length of her neck. She sighed and put both hands on his shoulders. She pushed him back gently and climbed onto the bed.

* * *

"You are very good, Mr. Borne," Honey whispered. She spoke so softly he hardly heard her. He chose not to acknowledge her compliment. For good reasons he did not feel up to idle chatter. He played with the idea that she had been sent by Sun Sun to find out his inner thoughts. He would draw her out with silence, which was often more effective than questions.

"Are you always so quiet, Mr. Borne? I got the impression earlier that you were a talkative man. You seemed to more than hold your own with the Doctor." Honey had spoken this last in a voice more than an octave above her sensual whisper. Sam remained silent. He rolled off her, then settled beside her. She took the opportunity to insinuate her head into the crook of his arm, her face lolling only inches from his. She leaned in and pecked him lovingly on the lips. He became more wary. He lay completely still, not wanting to make move one. He wanted to see where her strategy, if indeed she had one, would take her. After several minutes passed in total silence, she withdrew and sat up. She shook her head like a young filly, her mane of blue-black hair flicking from side to side in shimmering, radiant flourishes. Sam felt a quick stir rip through him.

"Since you are obviously through with me, Mr. Borne, I shall not trouble you further. Good night." Honey swung her feet over the side of the bed and bent forward to scoop up her peignoir and her slippers. Sam put a hand on her shoulder and kneaded it affectionately. She sat straight. He let his hand trip lightly down the length of her slender arm. He leaned in and kissed her as softly as possible on the back of her neck. She bent forward. Sam showered kisses on her nape as softly and steadily as a late spring drizzle.

"Do you have to go so soon?" he murmured against her flesh.

"No," she sighed.

* * *

That was how the predawn found them, in their own realm of pleasure and exhaustion. In the stillness, the changing light woke Sam; the light went from slate to silver, and the bird song clinched it. He woke and stirred slightly and Honey woke as well. She sat up immediately, spooked. She looked down at Sam and saw him looking up at her. He smiled slowly and reached out a hand for her. What ended one day well would start another better. Honey pulled back. She quickly kissed him on the mouth and whispered, "Sorry, Mr. Borne, I must go before I'm missed."

"By who?" he asked, though he knew.

"The Doctor," she answered. "He sleeps like an animal. He *is* an animal. But he mustn't catch me. That would be the end." She climbed over Sam and stood on the floor beside the bed. Before he could sit up, she had disappeared below the bed and emerged in a blur of motion, slipping on the peignoir and gliding into the slippers. He sat up and touched her gently on the arm.

She gave him a look guaranteed to give Zeus pause; she was paralyzed by fear, crippled with concern. She knew more than he could ever know, and he must listen. "I will never forget you, Sam."

"You may not have to. I'm liable to abduct you."

"Don't joke. He will kill you as easily as scratch his ear. You must listen." She was exposing herself in ways he couldn't realize; she was taking chances not only with her life but with those of her family as well. It was her family—two brothers on heroin, small-time pushers; two prostitute sisters, also addicts—that Sun Sun held over her like the sword of Damocles. One wrong move from Honey and it was bye-bye family.

Sam looked at her in a new light. He felt that Honey Pot was someone who would cash more than one chip for him. His mind formed a thousand questions. Before he could ask the first, she took his face in her hands and planted a kiss on his mouth you could build a dream on.

She turned and tiptoed from the room at a trot, the door clicking shut behind her like the closing of a book he would never get to read to the end.

He lay back in the silver light, listening to birds sing. He was in love.

A little over two hours later the phone rang. Bui answered it in the small secretary's alcove outside the big office Doctor Sun Sun kept in the front of the house on the second floor. He put the call on hold and went to the door to the Doctor's office. Sun Sun sat behind an ancient carved teak desk bathed in morning sunshine. Without looking up, he snarled, "What is it, Bui?"

"Hong Kong, Doctor. They say it's important."

"Okay."

Sun Sun picked up the phone on his desk. He listened intently, shaking his head in satisfaction, a slow smile spreading over his face.

"You're sure?" he asked. He listened. "Good," he said, "I suspected as much. This is good work. You boys will be well rewarded." He listened again. "Will do," he said, then hung up. He sat back in the chair like a man with a royal flush. He smiled his maniac's smile at Bui.

"You say our guest is a drug dealer, Bui, is that right?"

Bui hesitated. Finally he mumbled, "I believe so, Doctor."

"With geniuses like you around, Bui, I don't need fools."

"I'm sorry, Doctor."

"We'll see who fools who, Bui my boy. We'll see who gets the last laugh. Drug dealer." He snorted. "Drug dealer, my ass."

CHAPTER EIGHTEEN:
UP, UP AND AWAY

Sun Sun Compound
Central Highlands, Vietnam
August 24

The choppers sliced up into the blue sky and were away. Sam Borne rode on the port side near the window in the lead Bell UH-1D transporting Sun Sun, Honey Pot, Bui and the other members of the inner sanctum. The trailing chopper, also a Bell UH-1D, carried a phalanx of sentries and bodyguards who had ridden out that morning in the Doctor's caravan to the Ton Son Nhut airport from the old merchant's house in Cholon. The entire contingent had assembled in the narrow street outside the old house, looking out of place crowded in the street like a small army, lined up as most of them were in old jeeps left over from the police action. Sun Sun seemed to have outfitted his operation entirely with old United States armed forces matériel. The chopper Sam rode in was converted, with stuffed bench seats across its midsection and a small bar inset into one side of the bulkhead behind the pilot's compartment. It was Sun Sun's version of the corporate chopper used in the States.

Sun Sun now sat regally on the bench seat facing the passenger compartment from the front; it gave him clear access to his audience. Honey sat to one side of him, Bui to the other. Sam sat across from them on the first bench facing front. The night Sam had met Bui in the Number 15 Bar, he'd met the two other occupants of his bench seat, but he couldn't remember their names, and when they'd shown up that morning outside the old house, Sam didn't feel inclined to reintroduce himself and they hadn't bothered either. The bench seat behind Sam was occupied by three armed sentries. Sun Sun held everyone's attention as he declaimed in Vietnamese.

Sam was grateful for the window seat. Below him the runways and outbuildings of the airport disappeared and the tile roofs of the old houses gave way to modern high rises and then they were flying over rice fields and old plantations and the asphalt highways spiraling away from Vietnam's first city snaked through greenery until even they gave way and the ground below turned into solid double-canopy jungle ribbed with narrow rivers and wide streams. No one who'd seen the Vietnamese countryside could fail to notice its natural beauty. That it had been the scene of so much carnage was, on a day like this and from a vantage like this, nearly incomprehensible to Sam. Anger twinged him like sunburn. It always did whenever he thought of Vietnam and the lives of American boys lost there in a no-good political debacle. It was an outrage.

Sam looked from the window to Sun Sun. It was disgusting war pirates, profiteers and other pigs like Sun Sun who had benefited from the sacrifices of so many courageous American boys. Sam could usually afford all the anger over this tragedy his metabolism could stand, but now it wouldn't pay. He went instead into a mild first-stage meditation and let his mind drift and ventilate. He needed to stay calm. He was going to stay calm and at least strike one sure blow for all the guys sold short by scum like Sun Sun. He would stay cool and square one account with the swinish former General Loftus R. Laidlaw. Sam felt his blood calm, his system cool. He held Sun Sun's marker for a lot of kids who'd been fucked over, and he was going to cash it or go bust himself. But to do that he had to stay in control. So he turned back to the window and the junglescape below and meditated.

Before long, the jungle sprouted knolls and hills and then there were mountains. They were in the Central Highlands. From his dossier Sam knew that they couldn't be too far from the compound Sun Sun had established here. The only words he'd exchanged during the entire trip had been to refuse a drink from the Doctor himself. Of course, Sun Sun had gone right on, sloshing gin and tonics like a colonial lord and holding forth in Vietnamese on God knew what. Sam was grateful to have been spared Sun Sun's spiel. Now the landscape below was turning brown, like someone's money when it was running real low, and Sam felt a charge bolt through him. On every assignment there was a spot when Sam got the charge. This was it. He would do Sun Sun, or Sun Sun would do him. Stepping into a duel, taunting an enraged bull or pitting themselves against a saber-toothed tiger, men must have known this surge.

"Now, Mr. Borne, your special surprise will not be long in coming." Sam turned back from the window to look at the speaker. Sun Sun was grinning broadly at him. He raised his drink to Sam in a mock salute. "We will reach our destination shortly," Sun Sun continued, "and I hope you are with us to enjoy it." He flashed Sam his deranged grin and spoke sharply in a loud voice in Vietnamese. The three sentries behind Sam rose on command and came around the bench on which Sam sat. The lead sentry grabbed the hatch on the side door and swung it open. As he did so, one of the other two sentries jammed the snout of his AK-47 into Sam's shoulder and motioned for him to rise. The third sentry pointed his Kalashnikov at Sam and nodded in the direction of the open door. Air whipped into the passenger compartment and whirled around Sun Sun, Bui and Honey, who had a stricken look on her face.

"Just a little rescue-mission training, Mr. Borne. I like to keep the boys sharp. You don't mind volunteering to play a downed flier, do you?" Sun Sun roared at Sam.

His twisted laughter rose above the blast of the whirling wind. "You know how important it is to know how to save somebody, don't you, Mr. Borne?" He laughed again, savoring his sadism. He gave Sam a big vaudevillian wink; he was a man who enjoyed another's misfortune, who liked to witness discomfort, who liked another's pain, especially when he'd caused the pain to begin with. Sun Sun flicked an index finger at one of the sentries.

The sentry jammed his rifle into Sam. One of the other sentries held a rescue collar in both hands. He slipped it over Sam's head and Sam wiggled both arms through it so that it held him under the shoulders, riding under his armpits. This was the kind of collar tossed down to fliers in the water. It was connected to a winch. The sentry who'd handed it to Sam went to the winch and played out about fifteen feet of cable.

Sun Sun laughed in Sam's ear. Sam turned and looked him right in the face. The surgery on Sun Sun's eyes was hideous. The Oriental flaps were obviously superimposed on a Caucasian face. His breath reeked of gin. Spittle foamed in the corners of his mouth. In flowered Hawaiian shirt and chinos he was completely ridiculous. Several gold chains glinted around his bulging neck. The wind blasted into him, billowing his pants and shirt and forcing him to blink his eyes wildly. He put a hand on Sam's chest and forced him backward, toward the open hatch. Even above the rip and roar of the wind, Sam could hear Sun Sun's sick laugh.

"Enjoy yourself, Mr. Borne. And remember, this is just an exercise. Hope to see you at the compound," Sun Sun bawled, then rammed into Sam with a mighty shove.

The shove catapulted Sam out of the chopper. As he fell, he somersaulted. When the cable snapped taut at fifteen feet, the momentum hurled Sam out of his somersault and swung him violently under the fuselage. The cable caught above him on the copter's skid and flung him back the way he'd come. He dangled fifteen hundred feet above the earth, swinging, spinning rapidly, tracing a huge arc, first under the fuselage nearly to the other side, then back out to the edge of the rotor's blades, which beat above him like the hammers of hell.

In front of Sam was blue sky, the pure empyrean. Below him was the fleeing geography of the earth. The chopper rolled, and there was sky. The chopper dipped, there was earth. On the wide swings out to the edge of the blade's trajectory, Sam could snatch a glance upward and see in the open hatch the gleeful face of the Doctor, who turned and shouted toward the pilot's compartment. The copter wheeled radically, spinning and swinging Sam. Everything passed in a rush, the earth whirling, the sky spinning, clouds and jungle mixing in a hellish kaleidoscope.

The chopper climbed, the chopper fell. The harness bit into Sam brutally, tearing at his armpits, straining to be free of him. Sam locked his hands on the cable, each hand overlapping and reinforcing the other. If he lost his grip even momentarily, he was a goner. Each time the cable bucked against the copter's skid, the jolt nearly knocked Sam from the harness, wrenching his back, biting into his shoulder blades.

Sam slipped farther down. The doctor was playing out cable, swinging Sam in ever wider arcs. Sam whirled now under the fuselage and rose on his upward arc on the other side of the chopper. At the apex of his climb, the centrifugal force nearly flung him out of the harness. On the downward swing he fought the natural instinct to let go, to surrender, to let himself be hurled from the sling and tossed to the earth in a death fall. In his heart he wondered how many more such wide swings he could survive.

As he swung out under the open hatch, Sam saw that above him the Doctor was waving his arms wildly. Sam whipped back under the fuselage and forced himself to grip the cable tighter. He was going to make the big loop again on the other side. The cable snagged on the skid and he started up. His body twisted with the torque on the line, his feet swinging wide, his arms straining to maintain their grip on the cable. He crested the arc and held on. He started down in a rushing whirl, the cable spinning him. Under the fuselage he righted the cable and swung out cleanly on the hatch side of the copter. He looked up.

In the open hatch, Sun Sun gripped Honey's head and neck like a man about to perform an immersion baptism. Her arms flailed against him, beating in vain. He forced her to look at Sam, laughing all the while. It was the last image Sam took with him as he swung down and under the fuselage again, gripping the cable mightily, steeling himself, reaching within himself for everything he had. He swung out again, but the chopper dipped and wheeled in the direction of his swing, breaking its impact. He started to swing back and the chopper maneuvered again in such a way to lessen his arc. It did this several times, adjusting the swing till he swayed steadily under the hatch side, about thirty feet down. In the respite he looked around. Below was thick jungle; above, blue sky, tranquil with hardly a cloud in it. His arms ached. His back hurt. He had lost both moccasins and his stockinged feet felt cold. His hands were raw and frozen. He had barked the skin of his palms on the rough cable, and he could feel blood trickling down his wrists.

The helicopter dropped steadily. Behind him Sam could see the other Huey. It was about four hundred yards back. It also dropped. Sam wondered if they might be coming in to the compound, but he knew from the dossier that the compound was ringed by mountains and below was only a river valley, the dark brown muddy river slicing between two green ranges on either side. They dropped lower.

Sam looked up and saw that the sentries were standing

in the hatch with no Sun Sun and no Honey. He thought this was a good sign. Then the chopper dropped swiftly lower, the Doctor appeared in the hatch, clutching Honey, and Sam got a panicky feeling in his stomach as they glided lower and lower, closer and closer to the river. They were only about a hundred feet above the river when Sam looked up for the last time, saw Sun Sun grinning wildly and bracing Honey like a calf about to be branded and knew that the ordeal was far from over.

The copter dropped swiftly. Sam clenched himself. He knew what lay ahead. He gripped the cable as hard as he could, despite his bleeding hands, and folded in on himself, summoning all the resolve he could muster. He took in air in huge gasps.

In a rush, his feet hit the water, then he was in up to his waist. The pressure of the water on his legs and waist was crushing. A small tidal wave pushed against him as he dangled half in, half out of the river. The chopper dipped and Sam gulped air. The pressure of the water on his torso and face was paralyzing, whiplashing his head as he disappeared beneath the surface. Underwater, he curled his head back as far as he dared, protecting his face as he tore along at better than a hundred miles an hour. His arms quivered with the effort of maintaining his grip on the cable. His legs and torso twisted and tumbled out of control. He held on from sheer will. His breath grew short. He was out of air. He was going to die.

Then the cable jerked and he shot out of the water. He gasped for air, got some, then dipped briefly back below the surface. The copter was adjusting itself slightly, looking for something precise. It found it.

The cable yanked Sam from beneath the water and skimmed him along its surface. His body hydroplaned along, fanning white vanes of water to either side. His chest and stomach planed along the surface of the river, burning with the sting of the onrushing water. His arms buckled. He braced his hands, yet they started to slip.

The pressure was excruciating. He couldn't hold on much longer, nor could he get out of the harness altogether. It bit into his back painfully, pulling him along like a child's toy.

Sam craned his neck and saw a natural dam of fallen trees about two hundred yards ahead. He would be killed instantly if they hurled him against it. He quickly sought to free himself from the harness, to cut himself loose and take his chances, but the force of the harness on his back made this impossible. He would be killed on the dam.

Suddenly he lifted free of the water. He rose about twenty feet above the river. The dam passed below him in a blur. He dangled again under the hatch. The chopper climbed quickly. In seconds Sam was five hundred feet above the earth, holding on for dear life, exhausted, certain he would die if the chopper started to roll and pitch and swing him wildly from side to side.

It didn't. The Huey held steady at five hundred feet and Sam held on. He looked behind him and saw the other slick about four hundred yards behind. He looked above and saw the hatch was empty, not even a sentry keeping an eye on him. He let his head loll back and felt relief. His hands were locked now, clamped and frozen on the cable. He could hold on, he was sure, if they only didn't put him through another trapeze act.

He looked upward and out, clearing his head, feeling the dizziness recede. His stomach stopped tossing. One hand at a time, he cautiously readjusted his grip on the cable, flexing his aching fingers, trying to get some circulation flowing in them. He reclamped his hand on the cable and felt the chopper borne upward on a slight swell.

Ahead lay a ridge. They climbed to clear it. Suddenly they topped the ridge and there it was. Below, in a natural amphitheater formed by the mountains, sat a cluster of buildings on a plateau. In the center was a parade ground, bare and brown and baking under the sun. The buildings ranged from modern structures of cinder block to plain huts of bamboo and palm that might have stood in this basin thousands of years ago. On the mountainsides people could be seen working. At one end of the plateau was a large heliport with revetments like the ones the American forces built during the police action. It all looked efficient, and sinister.

The pilot swung to the right and they glided downward, making their approach to the helipads. As they dropped lower, Sam could see the workers bent over their crop. Its harvest would yield dependency, delirium, and death. This was the operation Doctor Sun Sun had offered to cut Sam in on last night, an offer now Sam had to conclude was withdrawn. He had to consider that his cover was blown, or that the capricious doctor had decided not to use him for reasons of his own.

The chopper hovered over the helipad and started down, Sam dangling some fifty feet above the ground. He knew to hit the earth easily, to let himself fall naturally, not to try to break his fall. Twirling in the backwash from the big rotor, he tightened his grip on the cable, the strands of wire biting into his cut hands.

Slammed into the earth, he folded down into himself, tumbled once and was dragged a few feet on his back as the chopper drifted, sand whirlpooling all around him. He put his forearm over his eyes for protection. At the circumference of the rotor's blades, small twisters danced. The engines cut out. The sand settled.

Sam Borne was still in the game.

CHAPTER NINETEEN:
GRAND TOUR

On the ground, Sam was ignored. When the helicopter's doors swung open, Sun Sun stepped down to be met by a committee of midgets and sentries. Then he, Bui and Honey departed straightaway, ignoring Sam completely. They disappeared across the parade ground, Sun Sun riding shotgun in a golf cart, everyone walking briskly beside him, including Honey. Especially Honey, since Sun Sun seemed to take some perverse pleasure in having Honey try to keep up with him in her heels as they crossed the parade ground and stopped on the far side in front of one of the cinder-block buildings. Sun Sun slid off the cart and led the way into the building, a handful of sentries left outside.

Sam was ushered at gunpoint from the helipad and marched across the compound to a bamboo hut. Inside the hut the light was striated from the bamboo poles. In the center sat a rickety table with four matching bamboo chairs. Sam was directed by gesture to sit in one of the chairs. He did. About half an hour passed. His hands hurt, his back and shoulders ached; his whole upper body radiated pain. His pants were tattered, and his shirt, pants and socks were covered with mud. Sweat trickled down his face and mixed with the dirt on it.

It was hot in the hut. Flies buzzed. The sentries

guarding Sam talked occasionally in Vietnamese, mostly in short exchanges. There would be a quick burst of speech, the sentries would lapse back into silence, then only the flies would buzz.

Finally, the door to the hut opened and Sun Sun was back. He had changed into large khaki bush shorts and a khaki shirt. He wore a pith helmet. He looked like a mad imitation of an English lord on a safari, like a refugee from a Kipling story. Pained though he was, Sam bit back hard on first sight of him so he would not laugh out loud. Sun Sun crossed the hut and plopped down in a chair opposite Sam's.

"Well, Borne, now I'll show you this dream of mine up close. How does that sound?"

"It sounds great."

"You're a trooper, Borne. I appreciate your cooperation with the rescue training on the way up."

"You're welcome."

"You look a mess, son."

"It was a rough ride."

Sun Sun laughed.

"Can you tell me," Sam asked, "whether these are my accommodations here?" He gestured at the hut.

"Oh, no, not by a long shot. You'll be staying tonight in much more refreshing accommodations than these, I assure you." Sun Sun laughed his big laugh. It was not reassuring. Sam was tempted to ask to see his accommodations but thought better of it. For the moment he'd let the kitten have his ball of string.

Sun Sun clapped his hands and said, "Let's go, Mr. Borne. I'm in the mood to give you the grand tour. It's a real eye-opener."

On this, Sun Sun was as good as his word. The tour was a real eye-opener. He led Sam around the compound buildings first, stopping to show off a luxurious underground theater and video center, a suite of rooms where he lived that was nothing short of palatial, and a comfort-

able dormitory that housed more midgets than Sam had
ever seen in one place before. In the midget dorms, beds,
tables, chairs, everything was small or low. Sinks and
light fixtures, everything was set at a height to accommo-
date three-footers. It was bizarre. Next came the living
quarters of the sentries Sam saw everywhere. They lived
in two cinder-block buildings with finished basements
housing modern recreation rooms. The sentries had
adopted Ping-Pong with the avidity of their Chinese
neighbors and were every bit as accomplished, from what
Sam could see. Next they entered a first-rate dining room
with all the best accoutrements.

Lunch followed. Sam sat in his wrecked clothes and
ate ravenously, his aching body reviving under such good
food. They feasted on a medley of Chinese dishes, all expertly prepared by a Chinese chef in professional whites,
including a toque. To his embarrassment, the chef was
dragged out for a praising from Sun Sun. He stood obedi-
ently bowing and smiling while Sun Sun commanded
everyone to thank him. In truth, the chef's egg flower
soup, squab Cantonese, Szechuan beef, velvet prawns,
shredded chicken salad, braised eggplant, fried dumplings and fried rice were superb. During the meal, Sam
shot glances at Honey, who sat next to Sun Sun across
from Sam. Bui and his cohorts rounded out their table.

"How did that lunch suit you, Mr. Borne?" Sun Sun
asked as they left the dining room.

"Very well."

"Good, good. I'm glad you liked it. I always try to
serve the best meals here, since I honor the Western custom of making the last meal memorable, and I serve a lot
of guests their last meals." Sun Sun chuckled at this, as
did Bui and his lieutenants. Honey didn't.

Sam took the initiative. "That was truly fine Chinese
cuisine. I didn't realize you were so fond of Chinese
cooking."

"One look at me ought to tell you I'm fond of good

cooking," Sun Sun laughed. "I'm fond of it all. You name it, I'll eat it. And tonight, Mr. Borne, we're going to treat you to a magnificent French dinner, one you'll never forget." He laughed some more.

The threat in Sun Sun's words was stark. It served only to intensify the professional cunning of Sam's inspection. As they toured, he calculated. He considered every angle, every ploy and trick, the entire layout. He considered each and every way to get to Sun Sun and to kill him.

"Right now, Mr. Borne," Sun Sun announced, "I'm going to show you the rest of this dreamland of mine. Then we'll rest before dinner. How does that sound?"

"Wonderful."

"Good, but let's take a look at the rest of this place first, shall we?"

"By all means."

Sun Sun led the way out of the dining room and across to another cinder-block building that contained a tremendous swimming pool on its ground floor, a gymnasium on its second floor. A finished basement held a Jacuzzi, a steam room and a sauna. A separate massage room had no less than three tables and a full staff on duty. Sun Sun spoke briefly to the staff in Vietnamese. He turned to Sam and told him in English that once their short tour was over he could feel free to come back here and have a massage, with his escort of sentries, of course. Sam answered that he just might do that.

They left the building and traveled down the line of other buildings. On the way, Sun Sun showed Sam the barracks that housed the forced-labor contingent. It was despicable, filthy and disgusting. The men slept in bare wooden bunks lining the walls and in two rows down the center. There were no showers, only a trough urinal and two open commodes. It was primitive beyond belief and it was deliberate. If Sun Sun could live in such opulence, these men at least deserved minimal facilities. The Doctor was into psychological warfare, and these men were

his victims. He tried to provoke Sam into making some
comment on the condition of the buildings, but Sam saw
no point to it. He wasn't drawn in. Instead he concentrated on figuring out how these buildings were guarded
when the prisoners were in them. It looked like two sentries manned a small area at the front of the barracks.

Sam now added a dimension to his mission. This the
Committee discouraged, but he would do it anyhow. He
swore to himself to try to free these poor devils from the
private hell Sun Sun had condemned them to. Sam had all
he could do right now keeping himself from chopping
Sun Sun to his knees and flexing with well-placed thumbs
on his jugular all semblance of life from a man so foul.
This was a simple assassination run, but Sam would risk
the Committee's wrath to give these guys a break; otherwise they were doomed. He took a silent vow to go for
broke. He would eliminate Sun Sun, free the prisoners,
liberate Honey Pot, wreck the compound.

"Now I will show you my pets, Mr. Borne," Sun Sun
said, cutting in on Sam's reverie. "You will follow me
and see something you will never forget." Sun Sun led
the way, trailing Sam, Honey and a handful of sentries.
They crossed to a small bamboo hut with a palm frond
roof. Sun Sun swung back the bamboo door and entered
eagerly, like a kid on Christmas morning. Sam followed.
Honey remained outside with the sentries.

Inside, amid lines and shadows, the air hung heavy.
Nothing stirred at ground level, yet there was an eerie
sense of life present, an eerie cheeping sound, constant
and disconcerting. The feel of the place was creepy. In
the center of the room, a bamboo hatch about six feet
long and four feet wide rested. Sam noted a smaller hatch
near the wall. Sun Sun was making a billing and cooing
murmur like the one he'd made wooing the parrot. He
was on his knees in the dirt, pushing against the edge of
the hatch. He pushed the hatch aside and leaned over a pit
the size of a grave. He reached into the large patch

pockets of his shorts, extracted something and started to sprinkle it into the hole like a man sowing seed. The cheeping intensified; it grew louder, then louder still. Sun Sun continued to broadcast the stuff from his pockets, billing and cooing as he did so. Then he looked back over his shoulder at Sam.

"Come over here, Mr. Borne. Come over here and feast your eyes on this little sight."

Sam walked over and stood above the kneeling doctor. He could see over Sun Sun's shoulder that the pit was a riot of moiling rats, cheeping and climbing, scratching and rolling over each other in a frenzy. Sun Sun showered more feed down upon them, placing it just so in order to cause more chaos. It was a survival-of-the-fittest show, and he loved every minute of it.

"Aren't they beauties, Mr. Borne? Aren't they just the sweetest little beauties?"

Sam said nothing.

"I keep them on the razor's edge of hunger, Mr. Borne," Sun Sun continued. "I keep them just at the point where they're ready to tear each other to pieces, and sometimes do, and my reward is that they're ever responsive, ever on the ball. They are a source for me of almost endless joy."

He reached into his pockets and took out more feed. He sprayed a big handful into one far corner of the hole and then quickly, as soon as the rats had scrambled to that corner, sprayed another handful into a near corner. The rats scurried in waves from one side to the other. He laughed heartily.

"I love these little beauties, Mr. Borne. You should see them when I use them in support actions. They are magnificent then, simply magnificent."

He rose clumsily to his feet, slowly and magnanimously emptying each pocket into the pit, turning the pocket inside out and shaking it vigorously. He looked at Sam and smiled. He walked over to the side of the pit and replaced the hatch. Sam had the distinct feeling that Sun Sun could have stayed there all day, that he got an almost sexual charge from feeding the rats.

Back outside they picked up Honey and the sentries. They walked back across the parade ground to the Doctor's cinder-block residence. They waited while Sun Sun went inside. When he reappeared, the golf cart was brought up. He climbed into the shotgun seat and instructed Sam and Honey to sit in the back where the clubs usually went. Honey asked to be excused, but permission was denied. Sun Sun didn't take any sentries, but he had strapped two pearl-handled pistols on and the driver was armed. They started off in the direction away from the heliports, toward the mountainside where so many workers could be seen bent over their field chores.

They rode in silence. When they reached the foot of the mountainside, Sun Sun raised a hand and the cart stopped. Sun Sun jumped out and stood gazing at the workers, who labored at gunpoint. Sentries cradling AK-47s stood at intervals between the rows of workers. There was no hope of escape. A worker attempting to escape would be cut to bits. A sentry with a whistle on a lanyard around his neck descended to Sun Sun and exchanged a few words with him in Vietnamese. Sam looked from Sun Sun and his adjutant to Honey. She felt Sam's eyes on her and looked at him briefly before cutting her eyes back to the Doctor. She was no fool and she was under constraint.

"Come closer, Mr. Borne," Sun Sun called back to them. "Honey too, come closer and see the world's prettiest flower being grown."

Honey shot Sam a lightning look, then climbed down from the cart and joined Sam in sauntering over to Sun Sun. They followed Sun Sun and the sentry with the whistle up the hill to where the workers were digging with hoes. Some workers dug while others stood near with burlap aprons around their waists. The aprons were like carpenters' aprons, but instead of nails they held tiny poppy seeds. When the worker using the hoe had tilled the land sufficiently, the worker with the seeds would kneel down and carefully plant the seeds in the fresh furrows. It was primitive. Opium farming hadn't gone agrotechnical, though it was certainly agrobusiness, big agrobusiness. It marked the first stage in the most lucrative criminal enterprise known to man.

Sam's mind reeled under the sight of the workers. They were clearly men ravaged and abused to the breaking point. In their ragged outfits, they bent to their work, their tortured bodies able to perform even under the most adverse conditions. The track marks on their arms bore silent testimony to the addiction Sun Sun had enslaved them to, and the thinness of their bodies, the gauntness of their expressions spoke volumes about the effects of their poor diet of rice and water and the rigors of their long workdays on the mountainsides. Yet they endured, the fine fighting machines as they were. Ravaged though they were, Sam was sure they weren't beaten. He was sure they would rise to the occasion if given a chance to avenge themselves on their torturers. The sight of them blistered Sam, and he swore to himself that he wouldn't leave here without at least giving these brave men a chance at freedom and dignity.

Sam was not unaware of what was taking place, nor of what would follow. Still, his mind ariot with rage at what had been done to these fine men, he listened politely while Sun Sun showed off his knowledge of the opium process. Like any true egomaniac, Sun Sun stood ready to explain the meaning of religion to God. He told how poppy seeds were planted in late summer and early fall and how at maturity the poppy plant, now green in color, would sprout one main stem about three or four feet high, with maybe half a dozen to a dozen smaller stems shooting off it. About three months later each stem would produce a bright flower. In time the petals of the flower would drop off; underneath would be a green seedpod the size and shape of a chicken egg. No one yet knew why, but the seedpod would produce a milky-white sap not long after the petals fell away. The sap was opium. To harvest it, all you needed to do was make a series of parallel cuts across the pod's surface with a special curved knife. The sap would then run out of the pod and congeal on its surface, where it changed to a brownish-black color. The opium could then be scraped off the pod with a dull, flat knife.

"You know, Mr. Borne," Sun Sun bragged, "we have our own laboratory right here, and we refine our own stuff. We turn it into the best number-four heroin in the world. It's a point of pride with me that my heroin be the best. I got lots of it stockpiled right here, waiting. It won't be arms that knock America for a loop. No, sir, it will be good ole number-four heroin manufactured by the good ole doctor, *moi*." He lanced a thumb into his chest for emphasis, grinning his big grin, beaming it on Sam and Honey in turn before bringing it back to Sam. He went on, "I have given some thought, Mr. Borne, to what brand name to use when we—I use the royal we, not the we of you and me, Mr. Borne—market our product in the States. I love the brand names on heroin. My! but I love them, especially No Monkey Business, Foolish Pleasure, Ding Dong and the unequivocal Fuck Me, the greatest label ever put on any product, yes, indeed. So I need to think big. I've thought of Sunshine and of Sundae, of Sun God and Sun Dog, but the one I like best, even more than Sunstroke, is Sunburn." He fairly hissed this last. He leered. "Get it?" he implored, almost in a whisper.

"You're a poet," Sam deadpanned.

Sun Sun looked at him hard. "You think you're smarter than everyone else, Mr. Borne, and that's a mistake with me. I want you to know that it wasn't unusual in the adored ancients for a man to be possessed of military facility, political acumen and poetic genius. And I know in my heart, I'm in a direct line to people like Alexander the Great and Julius Caesar. So your sarcasm is a form of pissing in the wind, Mr. Borne. And I'll see to it that it blows back on you, bet on it.''

There was a long silence, then Sun Sun clapped his hands and the sentry with the whistle let out a shrill blast. The workers languidly leaned on their hoes or stood with their fists buried in the burlap aprons. They all faced down the hill to where Sun Sun stood before Sam, Honey and the sentry with the whistle. ''Men, fellow workers, I'd like you to take a look at a real live capitalist whore, Mr. Sam Borne of the United States, formerly home to many of us before our enlightenment. Mr. Borne here is a dyed-in-the-wool capitalist. He's ready to sell anything, from his soul to his country, in order to turn a buck. He has no cause, like us. He claims he's here to help us, to put us over the top—for a price, of course. He's the real article, pure through and through, like the best poison. Take a good look at him, Mr. Sam Borne.''

Sun Sun paused to let his words sink in. The men gave no sign they heard. They leaned on hoes or slouched on their feet. They were malnourished, listless, in the grip of blackest despair. They were wrecks. Sun Sun had clinically eviscerated them, one and all. They clung now to the basest level of life, hollow men strung out as far as the human spirit could be strung out. Sam knew looking at them that they were addicts from their soles to their crowns. With any kind of luck, Sam would give them back to themselves.

''Well, men,'' Sun Sun shouted like a man exhorting the stone deaf, ''we'll never harvest the future this way, will we? Let's get to work, asses and elbows all around.'' He clapped. The sentry blew his whistle. The men started back to work, no more agile than mummies, wrapped in their addiction, hostages to a living death.

Sam forced himself to bite back his disgust and his

rage. He held himself in check. Sun Sun looked at him to see how he was taking things. "We're set now for the *pièce de résistance*, Mr. Borne. We'll skirt the fields here, and I'll show you the most advanced laboratory you'll ever set eyes on." Sun Sun walked down the hillside past Sam and leaped into the golf cart. He tapped his knee impatiently and glared at Honey as Sam helped her down the hillside. When they climbed aboard the back of the cart, the driver pulled out before they could get settled, knocking them backward. It was his way of showing he was on the Doctor's side; everybody at the Sun Sun compound appeared to be very eager to come up on the Doctor's side smelling like a rose.

They circled the perimeter of the compound while Sun Sun pointed out how much land he had under cultivation. When they came around to the heliport side of the compound, Sun Sun proudly pointed out the fully armed Cobra gunship parked side by side with the two Huey slicks they'd flown in on that morning. The rocket pods on the short wings of the Cobra reminded Sam of gigantic quivers loaded with steel arrows. All they needed was the right Robin Hood. The Cobra was a fierce weapon; it could cause a tremendous amount of havoc in a short space of time.

As soon as they cleared the helipad, the driver cut the cart back into the compound. They rode the edge of the parade ground until they came to a simple bamboo hut with a palm-frond roof. The cart stopped and Sun Sun hopped out. Sam and Honey climbed off. Sun Sun walked into the hut without looking back. Sam and Honey automatically followed. Inside, the hut was bare except for a door in its center with a slanting shaft behind it. The shaft led below the ground. Sun Sun opened the door and started down the steps. Sam and Honey followed. The shaft led down two flights to a steel door the color of rust with a rectangular window cut into it at eye level. Sun Sun reached into his khaki bush shorts and pulled out a key ring. He opened the door, stood back and waved Sam and Honey through.

They entered a vast room. Overhead were row upon row of fluorescent lights set in padded ceiling tiles. The walls were immaculate, white and bare. Tables ran in rows along the floor; they were lab tables, complete with Bunsen burners. Interspersed among the tables were aluminum double sinks. On the tables themselves sat flasks and beakers filled with different colored solutions. At the extremes of the rows of tables, big institutional stoves stood, their flames raised, pots and glass containers heating on them. The room was full of midgets, midgets everywhere. They were tending the solutions on the stoves and on the tables. Some were carrying what Sam immediately recognized as morphine bricks from a stockpile at one end of the room to the tables and stoves. There they would begin the conversion process to the white powder, eighty to ninety-nine percent pure, that is known as number-four heroin, the heroin users in America are addicted to. None of the midgets looked up. Instead they kept working, impervious to whatever was happening around them. They were dedicated.

Sam and Honey followed as Sun Sun moved off among the midgets. They strolled down one big aisle, and Sam noticed how professional everything was. Every drug operation would have liked to be so integrated, the raw opium grown only feet from where it was converted into morphine bricks and then refined into the white powder of heroin. This was ideal. This lab looked like something out of Du Pont, so professional was it; it was perfect. Sam knew that refining opium into morphine bricks was easy. Refining morphine bricks into the white powder known as heroin was slightly more complicated, involving five basic steps, the aim of which was to bind chemically the morphine molecules with acetic acid and then process the compound into the white powder of heroin. In that state it was smuggled to America. It used to be brought in in false-bottom suitcases and other doctored containers, like the stuffed animals of children or in dolls or in any of a number of other clever devices. But lately the authorities were much smarter. So now there were shipments made by cutting surgical gloves into fingers and stuffing the fingers with heroin. Or condoms were used. The stuffed finger or condom was swallowed by a carrier. When the carrier got to the States, vomiting was induced and the finger or condom would fly out and there was the heroin. If the finger or condom broke en route, the carrier was dead. That was the risk, and it explained the high price for carrying. That was why during the police action it had been safer to ship the stuff home in the corpses of dead soldiers. Heroin was a nasty business. As it was, people from all walks of life had acted as carriers—diplomats, actors, stewardesses, lawyers, doctors, international businessmen. For an eight-hour flight, they could earn up to twenty thousand dollars. Of course, if the container broke, the price was death. Still, there was no shortage of willing carriers.

Once the heroin hit the States, the process from lab to street was simple. The big distributors set up labs where the heroin powder was cut. It was so simple it could be done overnight. Usually an apartment was rented in a good neighborhood, one outside the usual drug neighborhoods. The apartment was then used as a heroin mill, always heavily guarded to prevent raids by competitors. Usually women cut the heroin, working standing up in the nude to prevent stealing. They were heavily guarded while they worked. Sam had once seen a heroin mill in operation. It had seemed to him a scene out of Dante, hellish beyond description. Women worked over the heroin, cutting it with lactose, mannitol or quinine, all of which are white and have the powdered texture of heroin. All three chemicals were preferred over plain sugar, which would also work as a cutting agent; none of the three is as sweet as sugar—in fact, quinine is bitter—and they do not impart sweetness to the cut heroin. On the street, smart addicts often tasted heroin before making a buy. If the heroin was sweet, the addicts knew it had been heavily cut, or "stepped on," in street talk. In the mill, when the powder was cut to the desired solution and percentage, it was packaged in glassine pouches and sold by brand name on the streets by the point-of-purchase pushers.

Sam would never forget seeing the heroin mill. The women had stood beside portable wallpaper hangers' tables of bare wood and had cut the powder quickly. Beside them were boxes full of glassine pouches. They might have been attending culinary classes in a nudist colony, except that armed guards in an empty apartment signaled to even the naive that this was a criminal operation. It was also a thoroughly efficient operation, if twisted. It was as though General Mills or General Foods had gone into the business of distributing disease, malnutrition and death.

Even the distribution was efficient. The pushers were the distributors. These pushers, called mules, were often kids. Kids worked for less, could be intimidated easier and, if caught, were tried as juveniles and got off easy. The mules even had subdistributors. These subdistributors were called steerers and were often still younger kids, children as young as ten or eleven years old. They would direct the addicts to the mules. The steerers would earn fifty to a hundred dollars a day, tax free, like all heroin money. The mules sold the glassine pouches, called quarter bags, good for two or three fixes, for fifty dollars a pop. So a kilo of pure heroin bought by an international drug merchant for eighty thousand dollars would yield, once in the States, cut and distributed, an on-the-street take of one million dollars.

With his monster farm and refinery, Sun Sun was going to undercut everybody. He was going to put heroin out there like candy, knowing that with the right network, addiction in America would turn into an epidemic, one that would ruin the entire country—its youth, its dreams, its future.

Sun Sun stopped in front of Sam and talked rapidly in Vietnamese to a midget holding a clipboard. Sun Sun smiled a big smile. The midget showed him some figures, and Sun Sun nodded. He turned to Sam, his demon's leer in full flower. "Do you realize, Mr. Borne, that just ten square miles of opium fields can yield enough heroin to supply the entire United States addict population for a year? Do you realize what you've just seen? Do you realize what this operation can mean? Correction—what it will mean? Do you now?"

"Yes."

CHAPTER TWENTY:
SURFACING

Only the digits changed. They were on a clock on a night table. Sam Borne lay on the bed beside it in the attitude of a man hunching over a putt on a golf green, only he was on his side, hands clasped in front of his thighs. He was in a relaxed state, in a mild meditation, one that left him free on the edge of his own thoughts. There was much to think about.

In the laboratory, when Sun Sun had stopped smacking his lips in the refining room, he had shown Sam the large room attached to it where the morphine bricks were made. There were the usual big drums for boiling water, a large supply of ordinary lime fertilizer in hundred-pound bags and big containers of concentrated ammonia. On a long roller on one wall a bolt of flannel hung. In short, the morphine room was fully equipped for the simple process of boiling the raw opium into morphine bricks, which were then transported by the midgets on skids via a manual forklift into the refining room. Sun Sun's operation was completely self-sufficient; it was a complete monopoly, horizontal and vertical, from seed to powder.

All Sun Sun needed was distribution. But it didn't track. If Sun Sun could organize such an elaborate system and have it in perfect working order, it would seem that

he could also have organized a distribution network. Sam
would guess that one of the Hong Kong triad guys or one
of the Corsican gonzos would have been greedy enough
to be sucked into a scheme whereby he could undercut
everybody else and steal most of the American heroin
market out from under the goons who now controlled it.
Yet it was possible that distribution was the stumbling
block for Sun Sun. Historically, the distribution of heroin
in the United States was tightly held and strictly regu-
lated. Factually, it would be hard to crack the heroin
racket and get the product on the market. In its distribution in the United States, heroin was more than a monopoly, it was a cartel, and the guys who controlled that
cartel were emphatically not to be fucked with. It was
possible Sun Sun needed just such a renegade dealer with
the distribution setup Sam promised to implement his
mad scheme.

Sam could only hope he had figured this right. There
weren't going to be a lot of chances for him. He was
going to have to hit Sun Sun soon, fast and hard. Nothing
had convinced Sam of this as had the trip he'd taken after
the official tour of the laboratory. They had all followed
the midget with the clipboard and left the underground
laboratory through a back door leading out of the morphine room. That was when the full shock had come.

The entire compound was interconnected underground. Sun Sun had gloated and grinned as they'd all
followed the midget through an elaborate underground
system of tunnels and little caves. All of it, Sun Sun had
explained, had been set up years ago by the Vietcong to
facilitate their underground communications and escape
hatches when the compound had been a functioning village that had served as a supply base and clearing house
for troops and matériel launched into the South and along
the coast to the east. It had been a crucial settlement for
the VC, one they had built up over years of fighting the
French and then the Americans. The walls of the tunnels

and the caves were hard with exposed age. The passages had a stifling underground atmosphere, and they were dark.

The midget had had a big flashlight with him. It had cast eerie shadows ahead of them as they moved through the tunnels. In some of the caves, in niches dug into the earthen walls, there were candleholders of beaten tin which still held old half-burned candles. Sun Sun had stopped long enough in one of the caves to light a candle. It had cast an unsteady pall of yellow light into the cave. On the floor, the cave still had matting where generations of guerrillas must have lain while French and American troops had searched the apparently innocent agricultural village above. There were remnants of mess kits, a fork here, an old can opener there. In one niche along the wall, Sam spotted wooden rice bowls set atop each other like a carefully arranged still life. The caves and tunnels, though still showing signs of their wartime function, were tranquil.

Sun Sun had been all smiles and mirth when the midget had finally taken them, after many a twist and turn, to a trapdoor in the ceiling of one cave that led into a storeroom at the back of the impeccable dining room where they had lunched earlier that day. They must have traveled, Sam would estimate, five or six hundred yards underground, without a signpost or an indication of any sort, and yet the midget had never taken a false step, had never, in fact, paused for a second to get his bearings. He had strolled to his destination as casually, as surely as any *flâneur* out for a strut in the Luxembourg Gardens. And that was it. The midget had not had to stoop in the tunnels, as Sam, Sun Sun and Honey had to do. He had been able to walk through the tunnels at his full height. If he had wanted to, he could have sprinted. Sam realized that the tunnel system here was designed and manned by these midgets and that it probably had been since the days of the French fighting. The clever Vietnamese had not only

built an elaborate and almost unbeatable system below
the ground, they had even assigned a guard to it, a staff of
midgets. These midgets had been given to Sun Sun when
the compound was converted to the task of growing
enough opium and processing enough heroin to under-
mine America. And it all worked magnificently.

And now here lay Sam Borne, the missing link, the in-
gredient they needed, the man with the distribution
know-how, the man who could make it all work. Yet,
hunched up on the bed, Sam knew something didn't add
up, something wasn't right.

The phone beside the digital clock rang. Sam let it ring
three times so he would not seem on edge. He kept his
voice low-key, as though he had been roused out of a
nap.

"Hello."

"Hello, Mr. Borne, how are you?"

"I'm fine, Doctor, how about yourself?"

"Splendid. Couldn't be better."

"I'm delighted for you."

"Now, Mr. Borne, we are going to dine tonight in high
style, and I want you to know that the English are not the
only ones who dress for dinner in the jungle, understand?"

"Yes."

"Good. Then a man of your distinction will not mind
dressing properly, I'm sure. So, in a matter of seconds
there will be a knock at your door. . . . Ah, do I hear it
now?"

There was a knock on the door.

"Yes. Someone is knocking at the door," Sam said.

"Well, Mr. Borne, let this person in."

Sam put down the phone and swung himself off the
bed. He crossed the room and opened the door. One of
the midgets stood in the doorway. He bowed low to Sam
and gestured that he'd like to enter. Sam stepped back
and the midget walked into the room. As the midget

started to go around the room unlocking doors, Sam walked over and looked into one the midget had opened. It led to a dressing room worthy of a duke. Along one wall were rack upon rack of tuxedos, suits, sports coats and slacks, all hung with care, all impeccable. On the opposite side of the room were drawers built into the wall. The midget opened various drawers in this wall. He pulled them partway open and left them. He went to another door and opened it. It led to a bathroom the size of a handball court. It had a large sunken tub with water jets for a Jacuzzi and a small sauna built into one wall. There were sunlamps and heated towel racks. Along one wall was a counter holding two sinks. Another wall was all mirrored. It was top shelf all the way.

The phone was squawking. Sam walked over and picked it up.

"Yes."

"Borne, you have your visitor. Good. Now I must go and prepare myself for our little repast, but let me say that we are most formal tonight, tux and so on. You wouldn't call a tux a monkey suit, especially here in the jungle, now would you, Mr. Borne?"

"No."

"Good. Then in an hour you will be called to dinner. I know you'll enjoy this evening's entertainment. I shall say good-bye for now, then." Sun Sun hung up. Like many bastards, Sun Sun used formality as a taunt, as a reminder that he was in charge. Like chivalry, good manners in the wrong hands was nothing more and nothing less than choreographed hostility. Sam knew the type.

The midget gently tugged Sam on the sleeve. Sam turned and looked down. The midget was smiling a genuine smile. He was making an honest effort to make Sam feel at home. The midget led Sam to the cabinet built into the wall between the two doorways, one to the dressing room, the other to the bathroom. The midget was too short to reach the keyhole in the front of the cabinet. He gave Sam the key. Sam opened the cabinet. Inside was a fully stocked bar with a small brown refrigerator. Sam bowed gratefully to the midget. The midget bowed back, took the key from Sam, walked across the room and left, closing the door behind him.

Sam was alone with an hour to kill. He would make the most of it, he quickly decided. He made himself a healthy Scotch and soda from the bar, took a good, soaking bath and a reviving sauna, showered off and dressed in the tux the midget had correctly guessed would fit him. He was ready and waiting an hour later when the knock came on his door. It was the same midget, dressed now in a tuxedo.

The others were all seated when Sam arrived in the dining room. He stood in the doorway for a second, taking in the scene. Everyone in the room was in formal dress. All the men, including about twenty midgets, sported tuxedos. The only woman in the room, Honey Pot, was resplendent in a chartreuse cocktail gown by Cacherel with high collar, cutaway sleeves and flared skirt. When Sam appeared in the doorway, Sun Sun clapped and rose from his seat and everyone followed suit. All eyes were on Sam.

"We welcome you, Mr. Borne, our guest of honor," Sun Sun intoned from his place at the head table. The midget beside Sam nudged him on the arm, and Sam started forward down the aisle between the tables to the head table at the front where Sun Sun, Honey and Bui stood awaiting him with the two flunkies from the helicopter. Sam realized that he was to sit in the empty place to Sun Sun's right. Honey was on the Doctor's left. Sam stood behind his chair and instinctively bowed to Sun Sun.

Sun Sun lifted his champagne glass from the table and held it aloft. "I would like to propose a toast to our honored guest tonight, Mr. Sam Borne, who has come here to help us in our quest. Mr. Borne has come to us like manna from heaven." Sun Sun repeated himself quickly in Vietnamese, and they all lifted their glasses. Sam lifted his. Brandishing his glass at arm's length, Sun Sun kicked off the toast and everyone drank. "Now," Sun Sun continued, "we shall enjoy the best of dinners. May it not be Mr. Borne's last supper with us." He sat down and everyone else followed suit.

Waiters dressed all in white started to scurry around the tables. As an opening gambit, they brought small bowls of gray beluga caviar and little silver spoons with which to enjoy it. They washed down the caviar with iced Stolichnaya. A classic *petite marmite* followed, chunks of beef and chicken floating in a rich consommé, along with finely cut turnips, carrots and celery. Next came *paupiettes de sole Duglésé*. On scalloped silver salvers, delicate rolled fillets of sole swam in a creamy *velouté* sauce and were crowned with tiny tomato balls and garnished on the edges of the tray with little puff pastry crescents. Along with this came bottle after bottle of Les Clos *grand cru* Chablis. The Chablis was dry and crisp, fragrant and big; it played just right to the sole, counterpointing and augmenting it at one and the same time, standing up to, but not overpowering, the creamy richness of the sauce. Sam glanced at Honey. She gave him a discreet look. Instantly he knew she was enjoying this sumptuous meal no better than he. There was an uneasy feeling to everything being done here that went beyond Sun Sun's showing off his power, his sophistication, his worldliness. There was something in the air very definitely like danger.

"How do you like our hospitality, Mr. Borne?" Sun Sun asked, looking up from his food for the first time. He was on his second helping of *paupiettes*, his third glass of Chablis.

"It's like being at the finest Parisian restaurant."

"I knew you were a man to appreciate quality when you found it."

"This is a classic Chablis. How do you get it here?"

"We can't give away trade secrets, Mr. Borne. You understand, of course."

"Indeed."

"Wait until you see what else we have in store for you this evening." Sun Sun chuckled a low chuckle and cocked one eyebrow into a cedilla.

"I bet I'll just die," Sam said. This was a game two could play.

Sun Sun laughed in spite of himself. "You could be all wet, Mr. Borne. You could be correct. You could be both." He laughed again, a private laugh; he was a comedian in his own mind. Sam took a deep sip of the Chablis, savoring its flinty kick as it washed down his gullet. He would keep his own counsel. He enjoyed the last *paupiette* on his plate, and the waiter removed it and replaced it with a clean one. While the next course was served, he listened to Sun Sun chattering away to Honey in Vietnamese. He was all animation, she all indifference.

The *pièce de résistance* was all it was ever meant to be: *poularde Derby*. This was Auguste Escoffier's monumental invention. On big silver trays the waiters brought forth for each table twin roasted chickens stuffed with rice, truffles and foie gras. Around the edges of the chickens were columns of bread topped with foie gras and a thin slice of truffle. Here and there among the columns were big truffles sitting on scalloped pastry bases like frogs on lily pads. Sun Sun was putting on the dog. So Sam threw him a bone.

"You have served one of my favorite dishes, Doctor. I'm flattered."

Sun Sun turned from Honey and beamed at Sam. Then he belched loudly. He dabbed at his lips and belched again. He looked at Sam and defied him to expect an apology. Sam overrode his rudeness.

"It's one of the highwater marks in a gourmand's life

when he eats his first *poularde Derby*. Can you remember yours?"

Sun Sun took the challenge. "I was on my way to France on the *Normandie* with my parents. We ate like kings, and the last night before we hit Le Havre we had *poularde Derby*. I can still taste it."

"You must have led a fascinating life, Doctor."

Sun Sun caught himself. He realized that he was responding, not controlling. He scowled at Sam and retook control. "My life is my business. I will tell you this. What's left of my life will be more fascinating than what's past, I guarantee it. How many people do you know, Mr. Borne, who can make that statement?"

"Few. Very few."

"And you? Can you make that statement?"

"I will tell you this. What's left of my life will be more fascinating than what's past, I guarantee it," Sam deadpanned.

A mad sneer filled Sun Sun's face. He was bested, and he despised it. He turned to Honey, then back to Sam. "Eat your chicken, Mr. Borne."

"Thank you. I will."

Until the waiters served a light green salad with vinaigrette dressing, Sam did not so much as rate a raised eyebrow from Sun Sun, who spent all his time regaling Honey with tales of his exploits, plans and mad schemes; gesturing and pounding the table to punctuate his points. Throughout, he kept quaffing the superb Thenard Montrachet the waiters were now pouring liberally. Sam sipped the wine carefully, reveling in its robust assertiveness, its verve and daring, its power and glory. It was a crime a great Montrachet had to be drunk among such awful company, in such awful circumstances. There was so much at stake that Sam could not afford to enjoy himself, to let go, to relax his guard for even a minute. On the contrary, he was officially on the prowl for the right moment to kill the Doctor, the sooner the better. The more

the Doctor indulged his appetite for veiled threats and ob-
lique taunts, the more restless Sam felt.

Sam was eager to get on with the events of the night, so
he was glad to see the waiters wheel in several carts laden
with desserts. There was a raspberry charlotte, a peach
Melba, a chocolate mousse and fresh strawberries with
cream. Sam politely refused them all. Sun Sun sampled
each, picking at strawberries dipped in cream between
mouthfuls of the other three. He needed only a bunch of
grapes and a chaise to have done a great imitation of a decadent Roman emperor, tux or no tux. Now somewhat
soggy from the vodka, Chablis and Montrachet, he continued to direct his attention toward Honey. From time to
time Honey sneaked a glance across at Sam and commu-
nicated volumes. Sam was restless, bored and eager to
kill.

The cheeses came as a blessing, as did the espresso.
Sam downed two hot demitasses of strong espresso, sus-
pecting correctly that they were needed to dispel the effects of the wine. Sun Sun toyed with one espresso,
washing it liberally with the Montrachet, a wine much
too good to be sloshed this way. Sun Sun used his free
hand to clasp Honey about the nape, then squeezed and
manipulated her head proprietorially, in a way sure to
cause her discomfort, if not out and out pain, but she for-
bore from reacting. Sam could not tolerate to look at Sun
Sun as he did this. Instead he scanned the room. Many of
the diners were now tipsy, if not stone drunk. Some were
acting out extravagantly and were quite hilarious. No
matter, Sam was in no mood to enjoy them. The doors at
the far end of the room were suddenly flung open and two
columns of armed sentries marched in, one streaming
down each side of the room until the lead sentries flanked
the head table. Sam turned and met Sun Sun's leering
stare full face.

"How did you enjoy your meal, Mr. Borne?" the good
doctor slurred.

"It was eminently memorable."

"I hope so. It will have to last you eternity." Sun Sun burst out laughing, and the midgets and the full-sized toadies joined right in. They stopped when Sun Sun raised his arm. "What do you say, good comrades? What do you say?" he roared into the room at large.

The diners picked up their wineglasses and twirled them in their hands, smacking them down on the table upside down, in many cases spilling wine all over themselves and their companions. Then they picked up their spoons and started to tinkle out a beat on the wineglasses. They wore sodden smiles. Sun Sun was in his glory. He looked at his glass and at Honey's, both still upright. Sun Sun went into full pantomime. He looked from his glass to Honey's and back again. He looked up at Honey, down at the glass. He repeated this farce several times to rising laughter from the diners. Along the walls the sentries grinned and exchanged knowing looks. Finally Sun Sun raised his arm above his head. There was silence.

Slowly he took up his glass, twirled it, then slammed it down upside down. The room filled with laughter and cheers, hoots and catcalls. Sun Sun abruptly raised his arm, restoring silence. He waited, milking the moment like a master entertainer. He looked at Sam, back to Honey, then to Sam and back again. He looked out at the diners. He looked back. He spidered his hand across the table and touched the stem of Honey's wineglass, then pulled his hand back as though the stem were electrified. Laughter filled the room, along with hooting and catcalls, whistles and cheers. Sun Sun looked at Sam in mock disbelief. Sam tweaked the tip of his nose, curled his fingernails and calmly inspected them. Sun Sun flashed the diners a "get him" look. They roared.

Sun Sun raised his arm. He looked at Honey, then picked up her wineglass and moved it closer to her. She looked at the glass. The room filled with the clinking of spoons on crystal. Honey looked at Sun Sun. She did not look across at Sam. She reached out reluctantly, picked up her wineglass and turned it clumsily in one hand, almost losing it, then put it down gently on the table upside down. The room went wild.

Sun Sun let the uproar peak. Then he raised his hand for silence. He stared at Sam. "What we've got right here, Mr. Borne, is a unanimous decision."

"Congratulations."

"And what we're going to see is how good you are."

"At what?"

"Surfacing."

CHAPTER TWENTY-ONE:
CRYSTALLIZED

Through the glass, everything was clear. Sun Sun stood flanked by Bui and Honey, champagne glass in hand, beaming and gesturing. He might easily have been mistaken for the proud father of the bride at a lavish wedding reception. Waiters circulated among the diners, filling glass after glass with Perrier-Jouët champagne. Corks constantly popped; one even ricocheted off the glass through which Sam Borne watched the scene around him in 360-degree freedom. The feeling of cold water climbing up his legs chilled him through and through.

Sam was in a blown-glass cylinder twelve feet high and three feet in diameter. A bright green hose hung over the lip of the cylinder at the top. Cold water flowed from the hose; so far it filled the cylinder to the level of Sam's shoulders. Sam was still in evening dress, in black tie and tux, in patent-leather pumps, all drenched. He was riveted on the goings-on in the room around him, which was large and all in tile, the walls aquamarine and the floor yellow. The room was situated behind the large swimming pool Sam had seen that afternoon on his grand tour. Only, that afternoon he hadn't been shown this large tiled room and its bizarre blown-glass cylinder, ready all the while for this night's slow execution. Only a mean fuck would have thought of it, the cylinder; and only a sick fuck would have used it. Sun Sun qualified.

Sun Sun now presided in regal ostentation. He pointed from time to time at Sam and made wisecracks in Vietnamese. Each time, the room resounded with laughter, the tiles serving as natural amplifiers, the hoots and laughs reverberating and echoing back and forth, filling Sam's ears with distraction. This situation was perfect for rule number one of the Sam Borne philosophy: Staying calm is the best revenge. Induced panic was a means of control and a source of pleasure to authoritarians, sadists and torturers of every stripe the world over.

Staying calm was the antidote. Sam would lean into himself, resort to himself, wait for himself to rise to the occasion. That the occasion was hopeless didn't matter. Not only had Sam's training as a ninja conditioned him to reject despair, not only had his meditations prepared him to live within himself when necessary, not only had all the rigors of the commando's life taught him to cope with barbaric adversity, but something plain in Sam, something reinforced by his readings in literature and philosophy, something gleaned from Emerson and from Zen, something from the inner core of his character told him to kick injustice in the balls, to spit in the eye of compliance, to blow his own horn till the air was definitely out of him. If this was Sam's day to join the big blue, to add his spirit to the oversoul, so be it; but he wasn't going gentle into any good night. He was holding out; he was looking for a break.

The water was at chin level. Through the glass Sam saw Sun Sun raise his arm on high. Everyone quieted. The tinkle of bottle on crystal stopped as the waiters stopped pouring. For the Doctor it was show time.

"Mr. Borne, honored guest, how do you feel?" Sun Sun's words bounced around the room like rubber balls. Sam waited till they died away, then waited some more. Not for nothing had he worked his ass off at the Royal Academy of Dramatic Art, not for nothing had he toured

the boonies, the fens and moors of merry old England. If
he was going out, he was going out with class, a sound
mind in a sound body.

"Wet."

The few drunken diners who understood English
couldn't stifle snickers. Sun Sun kept his aplomb. Borne
might steal a scene, but he, the great Sun Sun, would stop
the show.

"All wet, you mean."

On cue the diners broke out in peals of laughter. The
Doctor looked left, looked right, reigned supreme. Sun
Sun grinned hugely at Sam, walked over and tapped the
crystal. "Do you realize, Mr. Borne, that I had this
gigantic tumbler blown especially for me in dear old
Prague?"

"I hadn't realized that."

"Are you experiencing any difficulty, Mr. Borne? I
can't help but notice that you're standing on tiptoe." The
water had just reached the level of Sam's mouth, so he
had begun standing on tiptoe to prevent swallowing water
when he spoke.

"I like to stay on the balls of my feet."

"Good, good. Stay on top of things, that sort of
thing?" Sun Sun was back to high colonial. He had more
modes than a good stereo. Like all true maniacs, he had
multiple personalities.

"Sort of." Sam had craned his neck back at a severe
angle, so he was now facing the ceiling. He hopped in order to see Sun Sun clearly.

"Well, I've a feeling we're going to keep you hopping
tonight, Mr. Borne." Just then Sam hopped again, from
one foot to the other. The water had risen to the level of
his scalp; he now had to bob to breathe. Laughter broke
out. The timing of Sun Sun's last line was perfect, Sam
had to give it to him. Sam bobbed again. Raising his arm,
Sun Sun spoke.

"Slow down the water," he said. Against the wall a

sentry turned a handle slightly, and the flow of water from the hose slowed, though there was still a good flow. The cylinder was filling, only not so rapidly. Sam would have to bob now just to breathe. Eventually the water would become too deep, eventually Sam would become too exhausted. The sheer wet crystal would afford no purchase. No form of resourcefulness, no matter how athletic, no matter how gifted, would get him out of this jam.

Slowly, horribly, inexorably, he would drown.

CHAPTER TWENTY-TWO:
DIAMONDS ARE A GUY'S BEST FRIEND

Sun Sun Compound
August 25

Sam conserved his energy. Each time he ascended to the top of the cylinder, he took a deep gulp of air; in between ascents he crouched in the base of the cylinder and took his own counsel. He counseled himself to remain perfectly calm, to cope with death if death was to be his lot. Yet his will roared in his ears to fight back, to make the ascent each agonizing time he arrived at the point of breathlessness, for to wait longer would mean becoming too weak to propel himself to the surface. There he would take the huge gulp of restorative air and float slowly back to the base of the cylinder.

The key was remaining in control, remaining calm. Sam had not perfected meditation only to turn himself into a screaming idiot in every crisis. So he reduced his heartbeat, quelled his central nervous system and squeezed every ounce of oxygen for all he could burn from it.

Still, as he well knew, he couldn't last much longer. He was now at the maximum point at which he was able to get oxygen. The water from the hose still dribbled slowly into the cylinder, ever so slowly, since Sun Sun had the flow reduced to the level guaranteed to give Sam the most painfully slow death. The Doctor had enjoyed himself enormously at the end; he had made gay remarks

and grand speeches, all designed to humiliate Sam and
the people who'd sent him. Finally, in his ignorance Sun
Sun had thrown around the call letters of dread for half-
assed Communists and crack-brained revolutionaries, assuming incorrectly that the CIA lay behind Sam. In the
tank Sam had thought, CIA, my ass.

And so Sun Sun had presided over the conclusion to his
evening soiree, with remarks and speeches and other self-
indulgences. Then he had instructed that the water be cut
back. He had told Sam to enjoy his immersion therapy.
He had laughed and taken Honey Pot by the arm and led
everyone from the tile room. Then in the royal manner he
had waved good-bye to Sam from the door and flicked off
the lights, leaving Sam to bob and gulp in darkness,
alone, wet and in the departure lounge for eternity.

And Sam had conserved his energy. He'd resisted despair, the worst program the human mind could run. He
had bobbed and gulped. And grown tired. He was tired
now in his bones. His arms and joints ached from the cold
water. By design, of course, he could not tread water.
The cylinder was too narrow for that. He was reduced to
relying on the thrust he could get from his legs with one
quick assist from his flicking arms. And he was nearly
too tired now, nearly too cold and achy, nearly too soggy
to make the effort to propel himself again to the brim for a
life-restoring gulp of air. As Sam felt his consciousness
come dangerously close to shutting down, he clenched
his mind and body. Then he coiled and shot upward. His
arms pushed down mightily, gaining the extra thrust he'd
need to surmount the surface. With his forehead he broke
the waterline. He thrust his neck back sharply. For an instant his nose and mouth cleared the water. He gulped.
Air rushed into his mouth, his throat, his lungs. It poured
through him, restoring him, rejuvenating him even as
he drifted back to the bottom. In the rush, Sam knew he
could do this leap again and again, and yet again, but he
also knew that his time was short.

Then the room flooded with light. It penetrated the water, disconcerting Sam, blinding him suddenly. He blinked and blinked. He closed his eyes and concentrated. He knew that the time had to be well past midnight. He knew that Sun Sun and the others must have passed out by now. But he also knew that a sadist like Sun Sun would not hesitate to come back to continue his drunken fun, to watch as a human being he could save with one stroke of a hammer slowly lost consciousness and suffocated at the bottom of a crystal cylinder of his own devising.

In the doorway stood Honey Pot.

She looked stricken and relieved and uncertain of herself. She could tell that Sam was still alive, but she could also tell that he wouldn't last much longer, and she appeared not to have a clue as to what she should do to save him. The room was bare of anything but the hose, the cylinder and Sam. Honey moved a few steps into the room, then stopped. She clutched her face in her hands and started to weep.

Honey was Sam's only chance. He watched her through the water and thought quickly how best to use her. He had first of all to reassure her, then to activate her. First, he had to get air, so he crouched, coiled and pushed off. He made it to the top and got a small gulp of air. As he floated back to the bottom, he saw that Honey had taken her face from her hands, though she still looked stricken. Sam had to handle her. He waved with his hand. She smiled. He motioned for her to come nearer. She walked across the tiles to the cylinder.

Separated by pure crystal, Sam stood face to face with Honey. He thought for a moment, but he did not know how to tell her in the time remaining to him to go out and find something to smash the cylinder with. He wondered why she didn't automatically turn off the water, slow though it was. That would be first. Honey looked into Sam's eyes, and without wasting energy in needless ges-

tures he pointed her with eyes and index finger toward the
spigot on the wall. Immediately she realized what he
wanted and ran over and turned off the water. That was a
start, but only a start. Sam would still drown within the
next couple of minutes if he didn't direct Honey correctly.

There were probably sentries about. Sam did not know
and did not care how Honey had managed to get past the
sentries in the first place. But he did realize that her options were limited. The huge pool was all that was in the
next room. There would be nothing there with which to
smash the crystal. And if the crystal smashed, it would be
heard. The guards would surely be drawn to them.

Honey was back. She looked at Sam longingly, still
stricken. He looked back at her. He needed air. He hoped
she would remain calm. He crouched, coiled and propelled himself upward. He managed to get a gulp of air
and to float down without panicking Honey. He floated
to one knee, and he thought. He stood up and looked at
Honey intently. Honey leaned against the cylinder, hands
clutching it.

It came to Sam in a flash. On Honey's left hand
gleamed the tremendous diamond Sun Sun had been at
such pains to boast about. Now Sam had it.

Carefully, Sam mimed what he wanted Honey to do.
He took his left hand in his right, turned it palm toward
his body and clenched it. Then he slowly moved his left
hand with his right, using it like a tool, describing on the
inside of the crystal cylinder what he wanted Honey to do
on the outside. He described a square the size of a chess-
board.

Honey looked at him dumbfounded. He needed air.
Sam held up his index finger, crouched and shot upward.
He gulped air and floated down. He let himself hit a knee
again. He told himself patience was the key. He started to
mime again what he wanted her to do.

She caught it. Immediately she started to incise the

square on the surface of the crystal. Sam smiled at her.
He gestured to her cautiously to lean into it a little more.
He showed her with his own hands how to steady herself
and to carve a groove. Sam left her to her task and went
up again for air. When he returned, every bone in his
body, every joint ached. He waited, watching Honey.
Then his mind felt sluggish with lack of oxygen. There
was little time left and no margin for error. Calmly, he
propelled himself upward.

When Sam floated back down, Honey had described
the letter L. She was about forty percent home. Sam
watched through the crystal, fighting the urge to move
about, to waste energy gesturing and encouraging her.
She would do it. He would wait. He would keep the faith.
When Honey had reached the parallel ascending line of
the box, Sam went back up for air. When he got down she
was topping off that line and completing the square with
the topside horizontal line. Sam kneeled down and
watched her trace the silver furrow in the crystal. He
fought rising excitement within him. He fought to keep
his pulse steady, his heartbeat down. He still needed to be
extremely careful. When Honey was halfway across the
topside horizontal line, he went back up. He got back
down in time to see Honey close the square.

The square was roughly waist high. Sam smiled encouragement at Honey, conscious that he must still handle her, modulate her, make her do what she alone could
do. He mimed running the diamond back over the surface, but quicker this time. This would deepen the
groove. Honey started in, determined and eager. She
clutched her left hand in her right and routed the hand on
the course already incised on the surface of the crystal.
Sam whirled his index finger, signifying for Honey to
route her hand again around the crystal. She started as
Sam shot himself upward for more air.

When Sam got back down, the square was pronounced.
Now he would try it. Placing both hands carefully on the

square, Sam pressed slowly, with a cautious, even pressure. The square didn't move. Sam pressed again. Still the square didn't move. The effort had weakened him. He'd used what oxygen he had. He felt his mind float up and fly around him. Dizziness swept over him. He took a second to recoup his energy, then crouched and shot upward. He made it, just barely, and gulped some air. He let himself drift down effortlessly, conserving his energy for the task ahead.

That's when he learned Honey Pot was golden. Without being told, she had run the diamond around the square again and again. The furrow was deep and shiny, with burls of glass gleaming on either side of the cut. Sam paused a second, then placed both hands firmly on the square and leaned into it, applying an even and steadily increasing pressure. Nothing happened. Sam withdrew. He looked at Honey, and she looked back. Sam fought off a rush of panic. The glass should clearly have given way, but it was of high quality, built to hold, built to last. All of this was not in Sam's favor. He needed air. He crouched and shot upward. He got only half a gulp of air, landed on the bottom and shot right back up. This time he got more air.

When Sam reached the bottom again, he was cheered to see that Honey was as persistent as he. She was tracing the line of the square, pressing and digging with the diamond as hard as she could. Sam drew strength from her. He would not have much chance after this. His legs were rubbery, he ached all over, his head felt like it would float off his neck any second.

Sam placed his hands carefully on the square and pressed. Nothing happened. He pressed harder. Nothing happened. He felt his arms start to buckle. He was faced with a crucial choice now. He could pull back and repeat his ascent or he could press on. He did not have strength enough left to negotiate again the crouching, the pumping, the thrusting necessary to get himself air. He pressed hard, leaning his weight into the task, arching his back, planting his heels against the base of the cylinder. Exhaustion and nausea rolled through him. He felt faint. He would soon lose consciousness.

Sam pressed hard, and harder still.

With a pop the panel burst. Sam's hands were in the air, water rushing over them. Water rushed over his body, sucking out at the opening. He fell to his knees. He felt himself spin. He felt everything go blank, and dark. He lay still.

Water rushed onto the floor, swooshing out of the cylinder with the sweetest rushing sibilance Honey Pot had ever heard. She found herself exhilarated beyond belief, up on her toes, bouncing ever so slightly. She had done it. She was on cloud nine. Till she saw Sam slumped in the water pooled waist high in the bottom of the cylinder.

She hesitated, then acted. Honey slopped through the water on the floor at the base of the cylinder, reached in and grabbed Sam by the hair. She shook his head from side to side, underwater. He didn't budge. She reached in with both hands and grabbed his head on either side. She shook vigorously. Nothing changed. Sam was unconscious, floating in the water like a fetus in the womb. Panic tore through Honey. She thought Sam had drowned. She thought she had won only to lose. Every nerve in her body trilled. Rage roared through her.

With a super effort, Honey leaned her elbows on the lower edge of the cut square. The glass cut into her flesh. She felt blood trickle down her upper arms and drip onto the floor. She pulled harder, digging her elbows in. She got Sam's head craned out of the water. Every muscle in her body twitching, Honey held Sam's head above the water. Out of desperation, she started to talk to him, imploring him to breathe, to open his eyes, to live. Sam's head lolled inert in her hands.

Out of anger, Honey started to rock Sam's head. She shook him powerfully, tears of frustration coursing down her cheeks and dripping onto the floor. Exhausted, working purely on adrenaline, she held him, she shook him. Her elbows screamed with pain, the glass edge biting ever deeper into her, the blood coursing steadily along her upper arms and off onto the floor. Spots of blood spattered on the yellow tiles like red gears. Her hands started to quiver and she feared she'd drop Sam's head any second.

Then his eyelids fluttered. It was all the encouragement Honey needed. She redoubled her efforts. Her will took over. She exhorted Sam to open his eyes. She saw his nostrils flare. He moaned. She shook harder.

Sam opened his eyes and saw Honey's smile. Then he saw the water with red streaks marbling their way through it. He saw her elbows streaming blood and his heart quickened. He pushed off with his hands and righted himself. He stood waist deep in the water, bracing himself on either side of the cylinder. He took deep breath after deep breath, restoring strength to his body. His head cleared.

"Sam, Sam," Honey said through the open square. Her voice was low, almost a whisper. Her face was in the square, her arms still bled, yet she was smiling ecstatically. Sam leaned down and kissed her. She reached in and touched him gently on the cheek.

"Your arms are a mess," he said.

"They'll be all right. They look worse than they are."

"Let's get something on them to stop the bleeding."

Sam took his suit coat off in the confined space, shucking it into the water. He pulled off his pleated formal shirt and tore it into strips. Reaching through the square, he positioned Honey's elbows so that he could tie the strips around them. He bound the strips into tight knots and stopped the flow of blood. Honey leaned down into the square and Sam kissed her again.

There was no question that she had saved his life.

There was no question that together they had won.

But Sam was still in the cylinder.

"Honey, take off your ring and give it to me."

Honey worked the ring off her finger and handed it to Sam, who tweezered it tightly between his index finger and thumb and started to incise the glass on either side of the open square. He cut steadily. He cut the sides. He cut the top. He enlarged the opening in outline to about twice its original size. Then he went over and over the lines, using the ring like a carpenter would use a router, digging a runnel into the crystal. He cut three more panels in the glass, then pressed and lifted them out. As each panel came free, Sam handed it to Honey.

Then he gave her the ring back. While Honey replaced the ring on her finger, Sam stepped through the opening in the crystal like a catman about to rob the palace.

There were questions to ask, answers to weigh, information to analyze. Honey would know the layout of the compound cold. She would know where the sentries were. She could tell Sam what he wanted to know, what he hadn't been able to learn on the tour today. They needed a quick huddle, a hasty plan, and perfect execution.

"Honey, listen carefully," Sam started.

CHAPTER TWENTY-THREE:
NO GREATER LOVE

Sam Borne had one objective. It was the same objective he always had when the Committee sent him out: he had to assassinate someone whose intentions were inimical to the interests of the free world. In this case, that someone was Doctor Sun Sun. And now Sam had Sun Sun right where he wanted him. The Doctor was passed out drunk in his bed after what he thought was the brutal elimination of the emissary from the West, Mr. Sam Borne.

Once Sam was out of the death tank, things had fallen into place quickly. He had learned in hasty consultation with Honey that the Doctor had passed out drunk from his revelry and that most of the compound was at half-mast, with many of Sun Sun's key players also passed out drunk. The threat of the West's nefarious capitalist plan had seemingly been foiled with the elimination of Sam Borne, which they all assumed had gone forth apace. No one had figured on Honey Pot's defection; no one had figured that she had had enough. As Sam had hastily learned, Sun Sun had kept her in thrall for years by heavily addicting all four of her younger brothers and sisters with heroin. At a word from Sun Sun, all four could have their heroin doctored; then they could be listed as just four more junkies who bit the dust from an overdose. By such blackmail had Sun Sun held Honey in check for years. But in the night she had quit caring. She had seen her two brothers and two sisters recently without Sun Sun knowing about it. They had had a stealthy family reunion in Cholon, and afterward Honey had wept uncontrollably for hours. Her siblings were living corpses, among the walking dead, totally beyond redemption. There was no way they could ever recover from their addiction and lead normal lives. In one way or another, Sun Sun had maimed all the children in Honey's family, especially her. Upon first learning her last name was Pot, he'd even cruelly branded her Honey though her real first name was Le, which in Vietnamese meant "tears."

And Honey had sworn her revenge. She had watched as Sun Sun and his sick legions conspired to murder Sam Borne, the one man in her life with whom she had managed to share a meaningful moment. It had been altogether too much for her. She had known in an instant that this was her main chance, that now was the one opportunity fate would afford her to even the score with Doctor Sun Sun and his followers. And she had taken it.

Honey had helped Sam to sneak up behind the sentries posted at the entrance to the pool building and to eliminate them. Sam had killed one instantaneously while Honey had flirted with the other. Then Sam had killed the one Honey was flirting with just as quickly. Honey and Sam had found themselves with two AK-47 assault rifles, a good flashlight and an open field of sorts.

Together they had descended into the ancient system of tunnels that ran beneath the compound. Sam had followed Honey, and she had led him deftly to the headquarters building. They had emerged in the building from the tunnel entrance, and from there it had been a snap to climb the one flight of stairs to Sun Sun's private suite, a set of rooms in which Honey had passed many a miserable night.

Now, from where Sam and Honey stood, they could see Sun Sun sprawled in his bedclothes like a beached whale. He lay in his pale blue undershorts, snoring loudly, his mouth hanging open and sucking air like a grampus. A nightlight cast a pale glow around the room. It was just like Sun Sun to need a nightlight to sleep, even when he was loaded, Sam thought. When you had seen as much of Sun Sun as Sam had, nothing could surprise you.

Sam stepped ahead of Honey and entered the bedroom. He crossed quickly to Sun Sun and pressed the cold steel barrel of his AK-47 against his forehead. Not an eyelash batted. The Doctor was well anesthetized. Sam looked back and saw Honey standing just within the doorway with her rifle at the ready across her chest. He smiled at her and motioned for her to keep her weapon trained on the door.

Sam put his rifle beside the bed, went into the bathroom and came back with a hand towel. He walked across to Sun Sun, lifted his lolling head and slipped the towel under it. Then he folded the towel into a rope and jammed it firmly into Sun Sun's mouth. The big man stirred, kicking out with his legs like an angry child. In seconds he would come awake, so Sam rapidly crossed the towel behind his head and knotted it securely. Sun Sun stirred some more, kicking and groaning. Sam reached out and took his rifle in hand once again, then stepped up onto the bed and straddled the gagged Sun Sun.

On the bed Sun Sun twitched. The oxygen supply he'd been getting through his mouth was cut off. He rolled from side to side, making a muffled groaning sound through the towel. Sam reached down and pressed the cold steel of the assault rifle against his forehead. His eyelids fluttered. Sam kicked him hard. Sun Sun jerked to the side. Sam kicked him forcefully again. Sun Sun opened his eyes, then blinked rapidly, trying to clear his vision. He was in a drunken stupor. Sam pressed the steel barrel against his forehead, and Sun Sun stared upward, uncomprehending.

Quickly his eyes shot open as far as they could. He yelled silently, the faintest sound rising from the fluffy cloth jammed into his mouth. He squirmed violently from side to side. Each time he attempted to squirm, Sam increased the pressure of the gun barrel on his forehead. In panic, Sun Sun tried to raise himself. Sam pressed his head back against the mattress with the gun barrel.

"Don't make a move, Doctor," Sam hissed. "Your play is over. All you can do now is follow instructions. If you don't, I'll blow your fucking head into a million pieces. My only job here was to kill you, and from here on out that's my option, to be exercised any time I see fit." Sam paused and smiled a big smile. "If you're going to be a good boy, blink twice slowly for yes and I'll know that it's all right to let you up and that you'll do as you're told. Now blink or die, your move."

Sun Sun blinked twice, very slowly, deliberately.

"That's very good, Doctor," Sam continued. "I'm glad to see you're still in control of at least some of your faculties. Now know this: you will be let up from this bed. If you so much as stumble, I'll kill you. You will get up and you will follow Miss Honey Pot. You will keep your hands clasped firmly behind your head. If they slip, I'll kill you. I will be right behind you all the way, which you'll be aware of every second since I'll have the barrel of this rifle in your spine. Are we clear on everything? Blink twice."

Sun Sun blinked twice.

"Okay," Sam said, "get off the bed."

Sam stepped back and Sun Sun rose on one elbow. Sam now stepped down from the bed with his rifle trained on the Doctor, who rose to a sitting position.

"Easy does it, Doctor," Sam cautioned. Sun Sun shimmied to the side of the bed and let his legs hang over the edge. Then, steadying himself with both arms, he pushed himself upright on the floor. He had the thick movements of a drunk. Sam gestured with the rifle and

Sun Sun walked toward Honey and followed as she moved through the doorway, Sam right behind him, rifle in his spine.

Honey led the way down the stairs and out the tunnel entrance. All three were soon crouching along the tunnels, Honey again deftly leading the way. They followed the twists and turns, and if Sun Sun figured out where they were going, he gave no indication. When they arrived at a crude bamboo ladder, Sun Sun must have realized where he was. He turned and looked at Sam, panic glinting from every cell in his eyes.

Honey started up the ladder. After she reached the top and opened the trapdoor, she hoisted herself up and out on the ground above. Sam prodded Sun Sun with the rifle barrel. Sun Sun hesitated, then he gripped one stanchion of the ladder as though he were going to make a stand.

"I think the wise thing would be to climb the ladder," Sam said firmly. Honey shone the flashlight down into the tunnel from above and Sun Sun stood under its cone of light like the truly condemned. His face was working with nerves, twitching and jumping. He blinked rapidly and Sam misunderstood it. "So you want to be a good boy now, Doctor. You probably want to heal people, maybe even want to go off into the jungle and care for the needy like Schweitzer, is that it?"

Sam studied Sun Sun's face in the half-light. He now realized that the blinking had been a feeble attempt by the Doctor to keep from shedding tears, which now coursed down his face in streams.

"I'm touched," Sam said, "and if you so much as attempt to wipe a tear from your fat cheek I'll blow your face into Cambodia. Now climb the ladder and don't miss a step." Tears pooled on the edge of Sun Sun's chin before falling off. Sam shoved the rifle barrel against him, and he turned back around and took a first step on the ladder. Sam waited while he climbed, prodding him from time to time by jabbing the rifle into his buttocks and then, as he got higher, into his legs. Sam could see that at the top Honey had her weapon trained on the Doctor. Still, Sam knew that if Sun Sun was going to make a move, it was now he'd make it. Sam took a step on the ladder while keeping his finger firmly on the trigger with the rifle poised to send a burst or two ripping into Sun Sun from stern to stem.

The Doctor got to the level where the trapdoor gave onto the ground above, and hesitated again. Sam reached up and jabbed him hard with the AK-47, and Sun Sun pressed both hands against the earth above and hoisted himself through. Sam watched as Sun Sun cleared the opening above and moved off to the side. Sam had given Honey explicit instructions what to do now. Still, he vaulted up the ladder and through the trapdoor and had control of the situation in moments.

Sam stood on the ground above. Honey had Sun Sun on his knees beside the trapdoor, just as Sam had instructed her to do, with his hands firmly clasped behind his head. Honey held the big flashlight down toward the ground so its illumination was not visible from beyond the hut. In the darkness Sam could just barely discern the cheeping of the rats.

Nodding at Honey to keep her rifle trained on Sun Sun, Sam walked over behind the Doctor and grabbed him by the throat. After adjusting his hand until he had just the right grip on Sun Sun's throat, he said softly, "With a quick and sudden pressure from my thumb, I can send you on your way, so do as you're told. Slowly, on your knees, start to walk over to the trapdoor covering your little pets. Remember, one slip and you're dead. Can you blink twice?"

Sun Sun blinked twice. Sam held him in his death grip as Sun Sun started to work his way across the hut on his knees, Sam moving nimbly beside him, one hand clutching the Doctor's throat, the other the assault rifle. Honey backstepped slowly in front of them, her rifle pointing at

the kneeling Sun Sun. When they reached the trapdoor
covering the oubliette, Honey stood to the side. The rats
cheeped below. Sam noticed that the hands Sun Sun held
behind his head started to fidget.

"Now would be a bad time to start to do what you want
to do, Doctor," Sam said. He turned to Honey. "Honey,
if the Doctor moves, you get your wish. You let go with a
burst from the AK-47 and damn the consequences. The
Doctor thinks we can't get out of here alive anyway, and
maybe we can't. But we know the Doctor can't get out of
his predicament, right, Doc?"

Sun Sun looked at Sam with the vacant terror of a condemned man. Sweat stood in beads along the top of his
forehead. His cheek twitched. He tried to speak through
the thick terry cloth of the towel. Only a groaning issued
from him, like a muffled death rattle.

"Now you just hold still, Doctor, and this little operation will be over before you know it," Sam said. He
handed his rifle to Honey, then reached into his pocket
and pulled out the straight razor he'd taken from Sun
Sun's bathroom, all the while keeping his death grip on
Sun Sun's throat. Sam flicked the blade from the holder.
"This," he said, "will be like having a little war paint
on, Doc. You know what the Indians looked like in the
old westerns, right? Just a little war paint."

Sam reached out and cut cleanly into Sun Sun's left
cheek above the roped terry cloth of the towel. He cut
deeply. Sun Sun's face spasmed. Blood lines blossomed
on the cuts and started to run down into the towel. Sam
slashed three times across Sun Sun's right cheek with the
same result. Pain caused the Doctor to shuffle his knees,
which movement Sam stilled with a thunderously hard
kick.

By violently shaking his head, Sun Sun tried to break
Sam's grip on his throat. Sam moved his thumb up and
in, and the Doctor stopped. "We're almost through
now," Sam whispered into the quiet of the hut, above the

cheeping of the rats. "We're almost there, good Doctor Sun Sun, we're almost there." Sam threw a leg around the Doctor's bent legs and straddled him from behind. Applying pressure with his hand on Sun Sun's throat, he forced his head up and back. Sun Sun now stared toward the roof of the hut. Sam jammed his knees hard on either side of Sun Sun, pinning his arms against his sides. Beneath him, the Doctor squirmed, sensing in an instant what Sam intended to do. Sam clamped his legs harder, exerted more pressure on his throat, then reached around and incised the razor down Sun Sun's sternum from Adam's apple to belly button. Blood streamed out instantly and the Doctor fought to free himself with the energy of the doomed. Sam restrained him.

Then Sam discarded the razor. It landed with a soft thud on the dirt floor in the dark. Sam swiveled his head and indicated with a nod for Honey to come forward. Honey walked to the edge of the oubliette; she held her rifle at her side, and shone the flashlight on the dirt floor from her other hand.

"Honey," Sam said, "shine the light on the Doctor's pets."

Honey pointed the big flashlight down into the pit. The rats cheeped louder. In the strong light they leaped and tumbled against each other and against the dirt walls of the pit. Their tiny, sharp teeth glistened in their red mouths as they cheeped. Sam reached behind Sun Sun's nape with the free hand that had held the razor, and jammed the Doctor's face down into the pit. Blood soaked the towel, rolled over it and dripped off the Doctor's chin on either side of his mouth. Sam handled the Doctor with care; he didn't want to kill him easily and without pain.

Sam looked around. Then he said, "Honey, step back a few paces." Honey took a few steps back along the edge of the oubliette. Sam watched. "A little farther," he said. Honey backed up a few more steps. Sam looked

from Honey to the Doctor and back. He was satisfied.
Honey still shone the beam of light from the flashlight
down into the pit, where the rats rioted in its glare.

Carefully, Sam set himself. He took one leg from its
position against Sun Sun's side and stamped his foot hard
on the back of Sun Sun's one ankle. All in one motion
Sam thrust the Doctor forward, then reached back and
snared him about the legs like a kid about to play wheel-
barrow. Sun Sun tipped over the edge of the pit and hung
there suspended, bleeding profusely onto the rats. Sun
Sun bucked himself upward like a man preparing to hit
the water in a swan dive. Suspended over the edge, he
tried with Herculean effort to twist his upper body
around and implore Sam to stop. His face and chest were
a bloody mess. The blood dripping from Sun Sun onto the
rats was driving them crazy.

Sam looked at Honey. Her face was a blank. For a moment Sam wondered what kind of animal Sun Sun had
been to make a woman so loving so hateful. Honey felt
Sam's eyes on her and looked up at him. "This is too
good for him," she said flatly as Sun Sun flailed away
over the edge of the pit. "May I step nearer?" Honey
asked.

"Sure. Only don't get where he can grab you." For
good measure Sam took a short step forward, driving the
Doctor farther over the edge.

Honey looked out at Sun Sun. "You . . ." she started
to say and broke off with a sob. Tears of anger welled up
in her eyes and streaked down her cheeks. She took a
deep breath and spat vehemently at him. "Feed your
fucking pets, swine," she choked out.

Sam took two steps forward. Sun Sun's torso disappeared over the edge of the pit. Looking down over the
edge, Sam saw the rats leaping acrobatically at Sun Sun,
who hung only inches beyond the reach of their gnashing
teeth. Sam inched him farther down. And farther. Then

he heard the first smacks as the rats started to get their teeth into flesh. Then came the tearing sounds.

Honey walked closer, since the Doctor's arms were now deep within the pit, clearly out of reach of her. She looked down and whispered, "You fucking pig." Sam took another small step forward and stood above the edge of the pit with Sun Sun's ankles in either hand. Sam saw a mad scrimmage below as the glistening black rats scrambled over the Doctor's torso and arms. His head had been denuded of flesh, and skull showed through, mashed with hair and blood. The torso had been ripped open by the razor-sharp teeth of the rodents and the inner organs were rapidly devoured. Blood ran like rain. The towel that had bound Sun Sun's mouth lay in red tatters on the dirt floor, visible only in snatches as the rats scampered over it.

Suddenly two or three rats got a good purchase and started to scramble up and over Sun Sun's buttocks. Sam, aware it would take only seconds for more rats to follow, heaved the ankles out over the pit and flung them down. The lower body, legs flailing, tumbled and the rats went berserk. They swarmed and scrambled, scrambled and swarmed in black wave after black wave.

Sam and Honey stood and watched. Sam did not want to make the first move to leave. He felt that watching was serving some therapeutic purpose for Honey, that it was helping to free her from the Doctor's evil grip; only this way would she really put him behind her. Sam swung an arm out and put it around her. She leaned her head against his shoulder and he felt her sobbing. He could see that she was slowly and tightly turning in her hands the shaft of the large flashlight, her knuckles white even in the dim light.

"I feel like I am waking from a nightmare," she whispered against his shoulder. "I feel like I have been set free. A moment's freedom is worth an eternity's bondage." Sam agreed. It made for a nice moment. But he could not savor it. The wheels were turning in his mind.

The target had been hit. The Doctor was through, but his plan was intact.

So the job was not done.

Sam nudged Honey.

CHAPTER TWENTY-FOUR:
BREAKOUT

In the darkness Honey crouched behind Sam. Each clutched a Kalashnikov. When the sentries patrolling the parade ground were positioned just right, Sam would shoot out ahead of her and she would quickly follow. They were scooting from the back of one building to the back of another, working their way along the perimeter of the compound. They had now successfully scrambled from one building to another over five times. They were one building away from being behind the prisoners' barracks.

After killing Sun Sun, Sam Borne had three objectives: to set the prisoners free, giving each a fighting chance to restore himself to freedom and recover his health; to escape the Sun Sun compound in the Cobra gunship, taking Honey with him; and in the Cobra to swoop back down on the compound, kill its garrison and demolish forever its death crop of opium and its heroin-processing facilities.

Like the perfectionist he was, Sam knew he must destroy not only Sun Sun but Sun Sun's apparatus. Like the strategist he was, Sam knew that freeing the prisoners involved risks and jeopardized his escape to some real extent. It would be easier to steal away to the heliport, commandeer the Cobra and wreck the compound, prison-

ers and all perishing in the holocaust. But he couldn't do
it. Sam couldn't abandon American fighting men. He
must help them. He must give them another chance at the
heady air of freedom. So he had told Honey his plan. She
had immediately agreed to help. And they had started to
scramble from the back of one building to the back of another, making their way to the prisoners' barracks.

Now they crouched together in the darkness, one
building short of their goal. All was quiet. The parade
ground out beyond the buildings was empty. Nothing
stirred. They listened intently and could not even hear the
footsteps of the men on guard duty. Sam reached back,
tapped Honey on the knee and shot out into the space between the buildings. In a crouch he ran, bent over like a
primate. Honey followed on his heels. Gasping for breath
they arrived on the other side, behind the barracks.
Above them, set into the end wall, three windows with
bars stood in a line about the height of Sam's shoulders.
The windows were dark. Sam turned to Honey and gave
her the thumbs-up sign with his right hand. She smiled at
him, touched her fingertips to her lips, planted a kiss
there, then carried it to Sam's lips and pressed it home.
Then she turned and disappeared around the side of the
building, walking upright. Sam leaned around the corner
and watched her disappear around the far corner. Then he
heard the front door open and close and the sound of
softly spoken Vietnamese punctuated with laughter.

He moved. Hugging the side of the building, Sam
scurried in a crouch to the front. There he held. He
waited. From inside he heard the sounds of Vietnamese
chatter and an occasional laugh. He stayed back in the
shadows far enough so that he wasn't visible from the parade ground in front, though he was clearly exposed from
his flank. If anyone patrolling the grounds came upon
him from the direction of the next building, they would
see him. What the hell, he thought, life was chance. Energy flooded over him, as well as nervousness, but the

nerves he controlled. He told himself to wait. He told himself Honey would deliver. He waited.

Sam heard the first creak of the door before the hand pushing it had been on it two whole seconds. His body tensed. Voices whispered. A man's voice broke into a giggle. Feet shuffled, then stopped. Then a snap hit the air as a match was struck. Sam inched forward out of the shadows. He was fully exposed against the building, a poised silhouette, waiting to strike.

The man and the woman giggled. Honey's voice was clear. Sam moved to the corner of the building and paused. The feet around the corner shuffled. Then he heard it. He heard it in the lilting sexy voice of Honey Pot. The phrase he heard was *C'est la vie*.

Sam struck. On the prearranged signal, he knew that the sentry was positioned just right. Sam came around the corner and clamped his hand over the sentry's mouth. Bringing his other forearm rapidly into position behind the man's head, Sam snapped his neck instantly, the sound like teeth crunching into a stalk of celery. The man went limp in Sam's arms. Dropping his forward arm, Sam wrapped the man firmly around the chest, then dragged him around the corner of the building. Sam pulled him into the shadows and dropped him softly onto the ground. He went back to the corner of the building and gave Honey the thumbs-up sign again. She nodded and went to the door, opened it and stepped inside. Sam was right behind her.

Inside the door, the other sentry sat at a small table. He looked up and grinned hugely at Honey, then scrambled too late for his automatic rifle leaning casually against the wall behind him. Sam flung his right hand in a swift wide arc across the plane of his body and, with a side-hand chop to the nape, dropped the sentry like a man poleaxed. He collapsed in a lifeless pile at Sam's feet, knocking his rifle to the floor with a clatter as he fell. Neither the sound of his falling nor the clatter of the rifle woke the sleeping prisoners, zonked on heroin and exhausted from slave labor as always.

Sam stood over the dead sentry and looked at Honey. Then he looked down the length of the darkened barracks. In crude wooden bunks built in tiers along the side walls and down the center in two adjoining rows, the prisoners slept. Now would come their last chance.

"Get the rifles," Sam said softly to Honey. She disappeared out the door to return in an instant with the two AK-47s they had left at the back of the building and the one the other sentry had leaned against the front wall. With the rifle Sam retrieved from the floor, that made four. Four rifles for some twenty prisoners, himself and Honey, Sam thought. They'd make some army. Not even a good guerrilla band would be this underequipped. But as they said, it was the size of the fight in the dog that counted, not the size of the dog in the fight.

"Stay here and watch the door," Sam instructed Honey. Smiling the world's shortest smile, he set off into the lurking darkness of the long room. He would now attempt to wake twenty men without incident, instruct them and organize them in the dark, and mount a campaign in the dark against a vastly better equipped and healthier enemy.

But, Sam consoled himself, not a superior enemy.

CHAPTER TWENTY-FIVE:
FREE-FLY

Sam Borne had made a mistake. Half the awakened prisoners were barely in good enough shape to get out of their bunks, let alone fight their way to freedom. Sam stood in the darkness at the back of the barracks and wondered what would be the best move now that he'd stubbornly made the noble one. On a battlefield, Sam would have been bad at triage; he would always have tried to save everyone, as he'd done now. But looking into the darkness and seeing the hulking sculpture of men rigid with exhaustion and burned out on drugs, he knew that he had to be realistic. He would offer everyone a chance, but he would also minimize the risk to himself and to Honey.

None of the figures leaning wearily against the bunks or sitting rigidly on them, their legs dangling over the edge, made a sound. Sam walked over to where Honey guarded the door and told her again to watch sharply while he briefed the men on how they would proceed. Sam did not want a confrontation with the forces manning the compound. His plan was to get the prisoners over to the heliport with the maximum of stealth and the minimum of trouble. He would deal with the guard around the helicopters before the prisoners arrived there by leaving first with Honey, entering the tunnel system, coming up at the heliport and jumping the guards, then loading the men systematically onto the two Bell UH-1Ds. That was the plan. Something told Sam it would take a large miracle for it to work. And two of the men in front of him in the darkness would have to have enough left to pilot the choppers out of there.

"I'd like everybody to form a tight formation in the front of the room here around me," Sam said, projecting his voice as best as he could without causing a detectable disturbance. "I realize the men in the back can't hear me," he continued, "so please pass the word back and start forward." The men toward the front pushed off from the lower bunks or got down from the upper bunks as word sizzled back to those in the rear. Darker against the darkness, the figures of the men moved forward. They huddled around Sam, their eyes vacant, their cheeks sunken, their bodies withered. Sam waited for them all to gather around him. While he waited he listened, hoping all the while that no one would come across the compound to check on the barracks. The men assured him that usually the two guards would watch them through the entire night without further checking or vigilance.

"Okay," Sam started, "here's the plan. Can everyone hear me?"

Heads nodded yes, and there were scattered murmurs of assent.

"Okay," Sam started in again, "we're going to peel off from here in pairs of fours. Each group will leave this building at ten-second intervals. Proceed then to the back of the building and sneak from one building to another until you reach the rat hut. Descend into the tunnel system there and come up across the compound all the way out at the heliport. Do this professionally, like the trained and dedicated fighting men you are. In the tunnels there will be no talking, no noise. Each group will follow the group ahead. We will form a relay, with a man stationed at each junction to guide the next group. The last man in each group will hiss the password "free-fly" at ten-second intervals. Listen for this word and key in on it. Follow it. I will lead the way with my friend Honey Pot. You all know her. Right now she's guarding us up front here. At the heliport, two fliers must pilot the Hueys. I'll fly the Cobra. We will do everything in an orderly fashion, with never an ounce of panic.''

Sam paused. He let what he'd said sink in. There was no time for a Q&A session. This plan had to be gotten on the first take; there would be no refresher courses offered.

''Are we ready?'' Sam hissed. Again the men nodded and murmured their assent. ''Okay, men, form yourselves into groups of four. I will leave two automatic rifles here. Two men man them and keep a watch out front. Leave last and function as a rear guard. You men know who among you is best qualified for this function. Pick the best marksmen.''

Again Sam paused. The men evidenced muted activity among themselves. It was encouraging. They could handle the natural selection of the marksmen. When this brief process had spent itself, Sam spoke up again. ''Two men at the front here fall in with me and Honey and let's go. Good luck to all of you.''

Sam went to Honey, leaned over her shoulder and scanned the empty compound beyond. Clutching an assault rifle firmly, he tapped Honey, saw the two prisoners behind him poised to go, nodded to them, pulled back the door and stepped out into the night. Honey and the two prisoners followed. They scurried along the side of the building, reached the back and ran, crouching, to the next building. Sam wanted to turn and make sure everything was proceeding smoothly, but he realized this wasn't possible. He had to lead and hope those behind would follow. By glancing back over his shoulder, he could tell that the prisoners were stiff and clumsy. And slow. That meant all the rest would probably also be clumsy and slow. This raised the ante. The possibility for detection was higher.

Sam couldn't worry. He couldn't do more. His job was to get them back to the rat hut and into the tunnel. He was a smuggler, smuggling life from slavery to freedom.

It was the hardest commodity to smuggle.

CHAPTER TWENTY-SIX:
SHARKS OUT OF WATER

Everything was going smoothly. In the dark tunnel the cone of light from Honey's flashlight illuminated enough space for her, Sam and the two prisoners to wend their way swiftly through the labyrinth laid so long ago by the VC. They swept past the hard dirt of the caked walls and through the little rooms with the candle niches, the old rice bowls in corners and the discarded chopsticks. Sam was elated. He felt that with luck all would go well. Back through the darkness at each turning the last prisoner would hiss the single word "free-fly." They would never wait for an answer. The plan would either work or it wouldn't. There was no play in it, no tolerance. The single word "free-fly" would be cast into the darkness; the responsibility of those behind was to pick it up and follow it. Sam could hear scuffling and an occasional murmur behind them so he knew the next group was in motion. They were more than halfway to the heliport and everything was going smoothly.

Then, suddenly, all hell broke loose.

Behind them came shouting. At first it was indistinct, then gradually it became clear. The group behind Sam's was shouting that a firefight had broken out, that the movement was detected, that the compound was coming alive. Either someone had come upon one of the groups moving in the darkness or someone had discovered, by whatever quirk of fate, that Doctor Sun Sun was missing.

It didn't matter. Sam went into overdrive, his mind spinning. There were only certain options open to him now. As always, the top priority was to gather as much intelligence as possible. He stopped dead, the two prisoners crouching in behind him.

"Honey," Sam called forward, "stop." About ten feet in front of Sam, Honey Pot came to a stop. She turned, the light of the flashlight washing over Sam, blinding him. "Come back," Sam said. Honey scrambled along until she rested on her haunches in front of Sam. "Shine the light behind us," Sam instructed. Honey shone the cone of light back the way they'd come. Out of the darkness came the crouched figures of the prisoners in the next group, all attempting to impart information at once; it created a bedlam.

"Quiet," Sam ordered. The prisoners fell quiet instantly. Now it was possible to hear the excited voices of others farther away. Sam listened. The voices were speaking English. That meant at least one other group had made it into the tunnel. For a minute Sam thought to wait and see how many prisoners had made it into the tunnel, then he flashed onto the consequences of that action if the enemy had penetrated the line and entered the tunnel. It could be a disaster. Above the din of voices, Sam heard the distant chatter of automatic gunfire.

There was only one thing to do.

"Let's go," Sam snapped, pushing on Honey's shoulder. She turned and set off quickly, Sam falling in right behind her. Behind him he heard the prisoners get up and start following. "How far to the choppers?" Sam asked Honey. In his eagerness, he had almost overtaken her. He was psyched now. He was going to salvage what was salvagable and damn the rest. It had been a pipe dream, he knew, to have figured on leading twenty men, ravaged from drugs and forced labor, out of a compound against a far better equipped and much larger force.

"We are almost there," Honey shot back over her shoulder. Sam must avail himself of what was available to him. With the firefight raging behind them in the compound, the sentries at the heliport would be up and alert, but they would not, Sam gambled, be expecting a force to emerge behind them. Sam planned to spring on them from the tunnel hatch leading up to one of the small sheds used for storing fuel and spare parts for the choppers. It was their one chance.

Honey moved as fast as she could, but Sam still kept climbing up her back. They passed through another small underground room and off into a spoke of the tunnel system. They were moving down this spoke when Sam came as alert as a man in full cardiac seizure. He thought he'd heard voices, voices not speaking English. He pinned Honey's shoulder and stopped her like death. The men behind him came up quickly.

"Quiet," Sam hissed. He listened. And heard nothing. He waited. He would give it a ten count, then roll. At the stroke of five, he heard it clearly, distinctly. Honey heard it. She turned to speak to Sam, but he instantly clamped a hand over her mouth. Her eyebrows rose. Sam slammed his index finger over his lips and she nodded. He removed his hand. Honey leaned over and whispered into Sam's ear.

It was the midgets.

Honey told Sam all he needed to know. The midgets were in the tunnel system. They were trained to rule it like tiny commandos. And they would.

The voices drew nearer.

There could be no question that the midgets were lethal. Not only were they armed, Sam well knew, but in the tunnels they were virtually invincible in hand-to-hand combat. They were another of Sun Sun's devious resources. Seemingly innocuous, amusing, the mere playthings of a madman, they were in fact a deadly weapons system.

Sam reached behind Honey, took the flashlight from her and put it head down against the dirt floor of the tunnel. He needed time. He needed to think. He needed to compensate. If he only thought, his ninja cunning would pull him through. Honey stared wide-eyed, panicked. She knew something Sam didn't. She was paralyzed with fear. Sam did not want to rely on her any longer, but he needed to get information from her, and fast.

Sam grasped Honey behind the neck and pulled her head forward against his chest. He leaned down and whispered to her. She strained upward with her mouth against Sam's ear and whispered what he needed to know. Sam squeezed her hand for reassurance, then whispered to the man behind him to maintain complete silence. The man turned to pass it on. Sam squeezed Honey's hand again and patted her shoulder. As Sam had instructed her to, she started off without the flashlight, in complete darkness. She moved with utmost quiet. Sam slunk along behind her, all of the prisoners now behind him. They moved along quietly in the darkness. Their one chance depended on not making noise and reaching the nearest room before the midgets did. Sam was operating on the principle that a shark out of water was not the same thing as a shark in the water. The midgets, if Sam could trap them in the open space of the room, would not be the lethal opponents they would be in the tunnels, though they'd still be tough.

As they moved along, Sam held the flashlight only inches off the ground, casting a tiny nimbus just ahead of Honey. It would be enough light for her to see when they approached a room. Ahead of them the voices continued, drawing closer. The midgets chattered in excited bursts, intent on their mission, confident they would meet and vanquish the enemy as they had always met and vanquished the enemy.

After about forty yards, Honey dropped to the floor and braced herself on her hands. Sam and the line of prisoners halted behind her. She leaned forward, peering intently into the almost total darkness. Then she turned to Sam, leaned back and whispered in his ear.

They were there, on the rim of the room, the excited voices of the midgets carrying to them intermittently. Sam shifted the flashlight to his left hand, still holding its beam close to the ground. With his right hand, he gripped his AK-47 firmly and checked that it was set on full automatic, ready to rip. Then he pressed the barrel against Honey's arm. Increasing the pressure on her till she scrunched against the wall as hard as she could, Sam squeezed past her, his back scraping the opposite wall.

The voices came closer, grew louder. The midgets were near.

Sam Borne was on the point, waiting.

CHAPTER TWENTY-SEVEN:
MELEE

A thin beam of light danced into the room and played across the opposite wall. The midgets were coming into the room from the direction of the headquarters building. They would enter to the left of where Sam Borne crouched waiting for them, assault rifle ready. The voices of the midgets could clearly be heard, then suddenly several beams of light played about the room like floodlights at a Hollywood opening, crisscrossing and combining at random and illuminating the room completely.

San had to estimate quickly how many midgets there were. From the different voices, he knew there were several. It was all a matter of timing. He had to wait till several were completely in the room, then jump them at the crucial moment that would spell victory. The sounds of their voices, the sounds of their feet scraping grew nearer.

Then the lead midget entered the room. He came across Sam's field of vision and started to move off in the direction of the heliport. Two other midgets entered on his heels. There were others behind them, it was clear, from the play of lights and the sounds of movement. Their lights, Sam saw in a flash, were fixed to miners' helmets. In their arms they carried Kalashnikovs that were too large for them, and from their hips, also too large for them, hung revolvers.

It was now or never.

Sam sprang to the mouth of the tunnel, stood up and sprayed a clip of AK-47 shells at the lead midgets. He chopped them like meat, the big shells tearing into them, sending chunks of their bodies flying, bone and flesh, muscle and gristle all filling the air in a shower of blood. They fell like dolls. Sam was aware that to his left, in the direction of the tunnel from which the midgets had emerged, a steady stream of them filtered into the room. Before he could reel on the midgets emerging from the tunnel, one of them flew across the room and took Sam down at the ankles with a perfect tackle. Sam's rifle went flying.

As Sam attempted to right himself immediately, another midget dived over the top of the midget who'd tackled him and slammed into Sam headfirst, grasping him about the nape and pulling his head forward to spear it with his own. The butt left Sam reeling. Fully supine, nearly unconscious, he was about to sample eternity.

Suddenly the room reverberated with gunfire. Muzzles flashed, shells ricocheted, dirt fountained from the walls and the floor. In the dimness of his blasted consciousness, Sam saw a midget, his hand raised to chop into Sam's throat, shot in the head from behind, the whole front of the midget's cranium lifting off like a toupee and sailing out in front of him even as he toppled for the final time.

Something still gripped Sam firmly about his lower body. In the adrenaline rush the body sends forth right before you die, Sam knew that he had to fight back, that he had to act or perish. He thrust his upper body to a sitting position and saw that the weight on his lower body was the torso of the dead midget who'd tackled him, his arms locked now about Sam's lower legs in a death grip.

All about Sam the room spun. The ripping sound of

gunfire was deafening as light rent the darkness sporadi-
cally, tearing brief holes in it that instantly drew more
gunfire. Sam realized immediately that what they had
was a standoff. The midgets were pinned in one tunnel
leading to the room and Honey and the prisoners were
pinned in another. Apparently, the midgets had thought
Sam was alone and attacked him, and in the light from
their helmets Honey or one of the prisoners had been able
to pick off the two who'd slammed into Sam. The rest of
the midget corps had held their position in the tunnel.

A light played on the wall above Sam, and he shifted
on the ground. Gunfire chased the light. The midgets had
tried to locate Sam with the light and plug him from the
entrance to the tunnel where they crouched. Sam was out
in the open, alone, exposed, the darkness his only cover.

To wait was to lose.

The gunfire would lead the cadre of sentries to the
room. The midgets knew this. They only had to tie down
Sam and his band for minutes and the cadre entering the
tunnel from behind would trap them in a classic pincer
movement. In his mind's eye Sam knew that he lay halfway between the tunnel opening leading toward the chopper port and the one in which Honey and the prisoners
crouched. The midgets would be off at an angle of nearly
ninety degrees. Letting his hands play at their farthest
reach, Sam fanned his arms back and forth, feeling in the
darkness for his weapon and those of the slain midgets.
He located two rifles and laid them quietly across his
stomach and chest, balancing them carefully. Without
them, he and his band had no chance.

Hugging the ground, supine, Sam shifted in the direction of the tunnel leading to the heliport, heading away
from Honey and the prisoners. With luck he would be
able to hump along the ground in the darkness to the tunnel opening. He kept his body close enough to the wall so
that at all times he could reach out and touch it, using it to
guide him around the room to the opening. He shifted

soundlessly, hoping, hurrying. It was only a matter of feet.

Finally Sam reached out for the wall and got air. He had made it. He shifted, still scraping along on his ass, and pushed himself toward the opening. He reached it, pushed in and crouched back, out of line of fire from the midgets' direction. He leaned one rifle against the tunnel wall and took the other in his hand.

Now came the kind of decision nightmares are made of.

Into the dark quiet Sam heard his voice bellow, "Make a break for it. Come out firing and get your asses over here. Fill the other tunnel with a stream of covering fire and go. Now." There was no question who had said this, no question of what had to be done. Every second Honey and her band hesitated was against them.

They didn't disappoint Sam.

In the darkness a red flash issued from the muzzle of an AK-47 and then another, this one rolling toward Sam. One of the prisoners had set himself squarely in the mouth of the tunnel where they'd been pinned down and was setting up a hail of fire into the midgets' tunnel. Another prisoner had recovered a fallen rifle and was blasting suppressive fire at the midgets as he sidestepped rapidly across the room toward Sam. Behind and around him the other prisoners scrambled out of the tunnel and tore across the room. Sam ripped several rounds at the midgets, then had to stop for fear he'd kill one of his own band crossing toward him.

Sam roared, "Here, here," over and above the din, hoping in the dark to give the scramblers a homing sound. The first scramblers hit the wall beside the opening with a thud. Sam leaned out and guided the first prisoner into the tunnel. Bodies slammed into each other and the wall. In a mad tangle of limbs and trunks, the prisoners and Honey squeezed into the tunnel opening past Sam. The room resounded with deafening gunfire, lights wheeling, muzzles flashing, dirt flying, shells rebounding.

Out in the room the covering prisoner continued to fire into the midgets' tunnel as he ran across the room. He never made it. He was about halfway across when return fire from the tunnel cut him down, hurling him backward through the air, his rifle flying, still firing on automatic, its red muzzle flame wheeling in the air like a berserk torch. Sam noted roughly where it landed. They needed the weapon; its firepower was crucial, especially if they engaged in further firefights, which Sam knew were almost inevitable. Sam shouted above the din for a prisoner to fire steadily at the midgets while he crawled out into the room on his stomach. Hugging the dirt floor, the suppressive fire ringing above him, Sam bellied out into the room, sweeping his arms in front of him. Return fire from the midgets stitched the dirt wall overhead, showering Sam with soil and spent 7.62mm shells. Finally his fingers contacted the wooden stock of the Kalashnikov, and he grasped it and backtracked quickly, still prone, dragging the rifle behind him.

Back in the tunnel, Sam stationed a prisoner with an AK-47 at the tunnel's mouth as a rear guard, and in the chaos of roaring automatic fire organized the survivors so that they took off after Honey, who, heeding shouted instructions from Sam, still holding the flashlight cautiously close to the ground, had scurried off in the direction of the heliport. Sam scurried right behind them. He had one of the four assault rifles they still had. One of the others was blazing behind him, holding the midgets at bay. Two forward prisoners had the other two. If the midgets entered the tunnel behind Sam's fleeing band, shooting them would be like shooting carp in a barrel for the prisoner forming the rear guard.

Sam Borne and company still had a chance.

CHAPTER TWENTY-EIGHT:
DEATH FLIGHT

Honey reached the hatch and stepped back. Above was the shed for storing fuel and spare parts at the heliport. Behind Sam the prisoners who'd made it this far fell in. From behind came the rattle of automatic fire as the last prisoner held the midgets at bay. There was no time to plan. Either they would be able to get out of the hatch and take the sentries at the heliport by surprise or they wouldn't.

Stepping past Honey, Sam reached up and pushed the hatch cover free of the opening. Looking up, he saw nothing but darkness. Still, it was a lighter darkness than the darkness of the tunnel system. At least they had not opened the hatch to find a gun barrel staring them in the face.

Placing a hand on either side of the opening, Sam jumped straight up, working his arms hard to hoist himself through. Then he was in the shed. It was empty. Reaching back down, he took his AK-47 by its barrel and pulled it up. Then he helped Honey climb through. She was followed quickly by the prisoners. They needed Sam's help to pull themselves through the opening. Sam grabbed each in turn under the arms and hoisted them like flour sacks onto the floor of the shed. When they were through, he reached down to help the last prisoner, the

rear guard. The man let the rifle rip one last time down
the dark tunnel, hoping to buy enough time to get up
through the hatch before the midgets were on him.

Sam took the AK-47 from the last man, the barrel so
hot he nearly dropped it back through the opening. Lay-
ing the rifle off to the side, he reached down and locked
his hands around the man's forearms like a trapeze artist.
Then he pulled up with all his strength.

What Sam feared happened. A shattering burst of gunfire rattled down in the tunnel and the man went limp in
his grasp. Sam dropped him immediately. There was no
need kidding himself. The man was definitely dead. And
the midgets were on their way down the tunnel. And the
guards at the heliport might now be alerted.

Sam took one of the AK-47s from the ground and
handed it to another of the prisoners. "Blast the piss out
of anyone who tries to get through this opening," he said.
The man would form a rear guard. The midgets would
not be able, Sam figured, to hoist themselves through the
hatch without forming some kind of pyramid of bodies
beneath it. The guard would prevent this, but there was
still the lost element of surprise for the sentries guarding
the heliport.

Sam grabbed his rifle and sprang to the front of the
shed, the others closely on his heels. He opened the
rolled tin door and peered through a crack. He saw two
sentries fanning out on the perimeter of a revetment,
combing the area as they stalked closer to the shed. There
would be others. But again, to wait was to lose. The
midgets were coming up behind, reinforced by the cadre
of sentries who had overrun the other prisoners, all of
whom could now be dead.

The two approaching sentries were twenty feet away.
Sam flung back the rolled tin door, stepped out and cut
them down. They toppled instantly, their torsos flopping
forward as their legs collapsed under them, their arms
flung wide. Their rifles crashed to the ground. "Let's

go," Sam roared into the hut. Honey and the prisoners stormed through the door. "Strip their weapons," Sam shouted. The prisoners sprinted to the fallen sentries and grabbed their rifles. Now Sam and his band had increased their firepower. And their chances.

In the darkness Sam could see the hulking black shapes of the choppers behind the waist-high revetments. He ran toward them, tossing over his shoulder a roared "C'mon." He wanted desperately to take Honey in hand. Though acutely worried about her, he elected instead to stay well ahead on the point, figuring he could thus nullify any threat from the front, relying on the man he'd left in the tunnel opening in the shed to protect his rear.

It would take them only seconds, Sam calculated, to haul themselves over the revetments and liberate the choppers. In the darkness the aircraft looked like hulking prehistoric insects. They stood in a line, each in its own bay surrounded by sandbags. Nearest the compound were the two Hueys. Beyond the Hueys, last in line, stood the Cobra.

Sam scanned the empty terrain in front of him. Then he shot a quick glance back over his shoulder. Honey was running beside him. He turned quickly. The field ahead was still open, empty, his. "Honey, follow me," Sam yelled, veering to the left, making a line for the Cobra. He would jump the Cobra and take Honey with him.

Off to Sam's right, movement occurred. Still running, Sam wheeled around. In a burst of gunfire the prisoner on the wing went down. Three more sentries had rounded the corner of the revetment and had come out blasting. "Dive," Sam screamed, hoping Honey would understand and hit the deck. He flung himself in a half arc, squeezing off rounds as he went down, spraying automatic fire at the sentries. Another of the prisoners fell to Sam's right.

From the ground Sam fired, cutting down two more

sentries like ducks in a carnival gallery. A trail of shells
lanced into the ground about ten yards in front of Sam and
ripped up to him. Dirt geysered into his eyes. Then a
shell tore into his upper left arm, brazing a burning crease
into it like a red hot poker. The arm smarted incredibly.
In the millisecond before he clipped the third sentry, Sam
felt his spine dance with terror. Even as he squeezed off
the rounds that would launch the third sentry into eternity, he felt Honey's mistake flash on his consciousness
like pain. She was upright in the right corner of his pe-
ripheral vision. Then, as the sentry toppled from Sam's
blast, Honey landed on him in a deadfall. The shells from
the third sentry's rifle had stitched their way up her torso
and blown out the side of her head. Sam saw all this instantly.

Like the ultimate professional he was, Sam scanned the
field before him. Again it was empty. He rolled Honey's
body off him and looked at her for the last time. Her face,
what was left of it, was hideous, contorted, grotesque.
Blood flowed from her wounds in torrents. Sam felt like
ice. He vaulted to his feet and saw that about ten of the
prisoners were still with him. Pointing to the Hueys, he
sped off to the left, still heading for the Cobra. As he ran,
Sam shouted that he needed a flier to follow him. One of
the prisoners broke off and scrambled in behind him.

As Sam and the flier reached the revetment around the
Cobra, sporadic automatic fire broke from the end of the
line nearest the compound. Sam could only hope that the
other prisoners were commandeering a Huey and protecting their flank all at the same time. If not, they had
damn-all for a chance.

Sam had his AK-47 in his right hand and planted the
left on the top row of sandbags forming the revetment.
Then he hurtled it in one bound, landing squarely on his
feet, and immediately scanned the revetment for sentries.
There were none, so he turned and grabbed the flier, who
in his weakened condition was belly flopping over the

sandbags. Grabbing him by the seat of his pants, Sam yanked him over and down. The flier landed at Sam's feet on all fours. Before the flier even caught his breath, Sam grabbed him by the scruff of the neck and pulled him to his feet.

"C'mon," Sam commanded, "let's get that Cobra off the ground." Sam tore across the short apron to the chopper, the flier staggering and fumbling as best as he could behind him. Sam reached the chopper, opened one side of its double canopy and looked back for the flier, who stumbled up to him. Hoisting him, Sam half pushed, half shoved the man into the forward gunner's seat. Then he hustled around the chopper's nose, flipped up the aft canopy, vaulted into the pilot's seat and snapped the canopy closed. The flier had had the sense to strap himself in, ready for action. Sam planted his feet on the pedals, hit the ignition and grabbed the two sticks, all before his rifle clattered to the floor. The big Lycoming T53-L13 engine coughed and wheezed, the rotor making halfhearted rotations overhead. Then it died. Automatic gunfire crackled to Sam's left, a few shells pinging off the copter's housing. Sam hit the ignition again. The Lycoming coughed and sputtered, then roared to life, the rotor whirling above them, all eleven hundred horses engaged. Coordinating both antitorque pedals and the two sticks, Sam lifted off. He had some trouble feathering the collective with his left hand, since his upper arm still screamed with pain from the wound where the shell had grazed him; the burning wound was shooting pain up into his shoulder and down into his hand. With will and effort, Sam steadied his hand, forcing his grip tighter on the collective, yet keeping his touch light.

As the Cobra rose, Sam glanced down. A handful of sentries were racing toward them, firing their rifles. Random shells thudded into the fuselage and one even nickered off the canopy. As the sentries drew nearer, the shells chattered off the fuselage like gravel on the under-

pan of a car. Sam took them up quicker, then he modulated the pedals, cutting away, putting the Cobra into a
roll out of range of the charging sentries, heading away
from the compound. He was going to swing out and come
back. When he did, a lot of people were going to catch
hell.

As he turned away, Sam saw with satisfaction that the
other prisoners had got one of the big Hueys airborne. A
host of sentries and midgets had dropped to their knees
under the Huey and were firing up at it. Only a lucky hit
would do any damage. Automatic shells had to strike just
right, in a crucial place, to knock one of these rugged
birds out of the air. The other prisoners were going to
make it.

And Sam Borne was going to come back.

CHAPTER TWENTY-NINE:
RETURN ENGAGEMENT

The Cobra was primed for action, Sam Borne at the controls. Overhead the big engine roared. In tubes on either side lurked four TOW missiles ready to go, eight altogether. In front sat the flier, his fingers itchy on the triggers of a 7.62mm minigun with four thousand rounds and a 40mm grenade launcher. They were armed to the teeth and raring to go.

As the Cobra cleared the ridge, Sam saw the well-lit compound come up below. There was movement on the ground. Sentries and midgets dashed this way and that, carrying weapons, securing their positions, digging in. Around the remaining Huey there was a hive of activity as a handful of sentries jumped aboard. Its rotors spinning, the big Huey was about to lift off. Dealing with it would be his first order of business. Sam quickly scanned the parade ground looking for missile launchers. Then he dipped the Cobra and leveled off, lining up directly with the Huey below.

"Stand ready, soldier," Sam instructed the flier in the gunner's seat. "Open up hard and don't let up till we're well out of there. Throw all the suppressive fire on these bastards you can."

"Roger, sir," the eager flier responded, hunching forward over his controls. It always amused Sam how read-

261

ily military men accorded him the term "sir." Not only was he not an officer, he was not even enlisted. He was strictly free-lance, but he had a facility for command that amounted to genius.

"Let's take out the Huey, spin off and come back and waste the place. How does that sound?" Sam asked.

"Great, sir, just great." The emotion in the flier's voice was nearly choking him. It was as though he were getting a chance at something he'd only dreamed of.

The Cobra was within range for the TOW. "Okay, open up," Sam ordered.

"Will do, sir."

Sam tracked the target through the gyro-stabilized sight. The Huey was right where he wanted it, just lifting up, its wheels glancing off the earth, dust swirling beneath it. To its side, all around the revetment, sentries and midgets took positions and started to fire up at the incoming Cobra. The flier immediately opened up with the minigun and the grenade launcher, spraying machine gun fire down on them and hitting to the side of the revetment with a grenade. Sam held steady, then squeezed off the TOW. He tracked it optically but had to make only a minor adjustment. The TOW tore into the Huey when it was no more than thirty feet off the ground. It careened away from the approaching Cobra, shattering on impact, breaking into a thousand pieces before what was left of the fuselage slammed in a flaming ball off the side of the revetment. Flaming bodies flew from it like bees from a blasted hive. A huge piece of the broken main rotor cartwheeled across the ground, slicing two sentries in half, hurtling through the sandbags and spinning to rest on the apron of the adjoining heliport.

Sam quickly swung the Cobra up and out, the machine gun in the turret firing away as he climbed. He flew out over the perimeter before banking hard against the dark mountainside and heading back in. Below, the main buildings came up fast, the parade ground still alive with activity.

"Open up all the while we're coming in, soldier," Sam snapped to the flier.

"Roger."

Sam sighted again through the gyro-stabilizer as the cluster of buildings moved swiftly into view below. When he had Sun Sun's headquarters lined up in the sight, he held steady. He bore in close, not releasing the missile till he was five hundred or so yards away. This time the missile needed no adjustment. It hissed out of its tube and darted into the cinder-block headquarters building, gouging a tremendous hole in its side. The wall shattered, the roof collapsed and a fire broke out immediately.

As they flew overhead, Sam saw some sentries in the parade ground scrambling around under the direction of a man in evening dress. He recognized Bui, still dressed formally from their black-tie dinner. The sentries were setting something up, positioning themselves. From their movements, Sam had a strong hunch what they were up to. He let the chopper roar off into the western sky, then cut it hard to the left. He would swing down on Bui and company and take them out before they had him in range with their missile launcher.

Dropping a payload on Bui would be sweetness itself. He owed Bui. He swung the Cobra back into the compound sharply. Below him the sentries around Bui flanked a man kneeling on the ground positioning a tube launcher on his shoulder. Sam had no doubt it was an SA-7 Grail man-portable AA missile, the kind that had played such hell with American aircraft during the police action.

Sam feathered the controls and leveled the Cobra off, sweeping in on a line to dissect the middle of the compound. He knew he didn't need a direct hit with the TOW. He needed only to lay it in nicely near the men clustered in the center of the parade ground. He peered down into the gyro-stabilized sight, lining the men up. The sentries around the kneeling man were trying to position him just right, Bui to the side yelling and gesturing madly. The SA-7 had a ten-kilometer range, but Sam wasn't about to give it a chance. He squeezed off a TOW missile. It shot out of the tube and tore down into the center of the parade ground. About fifteen yards in front of the cluster of foolish sentries, it exploded. Earth and fragmented bodies, one of them Bui's, and one SA-7 with launcher, flew into the air.

"Let's take the barracks, soldier," Sam said, knowing there could be no sweeter prospect to a freedom-loving man than smashing his former cage. He veered the Cobra to the right and swung into line with the buildings on the south side of the compound. They came in on a line with the prisoners' barracks. Sam sighted, triggered a missile and watched as it screamed off in a straight line and slammed into the barracks. Cinder blocks hurtled into the air as the wall shattered, the roof collapsing in a fiery heap. As they roared over the other buildings, the flier pivoted the turret gun and rained 7.62mm shells down onto the remnant of Sun Sun's cadre still firing up at them.

Sam climbed off to the east again and banked hard, curling around the compound to the north. Then he swung in on a vector with the barracks for the sentries. They were on the north side of the compound near the destroyed and still flaming headquarters building. Sam swooped in and took them out sequentially with two TOWs. All the while they passed within range, the flier in front blazed machine gun fire down on the few sentries and midgets still tracking them. The parade ground was littered with broken bodies and discarded weapons.

Sam let the Cobra drift out over the compound to the west. Looking back, he saw the burning rubble of the decimated buildings and the still smoldering skeleton of the Huey off in the distance to the east. It was a beautiful sight. But there was still the pool building where he'd almost bought it, still the sentries and midgets. One more good roaring blast at the compound would do nicely.

Then he saw the running lights of another Huey. It was flying over the ridge, descending toward the compound. Sam swung farther out to the west, then turned south and headed back. The Huey was coming in from the southeast. He would flank it to see what its intentions were. As he watched, the Huey dipped down onto the rim of the basin, flying low over the mountainside.

"That's the guys," the flier in front of Sam yelled, "that's the guys, I'm sure of it." His voice rippled with excitement. He was exhilarated. Sam reserved judgment, holding the Cobra on a line to sweep over the pool building and the parade ground.

"We'll see, soldier," Sam said. "For now, get set to fire on the parade ground and dump any grenades you have left into the center. Let's take out anybody left down there."

"For sure, sir," the flier replied, then added, "Sorry, sir."

"No sweat," Sam muttered, leaning in to line up the sight. He released the TOW, and it shot down toward the pool building, Sam adjusting the wires only slightly as it flew. It slammed into the building, demolishing its side. Broken cinder blocks exploded everywhere, the roof buckled and flames leaped up. Then Sam swung to the left and dropped lower, giving the flier a chance to spray the parade ground with machine gun fire and to blast away with the grenades he had left. The flier opened up on the few sentries and midgets left, overwhelming them with the all-out firepower of the turret weapons. Then, as they reached the compound's perimeter, Sam started to climb.

That's when the first starburst exploded beneath the Huey. What looked to Sam like napalm spread a ring of fire below the chopper in either direction. Sam watched, stunned. After the Huey had covered another two hundred yards or so, he spotted something hurled from its side door. Immediately another starburst exploded beneath the chopper.

"They're napalming the opium," the flier shouted, his voice loaded with glee. "They're wrecking the fucking crop, burning it the fuck up." He laughed at the top of his lungs. Sam smiled. Ahead the Huey moved in a slight banking turn following the curve of the mountainside. Another packet shot from its side. Flames mushroomed below and spread. Now nearly half the mountainside ringing the compound was an inferno, red and yellow flames leaping into the night sky.

Sam positioned the Cobra below the Huey and to its side so that he and the flier could see the Huey and the destruction it wrought even as they covered its flank. They held formation as the Huey worked its way around the basin, spreading its holocaust on the mountainsides as it went. When the Huey had worked its way back to the eastern end of the compound, the entire basin was a ring of fire, flames roiling and spreading, blazing against the dark sky, the opium crop incinerated and useless.

Sam revved the big Lycoming engine, twisting the throttle grip, and turned inward once more. He was going to make one final pass, insuring that the compound was a total wreck and all its forces killed or routed.

"Open up hard all the way, soldier. Let it all rip," Sam commanded, swinging the drab-green chopper down hard, zigzagging from one side of the compound to the other, turret gun spinning, the shells blanketing the parade ground and tearing into the bamboo huts and sheds. In the darkness below, the compound was a flaming mess, the light from the burning buildings and the flaming mountainsides illuminating the total destruction Sam Borne had inflicted on Doctor Sun Sun's dreamland.

Sam let the big Cobra wing out to the west, then turned

it hard and headed back. It was time to pick up the Huey and get the hell out of there. Below in the annihilated compound the fires raged out of control, their flames licking yellow and red against the black sky, all of the buildings broken and burning and on the ground the bodies of the dead sentries and midgets, sprawled in attitudes of agony where death had claimed them, many soaked in their own blood, some charred from the explosions and fires, many with limbs and trunks splayed this way and that, at unnatural angles, some wrenched apart by shrapnel, others torn by flying fragments from the demolished buildings. Nothing moved.

"Hot damn," the flier blurted out, then let a low, long whistle spool out between his teeth.

"You like that, soldier?"

"Yes, sir."

"Yes, Sam."

There was a silent pause while the soldier contemplated this.

"My name's Borne, soldier, Sam to you. What's yours?"

"Foster, sir. Joe Foster."

"You win."

Up ahead, Sam saw the Huey swinging out to the side, drifting slightly, obviously waiting for them to take the lead. Sam twisted the throttle and shot in ahead of it. His arm throbbing, he felt weak but elated. He charged ahead into the silver screen of a sky lightening with false dawn. They had maybe an hour before full light in which to clear Vietnamese airspace.

Then they were home free.

CHAPTER THIRTY:
NICE WORK

Ventana Inn
Big Sur, California
September 5

Things were slow. From the terrace of the Ventana Inn restaurant, the setting sun cast a purple haze across the mountains leaning into the surf for fifty miles down the coast. The water itself had turned a deep gun-metal blue. Off at the edge of the horizon the fiery sun streaked the sky above it red. It was all spectacular. California was spectacular. The view was spectacular. The Ventana Inn was spectacular. But Sam Borne was bored. Things were too slow.

Sam fished into the inside pocket of his lightweight blazer and tweezered a Gauloise from the pack there. What the hell, he'd jogged down the coast for five miles today and slogged back. He was entitled to a Gauloise. He lit the tangy French cigarette and inhaled deeply. The smoke pierced his lungs and rushed through him, adding a swift fillip to his blood. He smoked and gazed out at the view and grew more bored.

Then it happened.

From over his shoulder she asked, "Excuse me, may I trouble you for a light?"

Sam turned. She could have asked him for help with her tax returns and he wouldn't have minded.

She too was spectacular. Through the hazy purple light of evening, she smiled at him. Her face had the high color and enticing cheekbones that drove him wild. The face, so delicate and striking, was framed by tresses black as a raven's wing hanging on either side of her chin and curling slightly outward. Her eyes were green, and to get lost in. Her mouth was wide, sensual and inviting.

Sam took out his lighter and, cupping it in both hands, held it out for her. She bent slightly forward with one of those impossibly long white filter cigarettes American tobacco companies made especially for ladies. The filter end was ringed with a floral design. Sam had tried one once and nearly slipped a disk trying to get a hit out of it. She was wearing a black scoop-necked dress, and while she bent forward Sam enjoyed the view. Her breasts were full and magnificent. She puffed her cigarette to a red glow, straightened up and smiled.

"My name's Wendy."

"Is that short for Gwendolyn?"

"It's short for Wendy. This is California."

They laughed.

"What's yours?"

"Sam."

"Short for Samuel?"

"Short for Sam. This is America."

She laughed. Sam grinned.

"Of course you have a last name."

"Borne."

"So you're Mr. Sam Borne."

"Sam to you, I hope."

"Whatever."

"Would you like a drink?"

"Very much."

"What can I get you?"

"White wine."

"Be right back."

Sam went in, crossed to the bar, got a white wine and a Bushmills on the rocks with a twist. When he returned Wendy had walked to the edge of the terrace and stood with her back to him. Her legs, in black mesh stockings above black heels, were slender and exciting, with just a hint of muscle at the calf and just a wisp of curve. They were the kind of legs that made you turn and look back when you parted from a woman who had them. You watched them till they were out of sight, delighted all the while by nature's bounty. They were a great argument for the existence of God, Sam thought, and wondered often why Aquinas hadn't included "The Argument from Gams" as one of his *a priori* assertions for the existence of a Supreme Being. Maybe Aquinas was a tit man, Sam concluded.

"Here we are," Sam said, handing her the goblet of white wine. "Sorry to interrupt," he added, noticing that Wendy was absorbed in the view.

"It's quite all right."

"Obviously you're experiencing the renewal and rejuvenation the brochure promises."

"Do you often quote resort brochures?"

"No. But I often read them."

"How peculiar."

"It's in my line of business."

"Are you a travel agent?"

"No."

"Are you a developer?"

"Not really."

"You're so cryptic. I give up. What are you?"

"A troubleshooter."

"Where do you shoot trouble?"

"All over. And now that you know what I am, tell me what you are."

"A producer."

"Like in movies?"

"Like in television."

"I'm impressed. So, obviously you've come here for the ideal hideaway for writing and project development."

"Is that from the brochure?"

"Where else?"

Wendy giggled. It was a private giggle. Sam waited it out. When it was over, he asked, "Are you working on something here?"

"I hope so."

"Now who's cryptic?"

"Do you really want to know?"

"Yes."

"Then buy me dinner and I'll lay it all out for you."

"You're on. But can you give me a hint?"

"I've been sent up here by my boss to come up with a series with the appeal of the old *Mission: Impossible*. You know, male fantasy."

"Don't you believe truth is stranger than fiction?"

"Most of the time, but not in male fantasy."

"I'll try to persuade you otherwise."

"I hope it helps."

"So do I. Let's go in, shall we?"

Sam took her arm and guided her across the terrace and into the dining room. It was a large room with cedar walls and a ceiling supported by thick columns of pine. In the vaulted gables of the ceiling were large picture windows, and beyond one the dark outlines of the rolling foothills of the Santa Lucia Mountains loomed above them under the first stars of the night. The hostess led them to a table along the south wall, with a view out over the terrace and beyond to the Pacific.

They made small talk over their menus, and Sam selected a split of Schramsberg Pinot Noir to celebrate their good fortune in both coming to the Ventana Inn simultaneously. To start things off, they also ordered some smoked trout to nibble on while deciding about their main dishes. Over the champagne, as good as California had to offer—and very good—they chose their entrees—filet mignon for Sam and for Wendy a sole in saffron sauce. To accompany the meal, Sam chose a Stony Hill Chardonnay, aged seven years and just right for drinking.

During dinner Sam got to know Wendy. She did not get to know him. For years Sam had been having conversations in which he couldn't discuss himself frankly. In fact, he often wondered what life was like for those able to discuss themselves openly. Wendy knew. She'd gone to UCLA film school and had worked for several producers until now, when she'd "caught the big break in network" and was assigned to come up with a new *Mission: Impossible* "clone," as she called it. She would either make it or break it here, she said; this was a career challenge. If she came up with a big winner, it would be a bonanza. If she came up with a big loser, it would be bust. She knew her career was on the line, she said.

Sam discussed this problem with her. Over coffee and Remy Martin, he limned out a character and a series of plots that Wendy flipped for. She said the ideas made her feel "in the outer reaches of outer space." She thought *she* had done it. All she needed was a secretary to take it down in the morning. Something like this on paper would do the trick. Tomorrow she'd refine it. Would Sam be available to collaborate with her?

He would be available. And did she care to drive down the coast now and see the white surf curl and splash off the dark rocks?

She cared to. Sam signed the check, and they went out to the parking lot. Wendy oohed and aahed over the red Lamborghini the Committee had supplied Sam with this time. All told, they'd been good to him, though the absence of gambling at the Ventana was a subtle rebuke, a reminder that he'd taken great, uncalled-for risks in getting the prisoners out. He'd picked up the car at the San Francisco airport and had driven it hard down the coast to the Ventana. During the days, he'd been rereading Emerson, especially "Circles" and "Self-Reliance," two of his favorite essays. The last few nights he'd tooled around the coast road alone, thinking back over the assignment, glad he'd got Sun Sun, glad he'd freed the ten prisoners, sorry he'd lost the other ten, miserable that he'd lost Honey, longing for her and all the fun they could have had. Now there was Wendy.

When they were settled in the lush bucket seats of the Lamborghini Coutah, amid the elegance of its black interior, Wendy blurted out what was on her mind. "How much did this rocket ship cost?"

We are in California, indeed, Sam thought. He debated whether to answer her. The Lamborghini was one of the most exotic cars in the world. Built in the fabulous little northern Italian town of Modena, the same town that built the Ferrari, the Maserati and the DiTomasso, the Lamborghini was a marvel and, in Sam's estimation, a great bargain at one hundred thousand United States dollars.

"A hundred thousand."

Wendy let out an emphatic "Wow," putting about half a dozen vowels into it. Sam turned the ignition and the engine leaped to life with a full-throated roar. He backed out of the parking lot and swung onto the twisting road leading out to the coast highway. In the darkness they passed the soaring redwoods.

They whipped down the coast highway in almost total silence, each absorbed in its nocturnal beauty, each contemplating his or her own thoughts. After about twelve miles, the Lamborghini hugging the tight turns and twists of the highway like the truly thoroughbred machine it was, Wendy softly asked Sam to take her back. He didn't argue. He spun the Lamborghini into a turnoff and shot back the way they'd come. In minutes they were back at the inn. Sam parked and turned to Wendy.

"Would you like to share a nightcap?"

"Very much."

They walked back along the lighted paths past the main office and lounge to Sam's room. They entered and Sam fixed Wendy a Remy Martin in a big snifter and poured himself one, then went to the fireplace and fixed a fire. When the fire came up, Sam stood and walked over and joined Wendy at the big picture window overlooking the Pacific, now a dark pool under the stars.

"Beautiful, isn't it?" she whispered.

"Yes."

"Let's toast."

"To what?"

"The success of my new series."

"The *Mission: Impossible* clone?"

"What else."

"Do you believe in male fantasy now?"

"And how."

They clinked glasses and Sam sipped his brandy. It warmed him all the way down. He looked at Wendy and smiled. She reached up and touched his cheek, then rose on her toes and kissed him lingeringly on the lips. Sam kissed her back.

"I wish we had some music," she whispered.

"We do."

Sam left the window and flipped on his stereo. The angular piano of Thelonius Monk filled the room. What was it Monk used to say? Sam wondered. "The only cats worth anything are the cats who take chances." Monk knew something. When Sam turned, Wendy was standing directly in front of him. She leaned into him and kissed him again, long and tight. He took her in his arms, then gently lowered her onto the bed.

From the stereo came the mellow phrase of "Nice Work If You Can Get It."

Monk tickled the ivory.

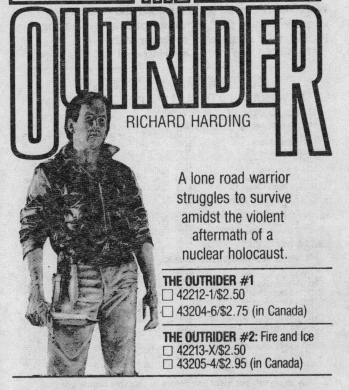
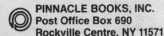

LEWIS PERDUE

THE TESLA BEQUEST
A secret society of powerful men have stolen the late Nikola
Tesla's plans for a doomsday weapon; they are just one step away
from ruling the world.
☐ 42027-7 THE TESLA BEQUEST $3.50

THE DELPHI BETRAYAL
From the depths of a small, windowless room in the bowels of
the White House, an awesome conspiracy to create economic
chaos and bring the entire world to its knees is unleashed.
☐ 41728-4 THE DELPHI BETRAYAL $2.95

QUEENS GATE RECKONING
A wounded CIA operative and a defecting Soviet ballerina hurtle
toward the hour of reckoning as they race the clock to circum-
vent twin assassinations that will explode the balance of power.
☐ 41436-6 QUEENS GATE RECKONING $3.50

THE DA VINCI LEGACY
A famous Da Vinci whiz, Curtis Davis, tries to uncover the truth
behind the missing pages of an ancient manuscript which could
tip the balance of world power toward whoever possesses it.
☐ 41762-4 THE DA VINCI LEGACY $3.50